MW01520036

STOCKER HILL | Dale R. Lentz

THANK YOU FOR
ALL YOU DO !

Dale

DORRANCE
PUBLISHING CO
EST. 1920
PITTSBURGH, PENNSYLVANIA 15238

The contents of this work, including, but not limited to, the accuracy of events, people, and places depicted; opinions expressed; permission to use previously published materials included; and any advice given or actions advocated are solely the responsibility of the author, who assumes all liability for said work and indemnifies the publisher against any claims stemming from publication of the work.

All Rights Reserved
Copyright © 2024 by Dale R. Lentz

No part of this book may be reproduced or transmitted, downloaded, distributed, reverse engineered, or stored in or introduced into any information storage and retrieval system, in any form or by any means, including photocopying and recording, whether electronic or mechanical, now known or hereinafter invented without permission in writing from the publisher.

Dorrance Publishing Co
585 Alpha Drive
Suite 103
Pittsburgh, PA 15238
Visit our website at www.dorrancebookstore.com

ISBN: 979-8-89027-191-4
eISBN: 979-8-89027-689-6

Chapter | 1

The morning dew put a pleasant aroma in the air that captured the peacefulness of the small town of Walcott.

Walcott laid at the foot of Stocker Hill and stretched from the basin of the Hill over Salt Creek and headed out towards Route 12. The town had less than 1,000 people and like all small towns; everyone knew everyone else's business—at least they thought so.

Life was simple in Walcott. There were two schools, a couple churches, and the downtown courtyard that hosted several festivals throughout the year. Central Park, which was the life and blood of all the young ones in town, was at the heart of everything. This was the place to be for the kids in the town—some not old enough to drive, but too old for all the kiddy games. While others were hanging on to their youth before the big step into adulthood.

Central Park was always packed on Sunday afternoons, though. Several pickup games of basketball were happening, and the teenagers would meet in the large parking lot to show off their cars.

The cool sounds of music engulfed the air while everyone enjoyed themselves. The taunting of the boys playing ball, the young boys playing tag, and the little girls in their Sunday best playing were common occurrences.

The local sheriff, Buck Hanner, did his Sunday drive through the park to catch up on any new gossip in the town. If anything was happening—you heard at the park. He was also keeping his eyes on the boys—John, Brad, Rob, and Reed. They were the kings of the town as far as the boys went and always stirring up some kind of trouble. Mostly unintentional, but trouble found them anyways.

Chapter | 2

It had been twenty years since the bodies of the twins were found on the Hill. No one knew what really happened—mostly just rumors now and it depended on who was telling the story too.

Ethel, who lived on the outskirts of town near Route 12, would tell you some hooligans came down from Cleveland and did the terrible crime. Others thought there was a local murderer in Walcott, while some of the town just blamed it on the Hill, blamed it on Stocker Hill.

Stocker Hill is not the official name of the Hill; actually, the Hill has no official name. Stocker Hill got its name from Stan Stocker, the multimillionaire who bought up most of the land around town and purchased all the land that made up the Hill.

The Hill, Stocker Hill, is the largest in the valley. Its rugged peaks and voluptuous trees and brush also make it the most beautiful. As other hills in the valley lose their identity as the summer comes to an end, Stocker Hill holds on to its personality far into winter. It stands powerful and sturdy over the other hills—like a general leading his men into battle, out front and in your face.

Stan Stocker was a tall, strong, rugged man who made his money in the coal mines of West Virginia and settled in Walcott. Stan loved the town of Walcott and the peacefulness the Hill brought him. His weekly routine, what he lived for, was to climb the side of the Hill, to conquer its peaks and valleys, to challenge the Hill and not to cower to what the Hill would throw at him. Every week Stan would climb the little mountain and take a different way to the top. Stan knew every inch of the Hill—every inch of Stocker Hill.

The legend of Stocker Hill goes: Stan Stocker found himself in Normandy in a bloody battle on a hill like the Hill that he loved. As Stan froze in battle, like a frightened schoolboy, his men became defenseless and died in a brutal battle without leadership. The once-rugged man that used to stand tall and powerful was defeated, defeated by the will and hunger of Hitler's soldiers. After the war, Stan Stocker returned to America a defeated man. America had won, but Stan had lost. He climbed his Hill one last time and as he stood at the top of the highest peak and asked forgiveness, his soul was taken from his body by the Hill. The town's men found him as he lay in defeat on the upper most peak of the Hill. Stocker Hill.

Urban legends—they sure had a way of changing through the years and through the eyes of the beholder.

Chapter | 3

"Hanner here," the sergeant barked back over the mic.

The sweet voice replied, "Just checking on you, Sarge. Are you heading out for the nightly rounds?" Becky asked.

"Sure am, Beck," the sarge replied. "Just making sure the boys aren't raising hell."

"You be nice to those boys, Hanner. They're good kids," Becky replied in the sternest voice her short petite body could muster. Becky ran her hands through her long blonde hair and blew out a big sigh since she knew the boys were probably raising hell, but they sure brought a lot of life to the town.

"Yes, Becky, I will be nice to the boys," Hanner replied in his usual grouchy tone.

Sergeant Hanner, an old grouchy son of a bitch, way to grouchy for a man with an easy life. Life was good in the little town of Walcott for the sergeant. Nothing major ever happened in Walcott, which made Hanner happy. He was too old for complications. Life was so simple in his town that he was not only the local sheriff, but also the town's funeral director.

"Frickin' boys. I bet they're on the school roof again throwing back some beers they stole from their papa's fridge," he murmured to himself. "Let's go and see." Hanner punched the old Ford and headed towards the schoolyard. He flew past old lady Ethel's house and shot her a wave as she sat on the porch. Ethel is a rather large grandmotherly type of lady whose body engulfed the plastic chair she was sitting on.

The sarge looked up at Stocker Hill and could see the tip of the sun sliding down the back side of the Hill. The sun was starting to set a tad earlier these days, showing a sign that summer was coming to an end. The leaves weren't changing yet or anything like that; the Hill just had a funny way of letting you know what was happening.

– – –

"Again," whimpered Reed, "we're going on top of the school again?"

"Stop being such a girl, Reed," bellowed John, "and hurry up before old ass Hanner catches us."

"Come on, Reed. You want me to carry you up there?" cracked Brad in his six-foot-four frame.

"Kiss my ass!" stammered Reed.

"You are so tough for a little guy! Coochie coochie coo!" Brad gushed as he sprayed the gulp of beer he just took. "I love you man!" he finished.

"Why are you two always bickering?" asked Rob. "Now, get out of my way and watch a real man climb this school. Did I tell you about the time I climbed the school because of the killer dogs chasing me?"

"You sure did, Rob!" barked John.

"Yeah, if I remember correctly, it was old lady Ethel's killer Chihuahua," Brad laughed out loud.

"You guys are such jerks!" Rob shouted out as he scampered up the side of the school with his lanky arms and legs.

Reed said with smile as he took a swig of beer and he looked back at the boys with his big blues, "Yeah, this is great once we're up here. Look at the Hill. So powerful in the background."

"Stop getting so sentimental on us, Reed," one of the boys snapped back as they looked on at Reed's short silhouette that was blocking the last of the sunshine.

Reed was right, though. The Hill was powerful in the background. The sun setting behind it, a sense of calm fell through the night with the breeze that carries the smell only the Hill can produce. Stocker Hill—the awe of the town.

The boys sat back and enjoyed their beer. John, the self-appointed leader of the group barked orders on what the group should do this weekend, but he was pretty much ignored. Everyone liked John, they just didn't get where a skinny, lanky guy with a bad complexion, big nose, and bushy eyebrows was the leader. A leader is usually strong and handsome like Brad—not a lanky Alfalfa-looking guy. They let him go on believing he was the leader, but everyone knew it was Brad. It was a lot easier that way.

"Oh shit!" one of the boys yelled out, "Hanner is on his way here."

"Why do you say that" Reed asked.

"Look where he is," replied John. "He only goes that way when he's heading towards the school."

"Well, shit, should we bail or let the old man catch us again?" asked Brad.

The boys decided to wait and let Hanner blow off some steam and make himself feel needed. Hanner whipped up to the school and let the boys hear his sirens as a show of authority. The sirens echoed through the schoolyard like a coyote howling in the Grand Canyon.

The boys were surprised because Hanner was way too loud for their liking.

"Boys, get down from there and bring down those beer bottles too," Hanner yelled over the loudspeaker.

"Damn it," barked John to Hanner, "why don't you announce to the whole town we're up here. All I need is my old man to crawl up my ass again."

Brad in his smartass way, said, "John, you don't think your old man knows we're up here? He's the one I bought the beer from."

"Hurry up, boys, hurry up" came over the loudspeaker again.

"Cool your jets, Barney!" cracked Reed.

"Good one, Reed, good one," Brad snapped back.

Rob murmured some comments under his breath like he always does as the boys slowly climbed down off the school and cleaned up their beer cans. Hanner stood there with his round belly hanging over his belt and a mustard stain over his badge. He sure was a goofy guy, but deep down all the boys liked him and he liked the boys. There was that "love to push each other's buttons" type of relationship. It helped keep the town of Walcott on its toes.

"Boys, how many times do I have to tell you to stay off the school?" Hanner questioned as he looked through the top of his glasses and wiped the sweat off his large forehead.

"Come on, Hanner. You know we only go up there so we can hear your sirens go off," Brad said while cracking a smile. "You're such an authority figure, I get goose bumps."

Hanner replied in an extra stern voice, "Brad, I am in no mood for your smartass comments. You always have to be a wiseass, don't you?"

"Yes, sir," Brad cracked back, and then he realized Hanner wasn't messing around this time. "Sorry, sir," he mustered quietly.

"Hanner, what's bugging you?" Reed asked.

"Oh, nothing you boys can help with," Hanner replied.

"The Hill getting to you again?" Rob asked.

"Boys, just get out of here," Hanner barked and then he jumped back in his squad car and sped away.

The boys looked at each other and wondered if the Hill was getting to Hanner again. It goes back to those urban legends that float around.

Supposedly, Hanner and his buddies went up to Stocker Hill one evening and something happened. No one really knows, but it messed them up pretty good back in the day.

Chapter | 4

The boys decided they had had enough and went their separate ways for the evening. Reed was buzzing pretty good as he walked home. It was a wonderful night, he thought to himself, *nothing better than a cool buzz, the moon being out, and not a care in the world.*

Reed walked down Main Street for a tad and then cut through some yards to the alley and headed towards home. He headed past the old manufacturing plant that used to employ the whole town and could still smell the burned oil that used to encapsulate the town when the wind was blowing right.

Reed's mind was really wondering now, as he strolled past Krista's house. She sure was a catch, especially around this area with all these cornfed girls. Reed giggled and decided to visit his girl.

"Knock, knock." The window rattled way too loud for Reed's liking as he tapped on the glass to get his girl's attention.

"Shhh," murmured Reed, "kind of difficult being quiet when you got a buzz on." Reed was eager to see Krista. Krista is a blonde-haired, blue-eyed beauty that stood about the same height as Reed. She is a tad less than five foot five and the eye of every boy in the valley.

"Boy, you are being way too loud, and you know my dad will skin your ass if he knew you were here at this time," Krista quietly whispered as she opened the window.

Krista and Reed have been a couple for a while now. Ever since the truth or dare game at Central Park. The two of them have always been enamored with each other; it goes back to when they were in grade school at Otter Creek.

"Darling, let me climb in the window; I'll be quiet," Reed whispered in his best boyfriend voice.

"Reed, boy, have you been drinking with the boys again?" Krista asked in a stern voice.

"But, but we were just hanging out at the school having a couple orange whips," Reed stammered back.

"You know how you get when you're drinking. Your horny ass comes knocking on my window for a little piece of perfection," she replied with a slight crack of a smile.

Reed shot back as he held the drool from dripping out of his mouth, "Perfection, you say? Well, that is correct, and you know all I want is to hold you and talk to my girl."

"I know what you want, you little sack of love. Get your ass in here and be quiet so my daddy doesn't tan your ass," Krista replied in an eager voice.

Reed finally dragged his drunken ass up through the window and was lucky Krista's dad was none the wiser. Reed and Krista lay in her bed and talked and laughed for several hours. Reed tried his accidental boob brush and hand roaming below the panty line, but Krista was not letting any of that happen. She was torturing the boy; she knew it and so did he.

"Hey, darling," Reed said.

Krista shot back, "No, you are not going below the Mason-Dixon Line tonight!"

"No darling, as much as I want to, no. You know old Hanner busted us again tonight," Reed moaned back.

"Tell me something I don't know," Krista replied.

"Anyways, I'm worried about Hanner," Reed said. "He was acting all strange, not his usual 'chew our ass' self, and Rob asked him if the Hill was getting to him."

"The Hill getting to him?" Krista replied.

"Yeah, the Hill getting to him; have you heard the old wives' tale about Hanner and his buddies going up to the top of Stocker Hill when they were teenagers?" Reed asked.

Krista replied, smacking Reed's hand away from her boobs, "Stop it, boy. And, yes, I heard something about it, but don't know too much about it."

"I heard a little bit about it too. I think Old Man Addy knows the story," Reed replied.

"Old Man Addy?" Krista questioned. "You mean Harold who runs the fixit shop downtown Walcott?"

"Yep, same guy, Harold," Reed replied. "I'm going to gather up the guys and we are going to make a visit to see if we can learn more about Hanner and Stocker Hill."

"You stay away from Stocker Hill, Reed. That Hill gives me the creeps," Krista demanded.

"Don't worry, darling. We'll be okay."

After Reed tried his hardest to get Krista revved up. She finally gave in and Reed and her enjoyed each other's company as the warm breeze rolled through the window. It was a perfect night for Reed and Krista. Reed hung out with his buddies, caught a buzz, and got to be with his girl. Krista couldn't help but smile with pleasure as she kissed Reed good night, and he slipped out of the window into the glow of the moonlight.

Chapter | 5

The other boys went their own way after the visit from Hanner since they knew where Reed was heading. John split off from Brad and Rob and headed home.

"John?" asked Brad, "you heading over to Suzy rotten crotch for a little midnight va-va-voom?"

"Wouldn't you like to know?" snapped back John.

"I just don't get it." Brad looked at Rob and said, "The son of a bitch is one dorky-looking guy and he gets to have his way with Suzy."

"I don't know, Brad," Rob replied as he rubbed his fed belly.

John walked off into the evening as Brad and Rob headed the same way. They walked for several miles before Rob finally spoke up.

"Hey, Brad," he said, "Hanner sure was weird tonight. He's never that nice to us. He's generally an asshole."

Brad replied, "You're right. Something must have crawled up his ass. Maybe his wife Martha crawled up his ass. Gross!"

"Damn, Brad. I'm serious here," Rob shot back.

"Okay, Rob. Take a chill pill—no need to get hostile. So, what's your concern? Talk to me, buddy," Brad asked in a normal voice as he wondered what crawled up Rob's ass.

"He just isn't himself and I think it's coming up to the anniversary of the Stocker Hill myth," Rob replied with a concerned look on his face.

"Rob, those stories are just urban legends to scare kids like us from messing around up on the Hill," Brad said.

"Bullshit, Brad!" snapped Rob. "Those stories are not urban legends. Shit really happens up on the Hill. Remember the twins went up there and they found them a week later all rotted up. They say the smell is similar to a putrid goat."

"Putrid goat—you're going to make me hurl. What? Are you going satanic? Anyways, the twins were slackers, and they crossed the paths of people they shouldn't have," Brad replied.

"I don't believe that, man. It's the Hill. The Hill will mess with you. Every time we go up there, I get the chills and maybe Satan does have something to do with it," Rob replied with intensity.

"Rob, you sound like Reed right now. Stop being such a little girl. Why do you get the chills? We've never even been to where they found the bodies," Brad shot back. "Tell you what. Tomorrow we'll grab the guys, and we'll go visit Harold over in the garage."

"You mean Old Man Addy?" questioned Rob.

"Yes," replied Brad, "Old Man Addy. We'll go see him. If anyone knows, Harold would know. Come on. Let's go have a night cap. My pop has some Old Milwaukee's Best in the fridge."

Rob and Brad headed down through Central Park towards Brad's house. They were hoping the old man was crashed out so they could have a couple more beers to end the night.

Chapter | 6

Hanner sped away from the boys with his mind in a funk. He had this itching feeling that he had not felt in years, and it bothered him more than he liked.

"Is that you, honey?" Hanner's wife, Martha, shouted from upstairs.

"Sure is, honey," Hanner replied, hoping his wife wouldn't catch the tension in his voice.

"Jack called for you tonight," she shouted again, "says it looks Mrs. Meyer is not going to make it through the night."

"Okay. I'll give him a call," Hanner said.

"What did you say?" Martha blurted.

"Damn it, woman!" Hanner shouted, "Get down here if you're going to keep yelling from upstairs."

Martha could hear the tension in his voice now. She had a stirring feeling something was bothering her husband. Martha did a couple more looks in the mirror and realized no miracle was going to get her boobs up where they used to be or turn her sparkling gray hair into the flowing locks of hair she had thirty years ago.

"You sure were a dish back then," Martha told her reflection in the mirror.

Martha was hesitant and took a few deep breaths before walking downstairs to her husband. Earlier that day, Martha noticed the date on the calendar and figured the anniversary of Hanner and the boys would be bothering him. She'd guessed right by the tone Hanner barked back at her.

"Here we go," Martha said as she strolled down the stairs to her husband. "I'll be right down" she blurted back to Hanner as she heard him mumble some more crap.

"Darling," Martha said in her ever-so-sweet voice, "What's wrong? Is it Gail?"

"Mrs. Meyer? Screw her," Hanner snapped back. "I don't care about the old hag."

"Honey, you know I don't like it when you talk like that in our house. Are you still mad at Gail because she dumped you for that football player in Elk Grove?" Martha replied in the sternest voice she could muster.

"*Please…*," Hanner dragged out.

"Well, honey, what is it?" Martha asked.

"It's the Hill, Martha. It is the Hill," Hanner stammered.

Martha patted Hanner's back and fixed his comb-over as he slowly sipped his coffee and ate the last slice of apple pie. The concern was racing through Martha's mind now. The last time the Hill was talking to Hanner, the twins died.

Brian and Doug Drucker were two ornery boys that were full of piss and vinegar. They were always in trouble with Hanner and starting shit within the town. Everyone knew they were bad boys and figured they would end up in jail or something. They were always rubbing knuckles with the wrong crowd. No one expected them to be gutted like pigs and laid out as if they were sacrificed for Satan himself.

"I'm going out back to enjoy the breeze," Hanner told his wife. As Hanner sat on the porch swing sipping his evening cocktail and enjoying the breeze that came through the valley in the evenings, he started to think about that day, the day they found the twins.

Hanner remembers that day like it was yesterday. Harold, the town's mechanic, went up on the Hill to work on the generator that is used to light the star.

The star was built as a dedication to Stan Stocker, for all his accomplishments and bravery in the war. The star is lit on special occasions—Thanksgiving, Christmas, Easter, and the changing of the seasons. The best night is when it is lit up, for the sign that the summer was over, and the kids had to go back to school. It glows like the sun, simply spectacular.

Harold was having problems and had to hike it back down the Hill to get some more parts. Instead of hauling everything up the Hill by hand this time, Harold decided to take his big Chevy up the east access road. He needed the four-wheel drive in that Chevy of his to get up the steep parts of the road. The Hill was a tough climb, even for a strong truck like Harold had. Harold was not too fond of doing this since the road is hardly traveled; the road had a look of a Mohawk with the weeds sticking up in the middle of the two gravel tracks. And he wasn't fond that the only place to park was by the grave.

Chapter | 7

Reed headed down the back alley away from Krista's house. "I better stay away from the front porch. Her daddy would have my ass!" Reed stated to himself and started to giggle. "Too funny, I'm here by myself and talking out loud. I must be losing it."

As Reed strolled out of the alley and headed toward Central Park, he could hear the crickets singing to him like a finely tuned orchestra. They were all in sync and they had a calming feeling over him as he continued his walk home.

"What is that?" Reed asked. "Sounds like a dog crying." Reed headed out of the park toward the sound. As Reed got closer to the sound, he picked up his pace and then started to run. The crying and whimpering were getting louder, and he could not believe he was the only person hearing this awful sound.

"Oh my!" Reed cried out. "You poor thing." There behind the old rotted-out garage was a puppy caught in a trap. Reed could not believe his eyes. As Reed approached the caught puppy, the whimpering dog calmed down in his presence. "I'll help you, little buddy," Reed whispered to the frighten puppy. "It is going to be okay," he said in the calmest voice he could muster as he held back his tears.

Reed reached down to see how bad the little retriever was hurt and noticed how lucky the dog was. The trap caught the puppy but did not fully get it. The puppy's little paw was stuck. As he tried his hardest to pry the trap open, Reed grunted, "Uhhh, damn, this thing is tough. Almost there, almost got it, little guy." Reed continued to grunt as he slowly opened the trap. "Okay, Buster, pull your paw out," Reed struggled to say as he held open the trap.

As the little guy pulled his paw out of the trap; Reed yelled out and startled the little pup, "Buster, Buster is your name. Since you couldn't bust out that trap yourself, I think you deserve the name Buster. If you got out of the trap all by yourself, I'd call you Spike. Spike is a tough guy. A guy that has tattoos and you can smoke with and drink whiskey, and… well, you know," Reed said happily to the puppy as he picked it up and cradle it in his arms.

Reed walked away from the rotten garage and fierce trap while holding the golden-brown puppy. "We'll fix you right up when we get home. Damn, you are so cute," Reed told the frightened little pup as it licked his nose.

As Reed walked into his house and checked the time. "Well, it is past midnight and I have had a full day," Reed said to Buster. "I bet you could use something to eat and some water, but let's patch you up first." Reed cradled Buster under one of his arms as he searched the downstairs bathroom for the first aid kit. Searching through all of his mothers' miscellaneous bins of crap, Reed finally found the kit. He was glad since his arm felt like Jell-O after holding Buster for so long.

"Okay, Buster, here is the thing, this is going to hurt," Reed said to the dog as he poured peroxide over Buster's paw. A little whimper came out of Buster as he looked up at Reed with his sad eyes. "Oh, you poor thing; it will be okay," Reed whimpered to himself as he knew he was hurting the little dog. As Reed fought back his tears, he put some cream on Buster's paw and wrapped it with tape and gauze.

"Let's just see how you get around now that you are all fixed up," Reed said gently to the puppy as he let the dog down on the floor.

Buster had no problem scampering around the kitchen floor and running into the dining room. "Shhh, Buster," Reed whispered to the pup. "Don't want to wake up Dad." Reed's dad had been feeling sick these past few days and Reed did not want to disturb him, especially with a little puppy running around the house.

As Reed turned from the sink to place a bowl of water on the floor for Buster, he could see the dog out of the corner of his eye with his leg lifted. "Buster!" yelled Reed as Buster began to pee on his mother's dining room chairs. "Awe man!" Reed started to chuckle as he realized he did not pay attention to the fact that the pup was a boy until he lifted his leg like a pro. "At least your name fits you," Reed said to Buster. "You have some frank and beans down there, don't you?"

Reed grabbed Buster and headed upstairs to his room. He closed the door ever so silently and began to talk to Buster as his best friend. "You see, Buster, when a woman loves you, you must give her your heart. There is nothing better in the world then the love of a good woman. Then again, an ice-cold beer comes pretty close to perfection." Reed silently laughed as he picked up Buster and put him on his bed. "Time to crash, boy… time to crash, time to cra—" Reed trailed off as he fell into never, never land.

It didn't take Reed that long to fall asleep that night; after saving a dog, the love of a good girl, and all those beers he had with the guys, Reed was spent.

Chapter | 8

"Uggg...," Brad moaned as he rubbed his curly brown hair. "Too many beers last night. I feel like shit."

Brad slowly rolled out of bed and headed downstairs. Brad's mother was cooking up some breakfast for his father and he needed to fill his belly to survive. As Brad walked into the kitchen, he got smacked with the smell of smoked bacon that his mother was cooking up. The sound of the sizzling bacon cooking on the stove was music to his ears. He started diving into the toast that was already on the table.

"Cool your jets, boy," Brad's dad yelled at him as he smacked him on the back of his head. "That toast is mine. You got it, boy?"

Brad murmured something as he stuffed another piece of bread in his mouth. "Mom, we have any juice left in the fridge?" he asked.

"Get your lazy ass up out of that chair and get it yourself," barked Brad's dad. "Your mother is not your servant."

"She should be," Brad cracked right before his mother smacked him in the back of the head. "Mom, my head is killing me."

"Too bad, who forced you to drink all those beers last night?" Brad's mom asked.

"My friends. By the way, you know I'm your little angel and would never do anything like that," Brad stated over the smirk on his face.

"Oh, angel, is it?" Brad's dad said. "Well, you better make sure the angel picks up those beer cans he left on the back porch. Plus, that angel owes me some cash for stealing my beers."

"Yes, sir," Brad replied as he started to stuff his face with the bacon and eggs his mother just put in front of him.

"What did you boys do last night?" Brad's dad asked.

"Oh, we went over to the school and harassed old ass Hanner," Brad replied. "Hanner wasn't himself, though. Rob is really worried about him. I think me, and the guys are going to go downtown and talk to Harold about Hanner and the Hill."

Brad's mother shot around from the sink and looked at her husband with her eagle eyes. Brad's father put up his hand and motioned he would take care of this.

Crack!

A loud thunderous thud came shooting out of Brad's dad's hand as he slapped the table. "You listen to me, boy, and you listen real good," Brad's dad yelled. "You boys stay away from Harold and the Hill. There are too many hidden secrets that the town just doesn't need stirred up. Harold and Hanner are good guys, so you and the boys back off!"

Brad's mouth opened in awe; he had never seen his dad get so heated over any topic. "What secrets?" Brad asked.

"Like I told you, boy—leave it alone," dad stated and stormed out of the kitchen.

Brad turned around and looked at his mother. The death stare shooting out of her eyes told him he better hush his mouth. "Umm'" Brad hummed. "Well, I guess I am going to go get in the shower. Thanks for the chow, Mom. Helped me tons," Brad said as he scampered upstairs.

Brad looked out of his second-floor bedroom window and could see his father in the garage. He could tell he was pissed off. *I must have really hit a nerve*, Brad thought to himself, and then he went ahead and called the guys.

As Brad got dressed in his usual T-shirt and jeans, he knew that he and the guys had to do some investigating. He was going to meet the boys in Central Park at 11:00 a.m. He better get going or he was going to be late. Brad left through the front screen door and let the door shut as quietly as he could. He had already stirred up the house enough that morning and didn't want any more trouble.

Chapter | 9

The sun shined through the little cracks in Reed's blinds and found its way to beam onto his eyelids. Reed brought his lifeless hands to his face and rubbed the sleep out of his eyes. He knew he had a good time last night; he could get whiffs of Krista's perfume off of his body and he could feel every heartbeat in his head. "Man, oh man," Reed said as he tried to gain a little clarity on the morning.

As life started to come back to Reed's body, he lay in his bed thinking about the day ahead and hooking up with the guys later that morning. As he contemplated whether he should drag his tired ass out of bed or not, he rolled over and grabbed his pillow and yelled into it, "MORNING SUCKS!"

"I heard that!" yelled his mom from the hallway. "Can you please control yourself?"

"Sorry, Mom," Reed replied as he ran his hands through his nappy bed head. "Son of bitch. I'm a tad hungover," he mumbled as he dragged himself out of the bed.

As Reed bent down and put on his shorts, he caught a glimpse of himself in the mirror. "For a short, fat guy you sure are a fine catch," he said as he looked at himself in the mirror and scratched his chubby belly. "I don't know what Krista sees in you, but you are one lucky SOB."

Buster tilted his head to the side and looked at Reed like he was crazy.

"Come on, boy!" Reed yelled at Buster while snapping his fingers. "We need to go introduce you to the Ps."

Buster jumped off the bed and scurried downstairs the best he could with his bandaged leg and introduced himself to Reed's parents.

"What the fu—" Reed's dad started to blurt out before his wife cut him off in midsentence.

"Don't say it, Bill, don't say it," Reed's mom said as she looked down at the cute dog that was looking up at her. "I guess our little animal lover brought you home last night. Reed, do you want to explain yourself?"

"Good idea, Katherine. Let's hear this one from the boy," Bill said to his wife.

"Well, Mom, Dad," Reed stammered out as he started to sweat from his nerves, "his name is Buster and he got caught in a trap behind the Corrigans' garage. I had to save the little fellow. Last night I had to do an emergency life-saving, I mean puppy-saving, procedure on his wounded paw. Plus, look how cute he is, and he needs a home."

"I don't care what he needs. You take that thing back and find out who he belongs to," Reed's dad said as he crossed his arms and oozed with disgust.

Right then Buster took off running right towards the father, lost his footing and slammed into Bill's legs. "*Yelp!*" Buster yelled out as he picked himself off the floor.

"Well, well… you sure are a cute fellow with a personality," Bill said as he picked up the little dog. "I guess we can keep you." He followed up with, "Enough with saving animals, Reed. Your big soft heart costs us too much money."

"Yes, Dad," Reed stated as he hugged his mom with all his affection. "I love you, Mom. This is going to be a good day."

"A good day? It would be better if you took a shower, son. You smell like an old whore house," she said as she pushed her son away from her.

"You know, Mom, you are the best mom in the whole wide world, and I am so lucky to have you as a mother, and Dad is the luckiest guy to have such a sweet, kind woman to come home to and—"

"Yes, I will make you breakfast," his mom said as she knew what Reed was getting at. "Go take a shower, stinky boy, and I'll whip you up something. Say, bacon and eggs?"

"Crispy bacon," Reed replied as he rubbed his hands together and made his way upstairs to take a shower.

As Reed soaked in the shower and enjoyed the hot water hitting his back, all he could do was think about Hanner. Reed began to wash his hair and body as the smell of breakfast snuck through the door. "Mmm, smells good," he said as the suds washed down his chubby body into the awaiting drain.

Reed hurried up, dried off, and got dressed in the best wrinkly clothes he could find and rushed downstairs to his awaiting breakfast. "I am famished," he said as he stuffed bacon into his mouth and gave a little piece to Buster who was looking up at him with his drooling eyes.

"I don't know what Krista sees in you, boy. You are a mess with those clothes on you and who matched those things anyway," Reed's mom said as she looked at Reed stuffing his face and sitting there in his mismatched, wrinkly clothes.

"It's pure love, Mom. Pure love," he explained as he took a big swig of his Diet Coke. "I got to go. What time is it? I need to meet the boys at the park as soon as possible." Reed finished eating and headed towards the door.

"Wait a minute," Reed's dad shouted at him before he could hit that door. "What are the plans today?"

"The guys and I are going to bother Harold," Reed replied. Bill asked, "Why?"

"Umm…," Reed hesitated, "because."

"Not a good answer," Bill replied. "What are you hiding?"

"Nothing," Reed said as he looked at the floor.

Bill looked at his son and crossed his arms while saying, "I know you, boy. You're hiding something. Unless you are looking for cracks in the floor, you're hiding something."

Reed looked up from the floor and glanced in his father's general direction as he took a few steps closer to the front door. His body language was… well, to escape. His father had the ability to make Reed twist in the wind. Reed got to the front door and said, "The legend of Stocker Hill—we want to know." As the front door was slamming, the last thing Reed's mom heard was "Watch Buster, Mom!"

Reed's father ran to the front door and opened it as he watched his son hightail it across the front lawn and yelled, "God damn it, Reed. You stay away from Harold. You don't want to open that door."

Bill slammed the front door shut and threw his hands up in disgust as Buster walked to the door to follow Reed.

Katherine peaked into the front room where Bill and the dog were and said, "It will be okay, Bill. You knew he was going to explore the legend someday."

Bill looked at his wife and smiled as he headed towards the couch. "Come here, Buster!" Bill yelled to the dog, who was sitting in a bucket of tears at the front door. "Come here, boy."

Buster whipped around from the door and made eye contact with Bill. Sure enough, Buster was excited and headed full speed towards Reed's father. "Whoa, boy!" Bill yelled out as Buster started to gain some speed and was heading his way. "You better slow down, or you're going to crash again."

Before Bill knew it, Buster was at full speed and was leaping onto his lap. As Bill rolled the little puppy over and started to rub his belly, Buster started peeing all over the place with excitement. "Son of a bitch. Buster, you little…. Katherine, the dog just pissed all over me and the couch!" Bill yelled with disgust as Buster looked at him with his little happy face.

"Coming, dear. I'll help you," Katherine said as she rang out a towel to clean up the mess. "You know puppies, darling. They have small, excited bladders and you always get the brunt of it."

Chapter | 10

The sunlight shined through Suzy's curtains the best it could, but it was enough to get her attention. As Suzy rolled over, she forgot that John was still there and started to get nervous.

"John, John," she whispered into John's ear. "John, John. Damn—he's is out cold." Suzy leaned up from under the covers and could feel the warm rays of sunlight hitting her bare breast. "Oh man, I hate when John does this," she said to herself while climbing out of bed.

As Suzy looked around the room for her clothes, John started to come to life and noticed his beautiful girl walking around her room naked. Suzy is a tall, lanky girl and a perfect match for John. Her fire-red hair flowed with curls that made her light green eyes sparkle in contrast.

"Oh baby," John said as he could feel the excitement rush back into him, "let's have some fun before I have to get out of here. I need to be cheered up before we head over to see Harold."

"No way, sir. If my daddy catches you in here or sees you walking down the road, he will know for sure you were playing with his daughter last night. Anyways, you mentioned last night about going to see Harold, but you never did tell me why," Suzy said as she stood over John naked.

"How am I supposed to tell you about what the boys and I are going to do as you stand over me looking so beautiful?" John questioned as he lifted the covers up for her to climb back in. "I'll tell you the entire story once you're back in bed and safe with me."

– – –

Rob rolled over on the couch to the sound of the TV going. It was 6:00 a.m. and he had hardly slept a wink. As Rob lay on the couch, all he could think of was Hanner and how his mother was doing.

Rob's mother worked the third shift out at the truck stop on Rural Route 71. She was the only source of income for the house since his father took his own life and never really could hold down a real job anyways. His father just couldn't keep it together after the Vietnam War and decided to take his own life one evening with a shotgun to the head.

Rob never really got over what his father did and seeing his bloody corpse changed him; it changed him deeply. Rob's emotions were uncontrollable at times and all he did was worry. If any person, he knew or any person in general showed any signs that they were not being themselves or sad for any reason whatsoever, Rob would worry about them.

That's what Rob was doing ever since their run-in the Hanner the night before—worrying about Hanner and his mother. There was something wrong with Hanner and he hated that his mother had to work third shift, but that is where she made extra money being the night shift manager.

Bam! The car door sounded as Rob's mother closed the door to the car. It was eight in the morning and Rob realized he just wasted the last two hours daydreaming as he stared into the crusted ceiling that lined the inside of the trailer that housed him and his mother.

"Oh, honey," Rob's mother said as she walked into trailer, "you know you can sleep in my bed when I'm not home."

"I know, Mom, but I just don't feel right. That's your bed and I want it to be nice and clean for when you crawl into it after a long night of working," Rob said. "Anyways, I just can't sleep in my room anymore."

"I know, honey, I know," Rob's mom said as she kissed him on his forehead. "You are so good to me, and I know you can't after what your father did."

"Why, Mom? Why did that coward have to blow his brains out in my room? Why?" Rob said as he slammed his fist down onto the coffee table causing his emptied pop cans to scatter.

"Rob, please don't call your father a coward, please," his mom begged as she ran her hands through his thick black hair.

"I'm sorry, Mom. I know. I know I should be proud of him since he fought for our country and stuff," Rob said as tears ran down his cheeks.

"I know it difficult, son. I know it is, but your father loved you, but he was a sick man—a sick man who was broken and couldn't be fixed. It happens to people, and some people aren't as strong as you and I are," Rob's mom explained as she gave her son a big bear hug. "Let's change the subject; what are your plans for the day?"

"Oh, me and the guys are going to visit Harold today," Rob replied to his mother who now was heading to her bedroom at the front of the trailer.

"That's nice, son. Please tell Harold that I said 'Hello' and you have fun today. I'll see you later and we can talk about your day," she concluded as she shut her bedroom door.

Rob lay on the couch until he could muster enough energy to take a shower. It was finally 10:00 a.m. and he headed for the shower. He tried to be as quiet as he could so not to wake up his mother. As the water dripped out of the shower head like a kinked hose, he daydreamed of better days for when he could get him and his mother out of the old white, rusted trailer they called home.

Chapter | 11

Harold glanced up from underneath the car he was working on, and the calendar that hung above his workbench caught his eye. He noticed it was getting closer to the end of summer and the anniversary of the twins.

"Damn," Harold said as he realized the time of year it was.

Harold crawled out from underneath the car and headed to the office for a drink. He couldn't get his mind wrapped around fixing the car with the sudden flashback of the twins. He grabbed a cold beer from the fridge and lit up a smoke to calm his wandering mind.

Harold walked out to the front of the auto shop, kicked over an old bucket he had, and started watching the town's people moseying by. *How lucky they are*, he thought to himself as he took a swig of his beer and flashes of the twins crossed his mind. "One of you poor suckers could have been them," he said out loud.

A slight mist flew from the top of the can as Harold cracked open another beer. "It's going to be one of those days, 10:00 a.m. and I'm on my second beer. Here's to ya," he said as he raised the beer to the sky. As Harold sat there on his bucket and watched the people of Walcott go on with their lives, he closed his reddened eyes and thought of that day.

— — —

A gray mask covered the sky that created a slippery mist that covered everything in sight. Harold knew his Chevy was going to have a hard time getting up the gravel road, but it sure beats walking his tools up to the star.

Harold fired up his old Chevy; him and his tools headed towards the gravel road that led up the side of the Hill. He came to a stop at the bottom of the Hill and jumped out to put the hubs into four-wheel drive. Nothing fancy here, no push button four-by-fours for this cat. *Good old work trucks are the best*, Harold thought. As Harold jumped back into his truck and reached down to pull the big four-wheel drive lever, he looked up the Hill and sat there in hesitation.

"I hate this fucking Hill," he said to the misty road he was about to travel. "I simply hate it, let's go," he said as he pushed the gas pedal down and started driving up the treacherous road. The truck bucked back and forth, wheels spinning, gravel flying as the truck slowly made the drive up the road. Harold's hands were as pale as he gripped the steering wheel with all his might. "Damn road! You can do it, truck. Don't lose your grip now. We need to fix the star," he mumbled between his clenched teeth while he guided the truck the best he could.

"Here we go," Harold said in relief as the gravel road started to lose its authority and the truck found its way. The road began to flatten and curved slightly to the right and faded away. A green, wet plateau lay to the right side of where the gravel road ended. Harold took a deep breath and pulled in all the oxygen he could hold. He let out a big sigh and tried to get his composure. Up ahead, in the green plateau was the grave. The only thing Harold was scared of—the grave on Stocker Hill.

The grave sat in the middle of the upper plateau. All alone it stood in a big, empty green space. It was outlined with large dark gray rocks—the color of death. Lying between the outline of rocks, the grave sat sunken into the ground a couple feet. At the bottom of the grave, the earth was black as night, black soot, a silky feeling dirt that held no signs of life. No weeds, bushes, or trees; no little animals, rodents, or squirrels—nothing lived in the dirt or dared to touch it. Anything in its surroundings knew to stay away from the grave.

Harold pulled his truck off the gravel road into the green plateau, just to the right of the grave. The plateau is surrounded by several large white rocks that are placed just at the edge of the green landing just in front of the woods. The white rocks mimicked seating, as if to hold an audience, as if the grave was the stage. Harold parked his truck and looked out of his front windshield in awe.

"What the hell is that?" he said as he shut the engine down. Harold climbed out of his truck and started walking slowly towards the rocks. As he got closer to the rocks, the blood rushed from his face and he started to shake, shake in fear of what he was looking at. "Oh my God, dear Lord, please no…!" Harold screamed in terror as he dropped to his knees and vomited in disgust.

Harold slowly got his composure, picked his pale body up off the ground and slowly walked toward the rocks. There, directly in front of him were the Drucker twins, disemboweled, sliced from their pelvis up to their throats. The white rocks were covered, covered in blood and pools of it had gathered at the base of the bodies. Blood splatter was everywhere, and it could be seen all over the green grass causing the grass to lose its vibrant color. As Harold looked in awe at the gutted bodies of the boys, the look on their faces was something Harold would never recover from—Brian and Doug Drucker were smiling as their gray, dead eyes stared up into the sky.

A cool breeze blew across the green plateau and wakened Harold from his trance. "Holy shit!" Harold barked as he turned and hightailed it away from the bodies. Harold started his truck, whipped around the grave and left tire marks through the plateau. As he frantically drove down the Hill, Harold reached for the CB radio and called for help. "Sheriff! Sheriff! I need your help! please help me!" Harold yelled into the CB radio as he maneuvered his truck back down the gravel road. "I need your help…," he whimpered again into the CB.

"Hanner here," the sergeant bellowed into the mic. "What is your problem Harold?"

"Hanner, Sheriff, the Drucker twins, they're, they're…," mumbled Harold as he slammed on the brakes to stop his truck at the bottom of Stocker Hill.

"For crying out loud," Hanner yelled as his patience started to boil over, "spit it out, Harold. What about the Druckers?"

"They're fucking dead!" Harold yelled back into the CB before he laid his head and hands on the steering wheel.

The gray mist that lay in the valley of Stocker Hill had become ever so eerie as the wail of Hanner's sirens blasted away in the distance. Every second that passed, the sirens slowly got louder. Harold sat in his truck waiting for Hanner to arrive. Harold was hoping no one from the town would arrive before Hanner did—he did not have the strength to explain what was going on, but the noise Hanner was making with his sirens was inviting everyone to come and play. Someone was sure to show up.

"Jack, you there? It's Hanner. Come in Jack," Hanner said into the CB as he raced toward Harold and the Hill. Jack was Hanner's side project. He was sculpting him to take over the town's funeral home along with him being his protégé Deputy Sheriff.

"I'm here, Hanner," replied Jack, "just typing up some reports in the office."

"You need to get to the base of Stocker Hill, Harold's out there and freaking out about something," Hanner replied into the CB as he made the turn off of Route 12 towards the town and out to the Hill.

"Got it, boss," Jack came back as he heard the sirens blasting in the background. With one leap, he was out of his chair, grabbing the keys and heading out the door to his truck. Jack jumped into his Blazer, started the truck, and reached down to the dashboard and flipped on the sirens.

"What is that?" Harold said as he looked up from the steering wheel. "Sirens—more sirens," he stated as he heard another set of sirens heading his way. "Hanner must have called Jack."

"Oh man, I knew it, I knew it," Harold said, wiping the sweat from his brow as he saw Dory approaching on his 4-wheeler.

"Holy shit, Harold, you sure are pale. Are you okay?" Dory said as he jumped off his 4-wheeler. "You must be the cause of all this ruckus."

Dory was a local guy, born and raised in the area and knew everything about everything. He was the owner and bartender of Lock 17 Tavern & Burger, being the town's bartender also made Dory the town's priest. He's heard everything.

"It's nothing, Dory. Go back in your hole," Harold shot back.

"Back in my hole?" Dory replied with disgust. "This coming from the guy who was crying on my shoulder the other night at the tavern."

"Sorry, but it's nothing, Dory, really, it's nothing," Harold said back to Dory as the sirens got closer.

"Well, Harold, something is obviously wrong. The sirens are getting closer, and you are sitting here at the bottom of the Hill looking like a ghost—I'm going up!" Dory stated as he hightailed it back to his 4-wheeler and headed up the gravel road.

"No, Dory, no, Dory, please, please—don't!" Harold yelled at Dory as he jumped out of his truck and chased after him.

Before Harold could get a grip on what just happened, Dory was on his way up the Hill, and Jack and Hanner were pulling up to where Harold was standing.

"What is up with you and who just went up the Hill?" Hanner asked Harold.

"Dory, Dory went up the Hill to see what was going on," Harold replied.

"Well… spit it out, boy!" Hanner demanded.

In his utterly shaky voice, Harold replied, "The Drucker twins… I found them… I found them dead up by the star."

"What did you say? You said the Drucker twins are dead?" Jack blurted out before Hanner had a chance to.

"They are gutted up on the Hill—they are gutted up on Stocker Hill. Do you understand what I am saying to you? They are dead!" Harold yelled out to Hanner and Jack in a voice filled with fear.

"Jack, Jack, let's get up that Hill now!" yelled Hanner. "We are taking your truck. My car won't make it."

Jack and Hanner jumped into Jack's Blazer and raced up the Hill. Harold stood at the bottom of the Hill and watched the two officers blaze a trail through the misty air on their way to the top of Stocker Hill.

– – –

"Excuse me, excuse me, mister," an elderly woman called out to Harold. "Can you help me, sir?"

"Huh?" Harold mumbled.

"Excuse me, sir, I have a flat tire. Can you help me please?" she repeated in an annoyed voice.

"What? What?" Harold stammered, dropping his empty beer can as he was jolted back to consciousness. "Sure, yes, ma'am, whatever you need. I am here to help."

"Are you sure you're capable of helping me?" the elderly lady replied as she handed Harold her car keys.

Chapter | 12

It was a little past 1:00 a.m. and Hanner's unconscious body swung back and forth to the rhythm of the breeze. The breeze was flowing through the valley while bringing along the cool air that lay at the base of the Hill. Hanner was out cold on the swing and his evening drink fell to the ground without him even noticing it.

Martha rolled over and could feel the emptiness in her bed. It was becoming a nightly occurrence; no matter if Hanner was in bed with her or not, he was somewhere else. His body was there, but his mind was adrift.

As she made her way down the old creaky stairs, she could see her husband fast asleep on the swing in the back of the house. "Oh dear," Martha said with a sound of concern, "he is going to catch a cold being out there and all this worrying he's doing is not good for his health. He's getting too old for this."

As Martha's foot hit the main floor, the phone rang with utter violence, *ring! ring!* The bellowed rings from the phone made it almost fall off the little stand it called home. "Oh my," Martha blurted out as she gained her composure and crawled back into her skin that she just leapt out of. "Hello, may I help you?" Martha said into the phone, "Oh, hello, Jack, you scared the bajesus out of me. You need him, don't you?"

"Please, Martha. It's Mrs. Meyer. She is on her last leg and they want Hanner to come out," Jack replied.

"Okay, let me get him," Martha said as she put the phone down on the stand and headed out back to get her husband.

Hanner's body began to twitch as he dreamed of the day of the twins. The sky was covered with a gray blanket with a slight mist in the air. The grass was green and slippery, Hanner could hardly keep his balance as he weaved his way through the woods toward the grave. "Hanner, Hanner, Buck, Buck," he heard the wind whispering to him through the trees as he walked up to the grave. "Hanner, Hanner, Buck, Buck," He heard again as he stood over the grave and his—

"What, what! Hanner yelped.

"Hanner, Hanner," Martha said as she shook his shoulder. "You're wanted on the phone. It's Jack, it's about Mrs. Meyer."

"Okay, okay, I'll be right there," Hanner said after he realized what he was dreaming about, and that Martha saved him from seeing the ending of that terrible nightmare.

"Jack," Martha said into the phone, "he will be right here." Martha strolled back upstairs and crawled into her sanctuary.

"Hello, Jack," Hanner said into the phone with an annoyance that would stop any killer in their tracks. "What is it?"

"It's Mrs. Meyer, the family wants us to head up there. They think that tonight is the night," Jack replied.

"Yeah, like last weekend and the weekend before that. She is not going to die tonight," Hanner replied. "I'm not going out there."

"You must, Hanner. You must," Jack insisted. "The Meyers have a lot of pull in this town and the people listen to what they have to say. If we don't go out there, it will be the talk of the town."

"What would they have to say? What? It's not like Stan is the Pope or something. Screw them!" Hanner yelled into the phone. "Before you say it, I am heading that way now," Hanner finished saying to Jack as he wondered where he put the keys to the hearse.

Hanner jumped into the hearse that was overwhelmed with the musty smell of death. Early that week, he had to go out towards Lock 17 and retrieve the body of a drifter that was found along the road. "I hate driving this beast. I don't know why I'm still doing this. The older I get the worse this job becomes," he said to himself.

Hanner made the fifteen-minute drive out to the Meyer's place and could see several cars parked all over the grounds. Jack was already there and was shooting the shit with one of the leeches waiting for old Mrs. Meyer to pass.

As Hanner backed up the hearse all he could think of was the past three weeks of this same routine and she always made it through the night. Hanner gripped the steering wheel to the big boat and tried to get his composure. The thoughts of death filled his mind. *Die, die, die* echoed through his brain. *"Die!"* is what the car door said to him as he slammed it shut.

"Looks like another false alarm, Hanner," Jack said as Hanner's feet hit the porch. "She's getting better, and the doctor and family think she's going to make it through the night."

"Great. Just great," Hanner replied. *"Die, die, die"* was what Hanner heard as everyone in the house said hello and thanked him for coming out.

"Thanks so much for coming out," Mr. Meyer said as he shook Hanner's hand with his soft, manicured hands.

"No problem, Stan. No problem at all," Hanner replied as he thought to himself of how he could lose this girl to this wuss of a man—he never worked a day in his life. "Can I see her?"

"Sure, sure, go right in. She's resting comfortably," Stan said as he showed Hanner into the room. "Don't mind the machine beeping—it's monitoring her heart and running the ventilator. She's doing good, though."

"Thank you. Thank you so much," Hanner said as Stan closed the door behind him. Hanner walked up close to the bed and looked over at all the equipment keeping Gail alive. As he stood next to the machine, he noticed the volume button and turned it down so that the beeping sound was a faint blip in the dark.

"Gail, Gail," Hanner whispered, "Gail, Gail, tonight's the night. I'll see you on the other side." And without hesitation, he unplugged the machine.

Chapter | 13

It was Saturday morning and the sun glistened over Central Park. The kids had started to gather, and a few pickup basketball games had begun. Life was generally pleasant on that Saturday morning for the town of Walcott and the park awaited the arrival of the boys.

Rob was the first to arrive at the park and found a seat on a lonely old park bench off to the side. As Rob admired the park bench, he was about to call home for a while, he couldn't figure out what was worse—the park bench or the decrepit trailer that him and his mom called home. As Rob sat down, the bench let out a whale of a creak that almost stopped everyone in Central Park in their tracks. "What was that?" Rob barked back at the bench. "I can see it's going to be one of those days."

Reed was happily strolling down the street as he crossed paths with John.

"What's up, little snapper head?" John cheerfully yelled out to Reed.

"Living the dream, buddy, just living the dream," Reed replied with a grin on his face.

"I see you're all smiley this morning." John answered back. "Is your grin the same grin that I have on my face?"

"You mean the, 'I just got some loving last night' grin?" Reed replied with a smirk as he held his fingers up in the quotation mark manner.

John came back with the same finger quotation gesture, "No, sir. My grin is from the double-dip action."

"Double-dip action?" Reed asked.

"You know; the late-night hurrah and the wham-bam thank you SUZY!" John bellowed out for the entire town of Walcott to hear.

"Thank you, Suzy," Reed giggled out.

"What did you do last night besides Krista?" John asked.

"Well, after I left Krista's house, I found a dog stuck in a trap," Reed responded. "Cute little guy, named him Buster."

"How did Bill and Katherine take having you bring home another pesky animal?" John asked.

"Who said I brought the dog home?"

"Come on!" barked John.

"So far so good. If they only knew the little shit pissed all over the place last night, things might be different," Reed replied.

John and Reed continued their stroll toward the park and chatted about nothing in particular, but they had a sense of excitement about meeting up with Harold.

Brad arrived at the park to find a couple basketball games happening and the young ones scampering around. He said his typical hellos, shook a few hands, and messed up a few of the little kid's hair with his powerful hands. The kids scurried away giggling, pointing, and yelling at each other, "He didn't get me, he didn't get me, ha ha…!" Brad loved messing with the kids. They are so innocent and full of life.

As Brad leaned against a big oak tree watching the basketball game that was happening, he noticed Reed and John walking toward him and waved them over in his direction.

"What's up, Mr. Bradmeister?" John dragged out as he and Brad bumped fists.

"Just suffering from a hangover and waiting for you losers to make an appearance," Brad replied as he wiped the sweat off his brow in an overacting manner.

"Where's Rob?" asked Reed. "Have you seen him yet?"

"Nope, nope—Hey! There he is," Brad replied, pointing in Rob's direction.

Reed and John looked in the direction Brad was pointing, and they could see Rob sitting alone on the park bench. They all knew Rob was having a tough time dealing with life in general but didn't want to stir the pot.

The boys headed towards Rob, and Brad murmured, "You notice Rob is hardly his 'know it all full of shit' self lately?"

"Yep," Reed replied. "Maybe he just needs a little sense of adventure."

"Well, he's going to get it, real soon," John answered back.

The boys met up with Rob at the bench and bullshitted about last night's adventures. It was peaking at noon at the park and the sun was at full blaze. The boys moseyed around a little and then headed to Harold's garage. There was a sense of excitement in the air.

Chapter | 14

It was 4:00 a.m. in the morning and Hanner pulled the hearse into the garage. Hanner had a slight giddy up in his step as he swung the back door to the hearse open and waited for Jack to arrive to help him unload this evening's body.

Hanner waited for a moment, and he could feel the tension leaving his body as he strolled to the garage fridge for a beer. *Crack!* said the beer can as Hanner opened it and a small evil smile whispered across Hanner's face as he took a big swig of the beer.

Jack's drive to the morgue after Gail Meyer had just passed was filled with utter emptiness. The evening was darker than usual, and the breeze had an eerie chillness even though it was still summer. "I can't believe what just happened?" Jack said to himself as he drove his squad car down the road, "one moment we were sad, and I was calling Hanner and then the doctor telling us all was well."

Jack got closer and closer to the morgue and was still contemplating the night's events. "Sad, happy, death. Death? What the f...?" Jack said while holding off on slinging swear words as he drove by Walcott's elegant church. Jack's last glimpse off Main Street before he took a right down morgue road was the church. "Something is wrong," Jack murmured as the church disappeared from sight. "Something is definitely wrong."

Jack pulled his squad car into the carport and sat there in the darkness for a moment. The sound of the engine running put Jack into a trance and his mind went blank. As he stared out of the front windshield, he caught a glimpse of Hanner moving about in the garage which brought him out of his daze, and he shut the engine down in his car. His squad car sputtered for a moment and then let out a big wheeze. Jack looked at the car as he climbed out of it, "You sound like death too."

"What?" yelled out Hanner.

"Nothing," Jack replied as he headed up the driveway into the garage.

"Okay."

As Jack walked up the drive into the garage and past the hearse, he noticed a smirk on Hanner's face that made his skin crawl. An evil smirk, as if, *you just got away with something and no one knows.*

"What's with the smile, Hanner?" Jack said to his boss.

"What smile?" Hanner replied.

"The smile that is on your fucking face. That smile," Jack responded in a pissy tone.

Hanner snapped back, "First of all, watch what you fucking say to me, Jack. Second, I don't have a smile on my face. It is called 'I slammed a few beers waiting for your ass to get here and I am a bit relaxed now.'"

"Sorry, sir, just a tad on edge," Jack answered back, lowering his head.

"What did you say?" Hanner snapped again even though he heard Jack the first time.

Jack replied to Hanner with a little more authority, "Sorry, sir, didn't mean any disrespect." In Jack's mind, he meant all the disrespect in the world, and he knew something was awry.

"Okay, Jack. I understand, a long night for all. I mean, damn, she died in my presence. That threw me for a loop too. I know I was grouchy on the phone earlier about heading out there, but I didn't really want her to pass on. She was a nice lady," Hanner spewed on in a pleasant voice trying to put Jack at ease.

"No problem, sir," Jack answered, "let's get Gail into the morgue. I'm ready to head home."

Jack and Hanner pulled Gail's body out of the back of the hearse. The wheels and legs of the gurney fell to the ground with a squeak that ran up Jack's spine. As they wheeled the gurney into the freight elevator, all Jack could think of was how the evening was just a little too eerie for him to handle. All the sounds of that night were frightening.

Jack hated going into the basement of the morgue, especially through the freight elevator. *This place is so creepy, and I am always afraid the doors won't open*, Jack thought on the way down to the basement. *Imagine getting stuck in this elevator with a dead Mrs. Meyer and Hanner. No thank you….*

The elevator hit the basement floor with a thud and the gurney's legs gave out. The jolt was enough to send Gail Meyers corpse off the gurney and onto the floor. Jack let out an "Oh God!" in fright and the shock sent Hanner crashing against the elevator doors as they were opening. He lost his balance and landed on the basement floor.

"Holy shit!" Hanner let out as he hit the concrete floor.

Jack lost all his calm, "What was that? I am telling you, ever since she passed tonight, this night has become really creepy. The dark night, the wind, the church, your smirk."

As Hanner picked himself up off the floor, he replied back to Jack, "Simmer down, buddy. Everything is fine, just a glitch in the system. Anyways, you always get spooked around dead bodies."

As Jack was about to respond back to Hanner, they both heard a clanking sound coming from the elevator.

"We have a problem," Hanner blurted out.

As Jack turned to look at what Hanner was cursing about, he saw the elevator doors opening and closing on Mrs. Meyer's dead head.

"Oh my…," said Jack as he ran to the garbage can to vomit.

As Jack retched his guts out into the awaiting garbage can; Hanner walked over to Gail's body and pulled it out of the elevator then dragged it along the basement floor to the awaiting embalming table. "Come on, Jack," Hanner said, "get your shit together and help me lift her up onto the table."

Jack walked over to the sink near the table and ran cool water all over his face. Once he had his poise back, he helped Hanner lift Gail's body onto the table and headed toward the stairs to get out of the basement as fast as possible. There was no way in hell he was going to ride in that elevator again. Before Jack hit the stairs, Hanner barked out to him, "You tell anyone about what happened here tonight, you'll be the next one on this table!"

After Jack had left the basement, Hanner began the embalming process on the motionless body. No need for an autopsy, everyone knew she was dying. As Hanner watched the blood draining from Gail's body, he could not help but notice how good of a mood he was in and wondered how long it was going to last.

Chapter | 15

The walk to Harold's garage was an uneventful one. The sun peaking and the boys had hardly talked at all. The sense of excitement and intensity had wavered away with the wind off of Stocker Hill and the mood had changed to nervousness.

"Hey, guys," Brad said, breaking the silence that had engulfed the boys, "no mentioning this to my pop."

"Mentioning what to your pop?" Rob replied.

"What we're doing, going to see Harold about Stocker Hill and stuff," Brad responded.

"Oh, yeah, no, no—no mentioning this to the Ps," Rob stammered as he thought of the worry it would put his mother through. "Anyways, I'm not scared at all."

"Who said anything about being scared?" Brad asked.

"Well, I am a tad nervous," Reed said.

"No shit. Reed a tad nervous? Tell me something I don't know. Relax, guys, relax," Brad annoyingly replied.

"Brad don't be a dick," John said, as if to let everyone know he was still there.

The boys continued their stroll towards the garage and decided to stop at the local Goshen Dairy for a drink and a hot dog. They were minutes away from Harold's garage and no one spoke as they shoveled in the hot dogs and slammed their sodas.

BBBBUUUURRRRRPPPP! Reed bellowed out a huge belch.

"Damn!" John replied as he choked down the last bites of his hot dog.

"Perfect timing," Brad said as he smiled and took a swig of his drink.

A noise started rumbling from Rob's gut and all the boys were looking at him. His belly was shaking, and he couldn't get a word out. At first the guys thought he was choking, but the noise changed to a giggle and then to a full-out laugh. Soon, all the boys were in a full belly laugh that they could not control.

"We needed that," John said after they all got their composure.

"Sure did," Rob replied. "And, guys, I really am not scared."

"Really am not scared?" Brad sparked. "And you don't go to school on that small yellow bus, do you?"

Reed started giggling again and they were all full of laughter again. The nervous tension had subsided, and the excitement of the adventure ahead had returned.

The boys left the Goshen Dairy and made the short trek over to Harold's garage. As they rounded the corner, they saw Harold drinking a beer and watching the people of Walcott walk by.

"This is great, guys," Brad exclaimed. "He's probably already half in the bag, which means we're going to get some free brewskis."

"Awesome," Reed bellowed back, "I could use a pick-me-up myself."

John spoke up too. "I bet we can get him on a roll, and he'll spew all the info we need."

Rob didn't say much at all; he just followed the boys through the parking lot up to the garage.

"Hey, boys." Harold said through his glassy, bloodshot eyes.

"You don't mind if we grab a few beers, do ya?" Brad asked.

"Help yourself," Harold replied as he motioned his hand in the air.

The boys went to the back of the garage to the fridge and helped themselves to Harold's finest—a few Old Milwaukee's. They really didn't care what kind of beer Harold had as long as it was cold and free. As the boys sat in the back drinking their beers, they could not keep themselves from looking around and taking in the full history of the garage. Harold's garage had been in the center of Walcott for as long as there have been cars on the road. Full off history, WWI and II, the return of Stan Stocker, the British evasion of the Beatles, the Mustang from Ford—just full of history.

"Can you imagine how many different cars and people have ventured through this place?" Reed said as he cracked another one of Harold's beers.

"You're not getting all sentimental on us again are you, Reed?" Brad asked as he tossed a few cold ones to Rob and John.

"Me? Sentimental?" Reed replied.

"Hey, guys," John said as he motioned to the front of the garage, "let's get Harold back here and get him talking. Hey, Harold, come have a beer with us."

Harold stumbled up off the bucket he was sitting on at the front of the garage and made his way back into the garage to where the boys were. He had well over a six-pack in him and was sick of daydreaming about the Drucker twins.

"Toss me a cold one and get out of my chair," Harold barked out as Rob scooted out of his chair and stood next to the fridge. "What brings you boys out here beside the free beer?"

The boys sat there without saying a word. Every one of them took a sip of their beers waiting for one of the other guys to jump in and get the conversation rolling.

After a moment or two of silence, Harold spoke up. "Well? Cat got all your tongues? Okay, I am going to go talk to a man about a horse and the four of you can pull your heads out of your asses while I'm gone."

Harold headed off to the greasy bathroom at the back of the shop while the boys watched him walk away.

"Let's get out of here," Rob said as the door shut behind Harold.

"No way. One of us has to get this conversation rolling," Brad said pointing in Reed's general direction. "Reed, start talking."

"What? Why me?" Reed followed while pointing to himself.

"Because everyone likes you Reed and Harold does too," Brad replied.

As Reed stood there in place and contemplated what to do and say next, Harold marched out of the bathroom and headed back to where all the boys were standing. As Harold sat down in his chair, he asked, "So, anyone get any balls in this group yet? This is not like you boys; you always have something to say. You want me to get you some beer? You boys need money? Just standing there looking at me like I'm a f'ing idiot is not helping my confidence," Harold snapped at Brad to get him another beer, as he motioned he was drinking something with his empty hand.

"We want to know about Hanner and Stocker Hill!" John blurted out.

"Damn… I knew this day was going to come," Harold replied as he let out a big sigh and ran his hands under his greasy ball cap. "Sit down, boys. We are going to be here awhile."

Chapter | 16

The wind running through Walcott had a brisk sense to it. It hit Jack's face with a rush as he walked out of the basement of the morgue. Jack's short trip to his squad car was filled with fear and anxiety, vomiting and disbelief. Jack leaned up against his car and tried to understand what had just happened and spoke to the wind that was rushing past his face. "Did Hanner actually threaten me tonight? Really?"

After Jack sat against his car for a while and had gone over the night's events, he climbed into his car and headed out of town. He drove past the town's main church and past the Goshen Dairy and flew past Harold's garage. The in-town speed limit was 35 mph, but Jack was well past that by the time he got to the edge of town and headed up Route 36.

"Martha. Martha should know something about what's going on with Hanner. I have some time before he'll be done with Mrs. Meyer's body," Harold mumbled underneath his breath as his Crown Vic picked up some speed as he headed to Hanner's house.

– – –

Martha couldn't fall back asleep since she woke Hanner about Mrs. Meyer. Her thoughts raced wondering what was going on and if her husband was doing okay.

The sun was just about to make its daily appearance over the Hill, but it couldn't find the energy as of yet. Martha stood at the sink and watched the sun struggling over the tops of the trees. The coffee maker was percolating, and the smell of fresh, brewed coffee was encapsulating the house.

Martha made her way back upstairs to get herself cleaned up for the day ahead. She knew Buck would be home soon and she should be ready to make him some breakfast. She drew herself a bath and eased her old body into the warm water. As she soaped up the sponge, the sunlight snuck through the shades and glistened Martha's gray hair. Martha dipped her head under the water to rinse her hair and face, but swore she heard some movement downstairs. "Buck, Buck, is that you, darling?" she yelled from the tub.

Jack pulled into Hanner's driveway just as the sun started to peak over the Hill. He shut off his car and headed towards the front door. Jack knocked briskly on the front oak door and heard or saw no movement. "Come on, Martha. I know you're in there," he said as he hit the front door again. On his last hit, the front door jarred open, and the scent of freshly brewed coffee engulfed his nostrils. "Martha, Martha, you in there?" he asked hesitantly as the door swung open. "Martha?"

Jack slowly walked into Hanner's house and looked around. He could hear the coffee percolating in the kitchen. As he slowly tipped-toed farther into the house, he could hear Martha rummaging around upstairs. "Oh," Jack said to himself and then blurted out, "Martha, it's Jack, I'm going to get a cup of coffee." Jack walked into the kitchen and helped himself.

Martha, not hearing any response, climbed out of the tub cautiously. She wrapped her rather large grandma body in a towel and peaked out of the bathroom door and listened carefully. As she tipped-toed out of the bathroom into the hallway, she looked down the stairs and saw that the front door open. "Buck, is that you?" she asked in a shaky voice. "Buck?"

Martha turned around and headed to the master bedroom. She went to Buck's side of the bed and grabbed the pistol he had in his nightstand. She sat on the side of the bed and tried to hold back the tears. All she could think of is what Buck had told her, *Point and shoot, Martha, that is all you have to do, is point and shoot.*

Trying to get her composure was difficult for Martha to do. Tears ran down her face as she slowly slid on her robe and grabbed the gun up off the bed. Her voice was shaky when she bellowed out, "Buck?" Nothing, no sound coming from anywhere except the distant sound of the peculating coffee and then there was a sound from the kitchen. "What was that?" Martha said. "They're going through my stuff."

"Damn it," Jack said as he took a sip of the hot coffee and dropped the full cup of coffee on the floor. "Martha is going to kill me." Jack leaned down and wiped the coffee up off the floor with the towel he grabbed off the counter.

Jack threw the damp coffee-soaked towel into the sink and poured himself a new cup of coffee. Jack headed back to the kitchen table, grabbed some cream off the counter and began doctoring up his coffee to perfection.

Jack looked up from taking a sip of coffee as he heard some creaking coming from the hallway floor. "It must be Martha," he said to himself as he looked toward the hallway. Jack kept his gaze toward the hallway since he figured she should have been to the kitchen by now. He pushed himself away from the table just as Martha came around the corner from the hallway.

Bam, bam, bam! The gun echoed through the kitchen as fast as the bullets could exit the gun that Martha held in her hand.

Chapter | 17

The boys grabbed anything they could to sit on as they anticipated the story that was going to flow from Harold's mouth. Reed grabbed the bucket Harold was sitting on that now sat vacant at the front of the shop. Brad found another bucket and Rob grabbed one of the rolling stools that sat around the shop. John was so excited that he just leaned up against the old fridge and maintained Harold with a supply of beer.

"So, you boys want to know about the Drucker murders?" Harold asked as he cleared his voice.

"No, not the murders, we want to know about Hanner and the Hill," Reed said.

Brad chimed in, "Unless the murders have to do with Hanner; we'll want to know about that too."

"Umm, umm," Harold coughed as he tried to clear his voice again. "You see, boys, something major happened to Hanner and his friends."

"Hanner and his friends?" John asked in desperation. "What friends?"

Harold shot a look at John that put a chill in the air. The boys were all tense and so was Harold. Harold grabbed his cap and lifted it off his head, let out a big sigh as he rubbed his hair again. As Harold put his ball cap back onto his head, he looked over at John and mouthed, "Shut the fuck up!"

All the boys looked over at John; Reed put his finger up to his mouth and shushed John, Brad threw his hands up and tilted his head in disgust, and Rob sat on the rolling stool watching this all taking place while mesmerized by the look on Harold's face.

"If I could continue—someone get me another goddamn beer—there were four of them with that day, that day up on the Hill," Harold began, speaking about Stocker Hill and what went on. He began….

"It was Buck, Bill, Slick, and Dory. Not much different than you boys. Just a bunch of guys looking to have fun, drink some beer, chase some tail. You know, all in a day's fun. The boys loved to mess with Old Man Stocker. He owned the Hill and everything with it. They'd go up there and sneak around Stocker's barn, move his tools around, unhook the plugs on the tractor, put bales of hay in front of the barn door so he couldn't get in—fun stuff to mess with him. Boy, did Stan Stocker get pissed, though. The boys would watch from a distance and just crack up, about pee themselves with laughter. This one-day, Old Man Stocker was all riled up and pulled out his salt gun and took shots at us. I mean, took shots at the boys."

"Wait a minute," Reed said as he was catching a beer that John tossed him from the fridge. "Who is us?"

Harold came out with, "I did not say us—I said the boys."

"No, no, no…," Brad ran on.

"You said us," Reed shot back.

"Who is us?" Rob barked in.

John just sat there. No way he was going to speak up after Harold bit his head off with the friends' comments.

"Okay, okay, you got me, I said us," Harold came back like a beaten old dog. "I did not intend this to go this way, but with these beers in me, you boys are going to get the full truth and nothing but the truth."

Brad spoke up after he saw the defeat in Harold's face. "All right, spill the beans, who is us? You have Buck, who is Hanner;

you have Dory, who lives at the bottom of Stockers; who are Slick and Bill?"

"Slick is me. I'm Slick. It was my nickname because I was always messing with cars. Racing cars. Working on cars. Anything to do with cars," Harold went on to explain.

Before Harold could get anything else out of his mouth, Reed jumped in with, "Who is Bill? Harold? Who is Bill?"

"Funny you should say that, *REEEEED.*" Harold drew out Reed's name to make a point.

Reed looked at Harold like a deer in headlights. It was not just computing. Reed scrunched up his eyes for a second and then slowly opened them wider and wider. So wide that all the light in the room was sucked into Reed's big, blue eyes. "My dad?" Reed finally said.

"BINGO!" shouted Harold as he got up out of his chair and walked to the fridge to get another beer, but realized he was still grasping a fresh cold one in his dingy hand.

"Wait, this does not make sense. You, my dad, Dory, and Hanner were buds?" asked Reed. "Wait, this has never been mentioned to me whatsoever by my father, by my dad, by Bill."

As Reed sat there contemplating what was just told to him and the other boys were gazing at him, Reed blurted out, "This does not make sense! Why wouldn't this ever be brought up? Brought up that you were all friends."

"Were. That is the word that you need to emphasize—WERE," Harold said back to Reed as Reed sat there in utter amazement. "We decided a long time ago that the best thing is not to talk about what happened. In doing so, it also ruined the friendship we had. Still friends—just not like it was."

"Talk about what?" Brad said.

"What I am about to tell you," Harold replied.

Chapter | 18

Hanner looked up from his gaze as the morning sunlight crested through the blinds that hid the morgue from the outside. Hanner was finished with the embalming process and started to prepare Gail's body for the next phase of death.

Hanner walked over to the sink, hooked up the hose and got the water running. "Need to get going here. Too much time wasted with this bitch. Martha is going to be all up in arms on how much time I've wasted tonight," Hanner bellowed out as he grabbed the soap and began to wash Gail's body.

An hour went by, and Hanner found himself in a daze again. His mind was wandering, and he couldn't concentrate. Gail's cold body laid motionless on the stainless-steel table, and she had areas of dried soap that weren't washed off. "Son of a bitch," Hanner yelled as he turned on the water on again. "What is going on with me?" Hanner finished rinsing off the body, dried it off and put it in a locker. "There you go, Gail. Stay there until I have time to fix your face," Hanner said as the locker door shut.

After a quick bathroom break, Hanner washed up and headed out the door. The sun was pushing up into the sky and Hanner did not get any sleep that night. He fired up the old squad car to head home and realized something, a sick sense, a sick sense of accomplishment.

"Why do I feel so good right now?" he asked himself as he pulled onto the road and headed home.

Before he knew it, Hanner's car had brought him home. As he drove up the driveway to the house, the gravel underneath the tires was crackling with conversation as he noticed Jack's squad car sitting close to the house. "What in the world is he doing here?" Hanner said as his car finally came to a stop behind Jack's car. "Seems like he might have missed what I said earlier."

Hanner walked to the front of the house and could hear weeping coming from inside. As Hanner slowly opened the front door, the smell of gun powder rushed his nostrils, and the weeping was coming from the kitchen. Hanner picked up the pace towards the kitchen as he yelled out, "Martha? Martha? You there?"

Martha moaned, "Oh, Buck. I thought we had an intruder; he didn't let me know he was here. I was scared. I got the gun."

Buck rounded the corner and found his wife lying on the kitchen floor in a pool of tears. On the other side of the kitchen near the table lay Jack's body lying motionless on the floor. "It's okay," Buck said slowly to Martha as he knelt next to Jack's body.

"Is he dead?" Martha asked.

"Hold on, Martha. I am checking that now," Hanner replied to his frightened wife.

Hanner reached down towards Jack's neck and felt for a pulse. As Hanner's hands touched Jack's neck, Hanner let out a gasp, "Oh boy!"

"What? What? What is it?" Martha shouted.

"He's warm and has a pulse," Buck replied as he thought that life would be easier if Jack was dead.

"Oh, thank the Lord!" Martha cried with excitement, "I couldn't live with myself if I killed Jack."

Hanner got up from Jack's body and noticed he lost a lot of blood based on what was on the floor and now all over his pant leg. "I'm going to go call for help. See if we can get an ambulance out here right away," Hanner said as we walked towards the phone in the hallway. As Hanner walked to the phone, in no particular rush, all he could hope for was the ambulance taking too long and Jack dying on the floor.

Hanner walked back into the kitchen and told Martha the ambulance was on its way. It took all of Hanner's energy to pull his emotionally wrecked wife up off the floor and get her into a seat at the kitchen table. "So, what happened here?" he asked his wife and as they both looked on at Jack lying on the floor.

"Well," Martha started off, "I was worried about you, and I couldn't sleep. I was fumbling around the kitchen and decided to get cleaned up for the day ahead, for you. When I was upstairs, I heard something, something coming from downstairs. I called out and no one answered. I got scared. I got the gun and *bam*... I shot Jack."

"Did you realize it was Jack when you started shooting?" Hanner asked as he admired the few bullet holes spattered throughout the wall.

"No. All I did was point and shoot. Point and shoot, just like the way you taught me," Martha said as she began to weep again.

That faint sound of sirens shouted from the distance. The sirens got louder and louder, as the ambulance raced towards Martha and Buck's place.

"I sure hope they're not too late," Martha said as she put her head in her hands again.

In too fast of a response, Hanner bellowed out before he could catch himself, "I do!"

Chapter | 19

The boys sat in anticipation of what words were going to flow from Harold's mouth next after they learned Reed's dad was part of the story.

"Makes sense now," Reed said out loud as he gazed at the floor.

"What makes sense?" Harold replied.

"Well," Reed began to say, "this morning my pa got upset with me."

"My Pa? My Pa? Since when do you call your dad, you're 'Pa'?" Brad blurted out.

John jumped in, "Leave him alone Brad. If he wants to call his father Pa, then so be it."

"Father?" Brad said, snickering, "Oh Father, please pass me the Grey Poupon. What the fuck has come over you guys?"

"Knock it off," Harold hollered. "You want to hear this or not? And Reed, why was your dad upset?"

"Because I told him we were coming to see you about Hanner, and he got all upset," Reed replied.

Harold got up from his seat and walked towards Reed. Harold bent down slightly to look Reed right square in the eyes. As he sat there for a moment, a large gulp came from Reed as he tried not to break eye contact. Harold lifted his finger and poked Reed right in the middle of his chest and asked him, "You sure you can handle what you are about to hear, boy?"

Reed nodded his head in approval as he pushed Harold's hand off his chest. Harold slowly turned around and walked back to where he came from. All the boys were staring at Reed at this moment in time and the drip from the sink echoed through the shop.

Harold took another big swig of his beer as the boys looked on in desperation, desperation at the story that Harold was about to spill. Harold looked at the boys, shook his head in disapproval, and began to speak.

"It was a day none like today is. All of us were inseparable, Buck, Bill, Dory, and me. As I was saying before, Old Man Stocker was so pissed at us this one day that he took a shot at us with his salt gun. Scared the living shit out of us and we ran. While we were hightailing out of there, that son of bitch took another shot at us and grazed your pa's ass. He yelped like a little girl and started running faster. We could hardly keep up. We lost Dory as Buck and I tried to keep up with Bill. When we finally caught up to Bill, there he stood, alone, in the middle of the green plateau and next to the…."

Harold hesitated for a second.

"Goddamn it, Harold," John blurted out after being quiet most of the time. "Bill was standing next to what?"

"The grave!" Harold stated.

The boy's stomachs dropped, and Reed's face went pale.

Brad asked in an ever-so-soft voice, "You mean there is an actual grave on Stocker Hill? An actual grave?"

Harold nodded his head and replied, "You bet your sweet ass there's a grave on Stocker Hill."

"Who's grave?" the boys asked in unison.

By this time, the boys sat there waiting for the next thing Harold was going to say. Waiting for every word to flow out of Harold's mouth. Waiting like a bunch of dogs waiting for a treat—no movement, no sounds, just waiting.

Drip, drip, drip… the sink echoed as the last word Harold said was the grave and then he sat there not saying anything. He just sat there and looked at, looked at… nothing.

Reed finally looked around at the other guys and pushed his hands and shoulders up as he tilted his head in confusion. Rob moved his feet to get more comfortable and the rolling stool he was sitting on moved a bit and hit a stand that had some of Harold's tools on it. The stand fell over and the tools bounced and slammed against the floor. The sound was so loud, so jarring, that all the boys leapt out of their skin and Harold, well Harold, Harold hardly moved.

The noise, though very loud, did jerk Harold out of his trance and he began talking like nothing had ever happened.

"There Bill stood in the middle of the green plateau and next to the grave. Blood was dripping off Bill's ass where Stocker shot him, but Bill didn't seem to care at that moment. Dory, as always, came up the rear and watched from a distance as we gathered around the grave and looked into the pit. It was weird, you know, the grass was so green, so green it almost glowed and the grave was deep enough to be freaky and the dirt was so dark. So black. And fine, the dirt looked silky and fine. Almost soft and—

In the middle of his sentence, Harold stopped, got up and walked out of the room.

The boys sat there in silence until they could not take it anymore.

"This is freaking me out," Rob said.

"I have chills," Reed replied.

"WTF!" John stated.

"Where the fuck did Harold go?" Brad asked.

After waiting a second or so, Reed and Brad jumped up and went after Harold. John and Rob looked at each other and then followed the other boys out of the shop to find Harold.

"Can you believe this is happening?" Brad said, "Right when he is getting to the good stuff, Harold bails on us."

"Let's split up and see if we can find Harold and get him back to the shop," one of the boys said as they exited the shop and started down the sidewalk.

Brad and Reed headed north and west respectfully while John headed east. Rob stood there in a daze and looked around like he was lost. He gently rubbed the back of his neck and put his head in his hands then let out a big breath of air. Slowly Rob turned and headed down the street the opposite way of the other boys.

Chapter | 20

The ambulance raced up the driveway towards Hanner and Martha's house and came to a stop behind the other cars that were already there.

Ray, the paramedic on duty, jumped out of the rig first and headed towards the back of the ambulance. Alex jumped out of the driver's seat and headed back to help Ray.

"A shooting at Buck's house?" Alex said as he helped unload the gurney out of the ambulance.

"I know, right?" Ray replied as they headed towards the entrance to the house.

As they entered the house and headed down the hallway towards the kitchen. They could hear whimpering coming from the kitchen. Ray was the first one in the kitchen and stopped dead in his tracks when he noticed it was Jack lying motionless on the floor.

"Jack, Jack's the one that got shot?" Ray said in amazement. "Officer down is what the call should have been."

Alex pushed the gurney into the kitchen and echoed what Ray just said, "Is that Jack? Jack's the one that got shot? Why isn't this all-hands-on deck? Jack is one of us."

Ray shook his head and shot Hanner a look that could have killed him if his eyes were loaded with bullets. "For the love of God, Hanner,"

Ray bitched out, "you could have covered and put pressure on his wounds. You know better than that. You're the law in this county for Christ sakes."

Buck looked back at Ray and basically told him where to go with his facial expressions as he slowly rubbed Martha's back.

Buck watched Ray and Alex get to work on Jack and all he could think of is it would be best for everyone if Jack bit the dust on his kitchen floor. *Sure,* he thought to himself, *Martha would be a wreck, but all-in-all it would end a problem I now have.*

Alex knelt down to help straighten out Jack's body and then felt for a pulse. His large hands felt around Jack's neck looking for a pulse. He pressed and prodded several places looking. He checked jack's wrist and found nothing. He went back to Jack's neck and found nothing. "Umm," Alex mumbled to Ray, "I'm finding nothing."

Hanner blurted out, "What? I just checked before you two got here and he had a pulse."

"Well, he doesn't have one now, Buck!" Ray shot back, "Alex, go back to the rig and get the captain on the line. Tell him to get out here ASAP and we need the f'ing helicopter too. You understand? Move it!"

Alex shook his head and raced out of the house. Ray leaned over Jack's body and cut off his bloody shirt. Once Jack's bare chest was exposed to the sunlight shining through the kitchen window, Ray placed a couple probes on Jack's chest hoping to pick up a heartbeat. The machine registered nothing and the flat line echoed in the tiny kitchen. *BEEEEEEEEEEP!*

"Starting CPR," Ray said as he breathed into Jack's mouth.

One and two and…. Ray counted to himself as he began chest compressions. Martha and Buck looked on as they watched Ray caving in Jack's chest with every compression.

"Buck. Get the paddles out of the bag and plug them into the machine. I'm going to shock Jack's body back into this world," Ray commanded.

"What for?" Hanner replied, "he's dead."

Martha let out a huge curdling wail as she heard the word dead come out of her husband's mouth.

"Because I told you to!" Ray screamed back at him.

Alex's footsteps roared down the hallway with every step as he headed back towards the kitchen. As he arrived and turned the corner, he saw Ray doing CPR on Jack and let Ray know the captain and the copter were on their way.

As Ray came up for another breath, he commanded Alex on the next steps to be done, "Get the paddles out and charge them now. Then get the IV line ready!"

Alex jumped into action and had the paddles ready for Ray within seconds. Ray placed the paddles on Jack's chest and yelled, "CLEAR!"

BEEEEEEEEEP, the machine replied.

"Charging!" Ray yelled, "CLEAR!"

The machine replied again with the same answer.

Ray directed, "Alex, up the machine and CLEAR!"

Martha and Buck watched on as Jack's body was being shocked by Ray. Martha was pale now and her weak legs couldn't hold up her body for another second. Buck made Martha sit in the closest seat as he looked at the machine, hoping it still registered death.

Ray was doing everything in his power to save Jack's life. Alex leaned over Ray as he was working frantically on Jack and said, "Maybe we should call it?"

"NO! CLEAR!" Ray shouted back.

Alex looked on as he watched Jack's body contort as Ray shocked him again.

Martha wasn't watching at this point and Hanner was standing against the counter studying over the commotion taking place in his kitchen.

Blip, blip, blip… the machine finally spoke up after its last conversation.

"Get the oxygen, Alex. We have a pulse!" Ray bellowed out as a wave of exhaustion rippled through his body. "We have a pulse."

Chapter | 21

Martha sat in the corner of the kitchen still stunned at what just took place in her home. One minute she was worrying about her husband and taking a bath and the next minute there was gunfire and blood.

"Buck, honey, I'm worried. I'm worried about Jack and that he is going to die," Martha said to her husband while she reached to him for a hug.

"Don't worry. Jack's a fighter. He'll be okay," Hanner replied as he gently patted her and looked at her face. Martha's face was worn, worn from the massive emotions she just encountered.

"Buck, I am not only worried, but I am scared too. Scared of what I heard you say," Martha followed as her old frail voice cracked with every word.

Hanner looked at his wife and all he could think of—*Hanner you have a problem here.* His mind began to race; what to do, what to say, what to do? All he knew was that if it was anyone else and he had a problem with them, it was easy—lights out. His wife, though. Now what?

Hanner finally replied, "Darling, I don't understand? What do you mean? What did I say?" But Hanner knew; he knew exactly what he said.

"You said that you hoped the ambulance was late. You said that, Buck. I heard you. You wanted Jack to die," Martha barked at her husband as she found the strength to stand up.

"Bullshit. Complete bullshit," Buck stated back to Martha. "I said nothing of the sort."

"YES, YOU DID!" Martha yelled.

"Listen here, all I want is for you to be okay. Yeah, maybe I said that, but it's because I was worried Jack was going to hurt you," Buck came back as if he just lied about stealing cookies from the cookie jar.

"Jack, hurt me, what?" Martha asked as she looked at her husband with disgust.

Buck's face started to get a tad red as he replied to his wife, "Yeah, like I said, hurt you. See Jack and I got into an argument back at the morgue. It was pretty heated, and he threatened me. He did."

Martha rolled her eyes at her husband and replied, "Jack is one of the nicest, sweetest people I have ever met. He would do anything for this family. For you and me. And you want me to believe he was coming here to hurt me?"

SMACK! Buck's hand declared as it crashed along Martha's face. "Don't ever question me, woman!" he loudly stated while his large finger pointed at Martha's face, which now looked up at him from the floor.

Martha lay on the kitchen floor and began to cry. The stream of tears flowed down her cheeks onto the kitchen floor and merged with the pool of blood that was already there.

Whip, whip, whip…. The helicopter's blades yelled as the copter was landing on the road next to the house to pick up Jack. The plan was to get Jack onto the helicopter and send him to the closest trauma center.

"I have to go outside, Martha. This conversation is done," Buck stated as he stepped over Martha who was still lying on the kitchen floor, "and clean up this Goddamn blood."

Buck stormed out of the house and made his way down to where the helicopter had just landed. By this time, there was a commotion brewing outside his house. The captain had arrived and was talking with Ray and Alex. His assistant was with them and was nodding his head as if he was following directions and headed back to the captain's vehicle.

Buck walked up and asked, "What's going on?"

The captain replied, "We're taking Jack to Dover for surgery. If we get him there quick enough, he will survive."

Ray and Alex stepped back from the conversation and stared at Buck with disbelief. Ray whispered into Alex's ear, "How can a guy be so callus about his partner?"

Alex looked at Buck and then back at Ray and said nothing. He stood there and said nothing. He was waiting for the captain to drop the bomb.

"Listen here, Buck. This situation is not good for anyone, and we feel for your wife dearly, but why didn't you let anyone know it was your partner who was shot?" the captain asked.

"Well, sir," Buck came back with, "since you're with the fire department and not the police department, I am not going to answer that question."

"Well, officer," the captain replied in utter disgust, "after hearing Ray and Alex's accounts of this morning events, I figured you would answer that way. So, I took the privilege of calling the County Sheriff's Department and let them know the situation. They are on their way out to question you and Martha."

Buck looked the captain in his eyes without any hesitation and took several deep breaths before turning around and heading back towards the house.

"That was intense," the captain said to Ray and Alex. "I've known Hanner for a long time, and he has always been pretty much of an asshole, but I have never seen such a soulless stare as that before in my life."

Chapter | 22

The boys found themselves all back at the Goshen Dairy. The afternoon sun was taking its toll on the boys, and they all needed something to drink.

"I have to tell you boys," Rob said as he watched John, the last one of the gang to stroll up, "all those beers with Harold and walking in this sun whopped my ass."

"You can say that again," Reed replied as he picked up his T-shirt to wipe his brow.

"All those beers with Harold and walking in this sun whopped my ass," Brad replied in his smartass way as a grin developed on his face.

"You walked right into that one Rob," John told the crowd as he patted Rob on the back.

The boys stood in front of the Goshen Dairy, talking about where they went, where they looked, and having had no luck with finding Harold.

"Well, well, look what we have here, Reed," John said as he pointed towards the front window of the dairy.

Reed looked up at John and followed his arm towards the front of the store. Sitting inside the Goshen, at the counter, were Krista and Suzy. Both sipping on a shake and giggling.

Brad looked at Rob and motioned for him to get closer and whispered in his ear, "Two too many dicks hanging at this place. Let's leave these saps and go back to the garage. Seems like they'll be busy for a while with the girls."

Rob agreed with a nod of the head and said, "See you boys back at Harold's. Don't be too long."

A smile came across Reed and John's faces as they walked into the Goshen Dairy to meet their girlfriends.

"Don't I know you?" Reed said as he walked up behind Krista and kissed her on her neck.

"No, sir, you do not," she replied with a slight grin. "My boyfriend will be here real soon and would not like me fraternizing with the likes of you."

"I see how you are. No big deal. I'll just go see if Amy needs any help behind the counter and see if she wants some of this," Reed joked as he tried to climb the side of the counter.

"PLEASE!" Krista replied as she landed a big smack on Reed's cheek. "Whoa, boy—you been drinking again? You smell like brew," she said.

"Yeah, mister," Suzy chimed in, "you smell too and you, by the way, must have forgotten to tell me what your plans were today. Krista told me you boys were going to go see Harold."

John leaned in toward Suzy and murmured, "Sorry, I was busy doing other things to you this morning then talking about Harold."

Suzy turned her head and blushed as she pulled John closer to give him a kiss. "Yuck. You taste like stale beer," she said as she pushed John away from her.

"Alright, boys," Krista said, "we are done with you stinky degenerates. We have places to go, people to see, boys to kiss."

"Speaking of kissing boys," Suzy replied, "what happened with Harold?"

"He kind of freaked us out," Reed followed.

Krista jumped in, "Reed freaked out. Tell me something I didn't know."

Reed stuck his tongue out at Krista while putting his hands on his head and wiggling his fingers.

"Seriously. He freaked us out," John replied as he pushed Reed out the front door of the store. Reed threw his hands up and made it look like he was dialing a phone and mouthed to Krista, *"Call me."*

Reed and John headed out of the parking lot and down the street back to Harold's garage. The day was getting later, and the sun was starting to drop out of sight behind the trees. The weather was warm, and the breeze was blowing ever so gently through the valley.

– – –

Brad and Rob made their way back to Harold's garage hoping to find him there. Their walk back to the garage was silent. Both boys were more bummed about their buddies having girlfriends than they were not being able to find Harold earlier in the day.

The sun dipped behind the trees as Brad and Rob walked back into Harold's garage. As they rounded the corner, they found Harold sitting in the place he had abandoned a couple of hours before. His motionless body sat there as the breeze from the front of the garage ruffled his hair.

The boys stopped in their tracks and watched Harold. Brad motioned to Rob with his finger to be quiet and they stood behind him to see if he was going to move.

The sink's drips were still echoing through the garage and the warm breeze turned to a chill as the boys waited. There was no movement in the garage. The boys stood there waiting for Harold to move, but nothing of the sort happened.

Rob couldn't take it anymore and pushed Brad with his left arm. "Is he dead?" he whispered in Brad's direction.

"NO, HE IS NOT DEAD!" Harold yelled at the top of his lungs.

Brad and Rob jumped, jumped as high as their legs could get them off the ground. As the two boys landed on the ground whiter than when they left it, Rob wailed, "BA-JESUS !"

Brad leaned down to catch his breath, his muscular arms gripping his thighs with all his might as he closed his eyes to catch his composure.

"I think I just shit myself?" Rob said.

"Hey, guys." John and Reed whispered into Brad and Rob's ears as they snuck up behind them, "watcha doing?"

Brad and Rob leapt out of their skins again and yelled, "WHOA!" The boys were on pins and needles at this point and could hardly get their wits together. Brad was shaking, and Rob went out the front of the garage to catch some fresh air. This whole time, Harold sat in the chair with his back to the boys without saying another word.

The breeze was still blowing through the front of the garage, and it was putting a chill in the air. Reed and John noticed it and began to rub their arms to warm up.

"So, what did we miss?" Reed asked as Rob was pushing his way past the other boys. Rob passed the boys and turned his head as he called them a bunch of assholes while making his way back to the seat, he owned a couple hours ago.

Brad finally gathered himself and followed Rob's lead. Reed and John stood there a second looking at the other two boys and the back of Harold's head before making their way back to where they were before.

As the boys settled into their spots, Harold asked, "Where did you boys go?"

Chapter | 23

The boys looked on at Harold with confusion. They were lost with what just happened, and how Harold was acting had them all on edge.

"Where did you—?" Rob started to bark at Harold. At that moment, Brad shot up his hand to stop Rob in his tracks. He shook his head no and looked back at Harold.

"So, ah, Harold. What were you saying?" Brad asked like he was asking for the car keys.

Harold looked at the boys, all of them bright eyed and looking back at him, and began speaking like nothing had ever happened, almost soft and inviting.

"We just stood there looking into this grave. We heard stories about it. Legends about it. They say something about townspeople would go there to die and of course the stories about Satan himself. I have even heard about a warlock being buried there. No one knows. All I know is whatever it is, it's pure evil. So, here we are, the three of us looking into the grave and Dory watching from a distance. I do not know what happened next, but Bill fell in. Fell right into the grave. Like someone pushed him, but none of us touched him and then he screamed. A bloodcurdling scream like none ever heard before. It was pure terror—it came from his soul that scream did. The funny thing though, the shot in his ass from old man Stocker, the blood was gone. All gone. Not even a little nick. It was like it never happened. The blood was… well, like it was, um, taken by the grave. The grave took the blood."

Harold paused for a moment and motioned for another beer.

Reed spouted, "Fuck me."

"Unbelievable," Brad responded.

"Wrong answer Brad. This is a true story!" Harold snipped back at Brad.

"No, Harold. You got the wrong idea. I was just commenting. I believe you. I truly do. I was just remarking. I mean, please don't take it the wrong way. Seriously," Brad stammered through his entire response.

Rob jumped in, "Dude—relax."

Harold took a swig of his beer, a big swig and stared out at the boys with his glassy eyes. The boys did not say another word. They sat there waiting for Harold to begin again. Harold sat back in his chair and wiped the excess beer off his chin that was having a hard time finding his mouth and began again.

"We were totally freaked out at this point, and Dory from his point of view thought he saw something sizzling or heard something sizzling. We all missed this if it did happen, but Dory swears that it did. Bill has no clue what happened. But, you know, to this day the thing that surprised me the most was—"

Harold stopped again in midsentence and got up from his chair.

"Not again. Harold, you better not leave us again," Brad beckoned at Harold with his fist raised in the air.

Harold replied, "Relax. I'm just stretching my legs. What do you mean leave you? You're the ones that walked out on me."

The boys sat there in doubt. "You walked out on us, Harold. You got up in the middle of your story and walked out on us. We couldn't find you," Reed replied to Harold as he looked around at the other guys.

"Reed, I was here the entire time. You're the ones that got up and left me. Remember? You found me sitting here. Sitting here waiting for you four fuckups," Harold stated as he was starting to get annoyed. "Whatever it is that you guys are smoking, you need to change your brand," he finished with.

Harold reached into his pocket to get his smokes. As he lit his cigarette, he looked at the boys who were starting to piss him off a little and took a big drag. As he blew out a huge puff of smoky air, he continued.

"To this day, the thing that surprised me the most, that surprised all of us, was that Buck lay down in the grave. He jumped down into the grave, not saying a word that he wanted to do this and lay down in the grave. Dory got so scared that he bailed. Didn't want anything to do with the grave anymore. Bill and I looked on. Looked on at Buck laying at the bottom of the grave. No way was I going to get in there and Bill was so freaked he could hardly move. But, Buck, it was creepy, but he looked at peace laying there. Seemed like a lifetime, but he was out of there in seconds. The thing is, it changed him. I can't put a finger on it, but it changed him. We all changed after that."

Harold took a couple more drags off his cigarette and looked at the boys and finished up by saying, "Nothing was the same after that. Life in general. Our friendship. Everything changed. We went on our separate ways; four boys living in the same town who hardly know who the other one is anymore. Four old souls now."

The boys just sat there, sat in the place they called home while Harold told them the story about Stocker Hill and the grave. Each of their minds were racing. Not knowing what to believe and not to believe, but they all knew that something happened on the Hill that day.

"Thanks, Harold," Brad said as he motioned for the boys that it was time to leave. The boys got up from their spots and all walked past Harold without making any eye contact. All the boys headed home in separate directions not saying one word before they parted ways.

Chapter | 24

The sun finished its job from that morning and started shining on the front of the house. Since then, the back of the house cooled down a tad, which helped Martha clean up the pool of Jack's blood.

Tears rolled down Martha's cheeks with every scrub of the brush. Each scrub, as hard as Martha tried, only took a little bit of the blood off the kitchen floor. Her bucket of hot soapy water changed into a puddle of pink suds that lost all its heat.

Martha got up from the floor for the hundredth time and emptied the bucket of blood she had collected. With one pour, the blood rushed down the drain erasing any indications of what took place in the kitchen that day. The sweat slowly rolled down Martha's forehead onto her cheeks as she filled up another bucket with steaming hot water. She reached up to wipe it off and yelped with pain.

"Damn him!" Martha said as she gritted her teeth. "He didn't have to hit me." Martha turned her head and cried some more as the pain finally subsided from where the blow hit her in the face.

The bucket was full again with hot water, the suds and brush, whose job it was today of scrubbing up blood, was now floating on top of the water. Martha slowly poured some of the hot, soapy water out of the bucket onto the kitchen floor. She was hoping this would be her last adventure to the bloodstain that resided on the hard kitchen floor. As the water poured out of the bucket, the scrub brush followed and ended up bouncing on the floor. It bounced around and flipped a few times until it came to rest. The brush landed bristle side up with the back of it landing directly on Hanner's shoe.

"Oh dear," Martha cried, "I am so sorry, honey. I did not mean to splash you with the soapy water. So sorry, let me get you a towel for your shoes."

"Boy, you're really batting a thousand today, aren't you?" Buck replied as he kicked the brush across the kitchen floor.

Martha began to cry, an uncontrollable cry, her grandma body shaking with every whimper. "Why? Why are you treating me this way, Buck? Why?" she asked as she cried out.

Buck took in a big breath of air and contemplated in his head what to do next. He knew the County Sheriff was going to be here soon and he needed Martha on his side and to be cool and collected. *No wait*—he thought to himself. I need Martha to be a basket case for whatever dipshit flunky they send my way. He let out his big breath of air while yelling, "Because you fucked up my life today… MARTHA!"

Chapter | 25

The day was coming closer to an end and the County Sheriff was on his way to Walcott. The shooting of an officer in another officer's house was the biggest news to come out of Walcott since the Drucker murders. The news spread fast, from the gas station to the dairy along the river and through the park. Everyone knew that Jack had been shot in Hanner's house.

It was not only the people of Walcott that knew about the shooting, but the hill knew too. The breeze that flows off the hill, which is usually a nice effortless breeze, changed to a rushing chill—strange for this time of year. The town was on edge, and they wanted to know what happened and why.

Alex and Ray sat with the county sheriff and explained everything they knew about the incident that took place that day. About Martha getting spooked, grabbing a gun, and shooting Jack. Along with that, no one could forget the eerie presence that Hanner presented. The county sheriff took his notes and contemplated if he should run this up the ladder to the State Police or not.

"Thank you, gentleman, for your time," he stated as he walked out of the fire station that Ray and Alex called home for twenty-four hours.

County Sheriff Richard Callahan walked out of the fire station to his cruiser he had parked out front. He started the engine, rolled down the windows, and lit up a smoke before dropping the car into drive and heading out to Hanner's house.

"Dispatch, dispatch, come in," Callahan said into his radio mic.

"Here," a voice repeated out of the speaker on the dash.

"I'm done with the interviews at the fire station. Please note the time and that I am now heading out to Buck and Martha's place," Callahan responded.

The speaker spoke up again, "Yes, sir. Got it."

Silence now overwhelmed the interior of the car at this point, which was soon replaced with rushing wind flowing through the open windows. A little red glow would appear and disappear with every drag on the cigarette that Callahan took. A slight puff of smoky air exited the now-speeding police cruiser.

Callahan pulled up to Hanner's house before the last bits of sunshine disappeared for good that day. The air was chilly now, so Callahan popped open the trunk to get the jacket he had before heading up to the house. Callahan opened the trunk and pulled out a police issue windbreaker that stated in large letters on the back of the jacket—SHERIFF.

"Fuck me!" Callahan said as he closed the trunk of his car.

"Richard," Hanner said as he stood next to the car out of sight of Callahan's initial view, "Been a long time."

"You startled me, Buck," Callahan replied.

Buck looked around to see if anyone else was there and answered back, "Sorry."

"I have to tell you, Buck; this is not a good thing," Callahan said as he threw on his windbreaker and walked around to shake Buck's hand. "Sorry if this has put Martha through the ringer today, but I heard Jack's surgery went well and he is in intensive care."

Buck thought to himself for a moment, *should I put a bullet through this guy's skull or let him in my house?* After a second or so of silence, he spoke up as he shook Callahan's hand. "Thanks, Richard. I am sure Martha will be okay after she hears the good news about Jack."

"Great," Callahan replied, "let's go talk to her."

As the two officers walked to the house, no conversation took place and Buck was still wondering if he should take Callahan out or not. A few more steps and he would be too close to the house to put a bullet in the head, but a knife across the throat would work well. Hanner stopped for a moment as he acted like he was tying his shoe and slowly eased his knife out of its holster that rested right above his right ankle.

"Okay," Buck said as he positioned the knife in his hand to pull it across Callahan's windpipe.

"Okay. What?" Callahan asked.

"Okay," Hanner replied as he began to bring the knife slowly up, "it's time we get down to business."

"Yes. The business at hand. To be honest, Buck, after talking with Ray and Alex, I don't think you have to worry about anything. According to them, it was an accident. She was frightened. If her story matches theirs, case will be closed tonight," Callahan responded to Hanner's comments.

"Whoa," Buck whispered. *That's good news*, Buck thought to himself on how close this SOB came to meeting his maker.

The two officers walked into the house and made their way down the hallway into the kitchen. Sitting at the kitchen table was Martha, gentle old Martha, hanging her head low and sipping on a cup of coffee.

To control the situation, Buck spoke up first to get Martha to go his way. "You remember Richard, don't you? He has good news. Jack made it out of surgery and is doing really well. Looks like he'll be fine."

Martha looked up from her cup of coffee and Callahan caught a glimpse of her face. "Oh Martha, good to see you, oh my, what happened to your face?" he asked.

"She slipped while cleaning the floor and hit her face on the table," barked Hanner.

"Yes. That's what happened. Good news about Jack. Real good news. Coffee?" Martha replied.

Callahan nodded in approval and pulled out his little black notebook from the inside pocket of his jacket. Without hesitation he began to talk to Martha, "So sorry for your troubles today, Martha, but we just need to go over a few things on today's events. I need to know what happened."

Martha smiled nicely at Callahan and poured him a cup of coffee. She then began to explain the series of events. "I heard a noise… got scared… then got the gun… bam, bam, bam… Jack was on the floor… blood… paramedics revived him… That's about it."

"Thank you," Callahan replied as he finished up his notes. "I am going to close this case. No need to take this further."

Callahan got up from the table and took the last swig of his coffee. Gently placed the cup back on the table and then he shook Buck's hand. He smiled at Martha and wished her well as he began the walk back to his car.

The evening was in full bloom by this time, and Callahan's car had a coldness about it. He started the cruiser and picked up the mic to his radio and called to dispatch. "We have a problem here. The stories don't match. Ray, the paramedic saw Buck Hanner hit his wife and now—"

BAM! The single bullet thundered out of the gun and ripped through Callahan's skull. A large splatter of blood and brains hit the windshield with a mighty force.

Chapter | 26

The moonlight was gently shining down on Walcott that evening and lighting the boys' lonely walks home. The glow of the moon made it easy to see and the night was eerily still. The afternoon breeze that flowed through the town was now off in the distance and the trees stood in silence watching the town's every move.

As the boys separated and went their own ways, all they could muster was a couple nods of the head and a halfhearted goodbye. Their minds were reliving the story that was just told to them, trying to believe every word that Harold had said. It was hard not to believe him since it took a lot for Harold to spit it out and get through the story. All they knew was whatever had happened that day—it messed with Harold.

Reed's walk home was usually filled with delight after spending time with the guys. This night was different, though. The wind was let out of his sails, and he could find no joy in his thoughts at all. His normal left turn and cutting through the yards on his way home so he could purposely knock-on Krista's window was now changed to a straight beeline home.

Reed walked through the front door to find the house silent with no movement except for Buster whining at the backdoor. "Awe, poor guy," Reed said to Buster as he accompanied him out the backdoor of the house to the awaiting lawn.

Buster's run to the lawn was an adventurous one. His little excited legs took off faster than his body could handle, and he tumbled out of control down the steps of the porch. Buster jumped up from his spill and piddled right there. The normal routine of finding the perfect spot and spinning in circles until he was ready go was out of the question this time out. Buster had to go, and nothing was stopping him. "Whoa… racehorse," Reed said as the first smile he'd had in hours flashed across his face.

Reed sat at the end of the porch and waited for Buster to stretch his legs a little before he called him to his lap. "Come on, boy," Reed yelled out at Buster while snapping his fingers and throwing out a slight whistle.

Buster turned, got some momentum, and leapt into Reed's lap. Buster's big eyes looked up at Reed while he flipped over in Reed's arms to have his belly scratched.

As Reed slowly scratched Buster's belly, a tear strolled down his face as sorrow slowly set in. Reed pulled Buster up to his face and hugged him tightly. Buster's little nose brushed up against Reed's face and swallowed up the lone tear that was still making its way down his cheek. At this point, an overwhelming set of emotions set in, and he started to weep uncontrollably. Buster just lay there in Reed's arms motionless as his emotions took over.

Buster snuggled his little face into Reed's pudgy neck and began to lick it with his little puppy tongue. He looked down at Buster as the tears gushed from his eyes and said to the only friend he had in the world at the moment, "I feel like I have been lied to Buster. Lied to. Why didn't Dad ever tell me anything?"

Chapter | 27

Rob's walk home was as non-adventurous as the other boys' walks were. He did the normal cutting through the lawns to make up time and strolled past the creek where he would normally stop and launch a few rocks into the water, but not this night. With his head hanging low, Rob just walked home to the trailer.

The night was still silent, and the moon stilled glowed for Rob. Every step he made onto the rusty stairs to the trailer followed with a groan as the metal stairs flecked with his every step. As he pulled the screen door open before pushing his way into the trailer through the front door, the screen's large spring wailed under the tension causing Rob to yell, "Shut up! I hate this goddamn trailer."

"Nice language, Rob," Rob's mom, Ann, barked from the couch.

"Oh, Mom, sorry. So sorry," Rob replied.

"It's okay, honey. Just control yourself, okay?" Ann came back with.

Rob looked at his mother rather awkwardly while scrunching up his bushy black eyebrows. "What are you doing home, Mom?"

"I needed a break," she said as she picked herself up a little from the couch and moved to make room for her son to join her. "You look… you look like you have something on your mind, son."

"I do," Rob said as he pushed the pillows out of his way and plopped himself onto the couch.

"What is it?" Ann asked while grabbing Rob's hand.

"Well, the guys and I went to see Harold. He told us the story about him and Hanner and Dory and Bill going up to the grave on Stocker Hill."

Ann's face went white as she let out a gasp of air. "Oh my, Rob, you didn't, please tell me you didn't... you didn't go to the grave? Did you?"

"No. We did not. Why?" Rob replied.

Ann pulled her hand away from Rob's and buried her now-pale face into her hands. She slowly began to cry into her hands and Rob sat there watching his mother fall apart.

"Excuse me," she said as she got up from the couch and walked into the little kitchen at the front of the trailer.

"Mom, I don't understand. Why are you upset?" Rob asked in a panic as he followed his mother into the kitchen.

"Just give me a moment, just give me a moment, please."

Rob looked at his mother and turned back around and headed back to reclaim his spot on the couch. He sat there in silence waiting for his mother to return.

Ann reached into the upper cabinet and pulled out an old bottle of whisky. She slowly cracked the bottle open as the dust that once lived motionless on the cap was now airborne throughout the kitchen. She put the bottle up to her thin lips, rolled her eyes back into her head and took a big swig of the whisky.

Rob, watching his mother through the blinds that separated the kitchen from the rest of the trailer, was now overcome with fear. During his time on this earth and every breath of fresh air he has taken since entering the world, Rob has never seen his mother take a drink of alcohol.

"Mom, Mom!" Rob yelled out at her. "You're scaring me, Mom!"

Without hesitation, she took another sip of the whisky, slowly screwed the cap in place and put the bottle back in its hiding place in the cabinet. She looked down into the sink, closed her eyes, caught her breath, and then made her way back into the room where her boy was waiting.

"Don't be alarmed, boy," she said as she reentered the room. "We need to talk."

"Please, Mom. What is it?" Rob asked frantically.

"Okay. The first thing I am going to do tomorrow morning is go kick Harold's ass," Ann spouted off as she pointed at her son.

Rob sat there looking at his mother like she was a few degrees left of center and said, "*Ookkaayy*" in a drawn-out manner.

Ann looked at her son as she held back her tears, her lower lip fighting the quivers, but she was drastically losing that battle. She wiped her eyes with the sleeve of her shirt and asked, "Who did Harold say went to the grave?"

Rob replied, "Harold, Hanner, Bill, and Dory."

"Harold, Hanner, Bill and Dory—correct?" Ann came back with.

"Correct."

Ann shook her head in disgust because she didn't want to bring this up. But her emotions were getting the best of her. She was now well past the point of no return. Plus, the frightening look her son had on his face was too much for her not to explain herself. She began to speak, "Listen, son. Harold's story is partially correct."

"What do you mean *partially*?" he questioned.

"Harold said there was four of them that went up Stocker Hill that day, but that is not 100 percent true."

"Mom. What are you trying to say? Please tell me."

"There were five of them that went up the hill," Ann replied to her son. "There were five of them. He left someone out of the story."

"What do you mean there were five of them? Who was the fifth guy to go up the hill?" Rob asked as he shifted uncomfortably on the couch.

"Your father."

.

Chapter | 28

The echo of the gunfire ripped through the valley that cool evening and startled Hanner after he pulled the trigger. He stood there in silence as the sound seemed to travel on and on without any resistance. There was no wind or warm air to stop the sound in its tracks. It just traveled so the entire valley could hear.

Hanner heard the echo yelling out to him as it slowly faded away— *"KILLER, Killer, killer"*…. Hanner rushed back into the house after he blew Callahan's brains all over the inside of the windshield while catching his composure from the blast. *I sure hope Martha didn't hear that*, he thought to himself.

Martha found herself at the sink cleaning up the coffee mugs that everyone used. The steaming hot water rushing out of faucet muffling the gun blast that called everyone to attention and she was none the wiser that her husband had just killed again. Martha's spirits perked up after the conversation with Callahan. Jack seemed to be doing okay and no one was going to press charges. The case was closed.

All Martha had on her mind was her husband hit her; hit her rather hard in the face. She grimaced a little as she gently touched her bruised face but started to forgive Buck for what he had done.

"Well…," Martha said as she reached to turn off the water, "I guess Buck was rather stressed and lost control. I forgive him Lord. I forgive him."

"Martha!" Buck yelled as he entered the house.

"Yes, dear," she replied in her old gentle voice again, "still in the kitchen."

Buck hesitantly entered the kitchen and contemplated his next moves if Martha heard the gunfire. "You, okay?" he asked as he finally entered the kitchen.

"Yes, dear. I'm fine," she said with a smile.

Buck looked at his wife and instantly became at ease. He knew at the moment that she heard nothing, and she must have prayed to the lord. She always felt better after she had a conversation with God. "Oh darling," Buck said to his wife as he hung his head low, "I am so, so sorry. I feel so bad and—"

Martha cut her husband off in midsentence, "Shhh, shhh, Buck, darling, I know, I know." She walked to the middle of the kitchen to meet her husband and comfort him during his suffering, "I know, darling."

Buck held Martha in his arms and squeezed her tight. He gently kissed her cheek as he pulled away from her and looked her in her eyes and smiled. A sudden warmth rushed over Martha as she knew her husband was sorry for what he did. *He must have asked forgiveness from the Lord too*, she thought to herself.

Buck kissed his wife again and began to speak, "Martha, umm, Callahan is having car troubles. I am going to ride with him into town and get him to Harold's garage."

In her sweet voice, "Okay, darling. I'll hold down the fort since all the commotion is over. See you later, my dear." Martha hugged her husband once more and began the noisy trip upstairs to her bedroom.

Hanner walked out of the house and the front screen door slammed behind him and yelled at the tops of its lungs, *"KILLER, LIAR, KILLER, LIAR!"*

He grabbed his ears and tried to muffle the yelling that was piercing him in the spine. "I know goddamn it!" he yelled as he walked to Callahan's blood-spattered car.

Buck opened the driver's door and could hear the speaker calling out to Callahan, "Callahan, are you there? Come back. Callahan, we got cut off, are you there? Come back." Buck reached over Callahan's bloody body and turned off the radio. He pushed the corpse out of his way, so the faceless body now lay over the passenger side of the car.

Buck jumped into the driver's side of the car and turned on the windshield wipers and began to laugh, laugh out loud at himself. "You idiot," he said as he giggled like a schoolboy, "that blood is on the inside."

Dropping the car into drive, Hanner whipped the car around and pulled near his barn. With the car still running, he jumped out and found something to clean the inside of the windshield. As he wiped the blood and bits of skull off the inside of the windshield, he began to sing, sing a song, "Brain, brain, go away, comeback another day."

"There we go," Hanner said as he cleaned the windshield enough so he could see where to point the car. He dropped it into drive and made his way out of the driveway, onto the road and off to the morgue.

The moonlight shined bright in the cool air and Hanner's trip into town was effortless. The windows were down, and the air was rushing through his hair along with trying to blow the bloody mop that was left on Callahan's head. He drove through the middle of town that was quietly sleeping and made his way to the morgue.

Hanner pulled the patrol car as close to the building as possible. He made his way to the basement to get a gurney for Callahan's body. The elevator slammed behind him as he pushed the button to go up and the sound of the elevator whispered to him, *"Fire."*

"Yes," Hanner replied as the doors opened at the main floor, "Fire. We are going to light this f'ing thing up. In a couple hours; the name Callahan will be a figment of everyone's imagination."

The gurney moved effortlessly out of the morgue on its way to the car. Hanner kicked the lever and the gurney lowered a foot or so to make it easier to put Callahan's corpse on. Hanner opened the door and the body fell out of the car and its bloody stump of a head landed on the ground. "Damn it," Hanner said as he pulled the rest of the body out of the car which was now laying completely on the ground. With one quick action, Hanner reached down and pulled Callahan up off the ground and placed his body on the awaiting gurney.

Again, the elevator whispered to Hanner on his way down to the basement of the morgue, *"Fire."*

"Yep, FIRE, we have FIRE!" Hanner yelled as he turned the furnace on and cranked it up to 1800° to ensure the disintegration of Callahan's corpse. As he closed the door on the furnace, the flames slowly started to engulf the body and soon it was at full torch.

"Need to ditch this car now," Hanner said as he made his way out of the morgue. He looked up and saw the smoke slowly rising out of the stack, as he watched the smoke rise into the moonlight, he whispered with a slight smirk, "Ashes to ashes and dust to dust."

Chapter | 29

The morning sun rose slowly over Walcott that day. With every second that passed, the sun had to battle against the town to shed its light for everyone to see. Walcott did not want the sun to rise that day and neither did the boys. A restless night followed all the boys, and they did not have the mindset or the energy to face another day. Harold drained them of life the day before and now they had questions.

Reed awoke with Buster snuggled up against him. The morning light seemed to pass his window that day and the sounds of his mother wrestling with the pots and pans is the thing that brought him to life. Buster was ready to get up, but Reed contemplated every movement he made and decided to stay one with his bed. The safety of his bed.

Katherine's morning breakfast usually woke her son out of his sleep and within seconds his chubby body was ready to be filled. Not this morning, his spot was empty, and his father wondered why. "Where is your boy?" Bill asked Katherine. Katherine looked at Bill and without saying a word she had a full conversation with him.

"Come down, boy, not like you to miss a meal!" Bill yelled up to Reed.

The only noise that was heard was Buster's little collar moving when he was finding a new, warm spot on the covers.

"I said get down here!" Bill yelled again to his son.

"No!" Reed yelled back.

Bill's face started to turn red as he began to reach his boiling point, "What did you say to me?"

"I said no. N... O... NO!" Reed yelled with all his might as Buster scampered into hiding.

Bill pushed himself away from the table and started to make his way towards the stairs. Before he could take his first step up the flight, Katherine grabbed his arm and said, "He's testing you. It's his age."

Bill looked at Katherine and replied, "Testing me. I'll test him with my foot up his ass."

"Shhh... Bill... calm down. I'll go talk to him," Katherine gently said to her husband.

Katherine took one step towards the stairs and looked up the staircase before making the adventure. At the top of the stairs stood Reed, looking down at his mother, looking down with disgust, looking down with disgust of his father, a look of betrayal.

Reed slowly made his way down the stairs; with every step the stairs echoed his anger. Echoed the betrayal he was feeling. He loved his father dearly and could not understand, could not comprehend, could not grasp why something so important was never told to his only son.

Reed rounded the corner and looked his father straight in the eye. Without saying a word, Reed pulled the chair out from the table and told his father, "We need to talk, sir."

"Sir? SIR? You disrespect me in my house, the house that I provide you? The house that keeps you safe at night. Who do you think you are?" Bill yelled at his son as he stood leaning over the table from his chair.

"Sit down, Dad. We are going to be here for a while," Reed snapped back.

Bill looked at his son, looked with a state of awe, looked at a boy who would crumble with emotions if he raised his voice. Now, his boy stood in front of him as a man demanding respect. Bill slowly sat down and figured he would play Reed's game. "So, what's on your mind?" he asked his son in an ever-so-pissed-off voice.

"Dad," Reed said as the emotion slowly began to rise, "you lied to me."

"Lied? About what?" Bill replied.

"A little trip about four guys made to a grave up on Stocker Hill. You, Harold, Hanner, and Dory," Reed said as his lower lip began to give away.

Bill's anger drifted away quickly as he looked back at his son while watching his emotions start to take over. Bill rubbed his head slightly and waved to Katherine to leave the room. "Son, if I don't tell you something, it doesn't mean I am lying to you," Bill finally said.

"I think so."

"No, son," Bill followed, "I did not lie. I chose to wait to tell you when you became a man, and by how you are reacting, I was right. You are not ready for this. Drinking beer with your buddies does not make you a man. Having a conversation with Harold, does not make you a man."

In a full-out cry, Reed replied, "I am a man."

"Reed. What did Harold tell you about that day?" Bill asked.

Reed tried to respond to his father but was overcome with emotion. He stood up to his father and demanded information. Stood up to his father like a man and now he was sitting in front of him crying like a boy.

"Hold on. You need to relax. Take a few breaths. Let's go outside and talk," he told his son as he walked around the table and headed towards the back door.

Reed got up from the table and followed his father out of the house towards the garage. The garage stood alone away from the house. It was its own entity that would become Bill's home away from home when he needed to escape reality. Homed in the corner of the garage sitting on top of the workbench was a little brown fridge.

Bill walked towards the fridge and motioned for Reed to sit down on one of the stools that were scattered around the workbench. He slowly opened the fridge to reveal several cold beers. "So, you think you're a man now? How about a beer at 9:00 a.m.? Think you could handle it?" Bill asked his son.

Reed smiled with delight, "Sure."

"I think not," Bill replied as he threw his son a Coke.

"Dad. Come on," Reed said with disappointment.

Bill cracked open his beer, and with a slight grin, nodded to Reed that it was okay. Okay to talk to him as a man, okay to sit and talk with him and drink a beer like a man.

Reed got up from the stool, opened the fridge and grabbed a beer for himself. As he walked back to the stool, he passed his father who was now sipping on his own beer.

"So. Reed. Again," Bill slowly blurted out, "What did Harold tell you?"

Reed took a sip of his beer that did not taste as good as he thought a 9:00 a.m. beer would taste and began to speak. Speaking in every detail based on what Harold had said. Telling the story back to Bill as Bill relived every moment again in his mind. Bill looked on without interrupting the story as Reed spewed the entire account back to him without missing a beat. At the end of the story, Bill looked at his son with a blank face.

"Dad?" Reed asked. "You okay?"

Bill shook his head as if to say okay and sat there for a moment as he collected his thoughts.

Reed looked at his dad and wondered what thoughts were racing around his mind.

"Reed," Bill finally said, "the story you told is pretty much true."

"Did Harold lie to us?" Reed asked in anticipation.

"Not exactly. Was Rob with you?" Bill asked his son.

"Yes, sir," Reed replied.

"Makes sense. Reed, there were five of us who went up on that hill that day. Five of us. Other than that, the story is true," Bill said to his son.

"I don't understand. Why would Harold leave someone out? Why did you ask me about Rob? What is missing…? Wait a minute," Reed said as he stared at his father.

"Figure it out yet?" Bill asked Reed.

Reed looked at his father a little more before asking, "Are you saying Rob's father was the fifth guy?"

Bill looked at his son and slowly nodded yes as he stood up from where he was sitting. As he walked past his son on his way out of the garage, he whispered in his ear, "This conversation is over—never to be spoken of again."

"But, I have so many questions," blurted out Reed.

Reed's father kept walking and did not say a word. He left Reed sitting there alone in the garage with his thoughts and a beer that was only missing a sip.

Chapter | 30

The morning sun finally broke free and shined into Rob's face as he slowly awoke from the couch. The night was full of worry and questions; questions on what really happened on Stocker Hill that day and worry on what he was going to learn.

Rob had a mission that day; even though he hardly slept, he wanted to talk to Harold as soon as possible. He slowly pushed himself out of the couch and stretched his body. As he made his way to take a morning shower, he heard rustling coming from his mother's room. Not to disturb her, Rob changed his mind and did what he could to get cleaned up a bit. He wanted to get out of the trailer before his mother was up. She did not need to know what his plans were for the day.

Rob slowly opened the door to the trailer and the spring on the door yelled out, *"I'M LEAVING!"*

"Damn door," Rob said under his breath as he leapt from the top step of the stairs to the ground. No need to allow the trailer to give him away anymore.

"Rob, Rob. Is that you?" Rob's mother yelled out as she raced out of her bedroom. "I knew he was going to do this," she said as she found the trailer abandoned by her son. *He is going to open doors that he will regret he opened,* Ann thought to herself as she slowly sat in the warm area her son had left.

Rob made his way out of the little land his mother and him had and headed towards town. The walk back into town was worse than when he left it the night before. The usual route he took was tainted with thoughts of Stocker Hill, the grave, and now five guys who adventured where they shouldn't have.

"Should I get the guys—should I not? Should I get the guys—should I not?" Rob repeated as he walked down the path until he got to the park. The park was quiet, not a kid in sight or a person around. It was eerily quiet for a sunny summer morning. Rob stopped in the middle of the park and looked around. As thoughts of his father raced through his mind, he decided at that moment to move on. Move on to see Harold without the guys—without the protection of his friends.

He walked out of the park and headed towards Harold's garage. He avoided the easy trip through the main part of town and past the Goshen Dairy; he chose the back way, the industrial way. As Rob walked behind a few of the small factories that were scattered throughout this part of town, he caught a glimpse of Donny, the local tough guy, starting up an old dump truck. The big diesel engine roared to life and blew puffs of dark smoke up into the clear, blue sky.

Rob hid behind a junk pile and some concrete barriers as he waited for Donny to drive the old rattling truck away. As soon as it was quiet again, Rob resumed his quest towards Harold's garage. The sun started to beat down on Rob, causing his forehead to glisten with sweat. Rob stopped on the side of Harold's garage to catch his breath and to tame the moisture that was rolling down into his eyes.

Rob turned the corner to the front of the garage and standing there looking through the front of the shop was Reed. Rob sighed and said, "What the fuck are you doing here?"

"Fuck you," Reed replied. "What the fuck are you doing here?"

"I'm going to confront Harold," Rob said as anger began to set in.

"Me too."

"What?"

"I said me too. All of a sudden, you're fucking deaf now? Me too," Reed snottily replied.

"Why? Asshole!" Rob asked.

"Harold lied to us you," Reed spouted.

"Why are we arguing?" Rob asked. "I know he lied to us."

"I am in a shitty mood, and I guess you are too. Let's stop. Okay? How do you know and what do you know?" Reed wondered as he responded back to Rob.

"My mother told me something last night."

"My father told me something this morning," Reed said.

"There were five of them," the boys said in unison.

"Damn," Reed stated.

"Yeah, five of them," Rob answered back to Reed as they stood and looked at each other. "There were five of them and the fifth was my father."

Reed replied, "That is what I was told this morning. I spewed the entire story to my dad, and it was all true. Word for word. Everything. Except the fifth guy. Your father."

"Why would Harold leave that off?" Rob questioned Reed.

"Don't know," Reed replied. "It was weird with my dad, though. The only thing he said was about your dad not being in the story and when he walked out of the garage, he said to me 'this conversation is over—never to be spoken of again.' He never mentioned anything about your dad, any specifics at all, just walked out."

"This is bullshit…," Rob hesitantly said.

Reed looked at Rob and did his little head shift while picking up his shoulders and said, "Yep, bullshit, let's find Harold."

"You got that right," Rob replied as he walked to the front of the shop.

Chapter | 31

The moonlight was shining down lighting up Hanner as he sat in Callahan's car. Every once and awhile the smoke billowing out of the stack would blow across the moonlight sending Hanner and the car into darkness. With each puff, the smoke would float up into the night erasing any existence of Callahan as it slowly dissipated over the town.

Hanner started the squad car and made his way out of the parking lot to the front of Harold's garage which was just down the street to the left. Hanner turned off the car, threw open the door and climbed out. With all his might, Hanner slammed the car door and kicked open the front door of Harold's shop. Pacing around in the dark until he found the button, Hanner swore with every step until he found the button to open the big garage door to the shop. He then jumped back into Callahan's car, started the cruiser up and pulled it into the lonely waiting spot at the front of the garage.

He shut off the car and it sputtered its last breath as the motor slowly went silent. Hanner shut the big door to the shop and made his way into Harold's office. He plopped himself into Harold's office chair and picked up the phone.

On the other end, Harold's home phone rang and echoed throughout the house. Harold hardly moved an inch as he sat quietly at the kitchen table. The empty bottle of scotch and scattered beer cans where the only witnesses to Harold's binge.

Hanner let the phone ring and ring without an answer. "Damn it," Hanner said as he slammed the phone down. "Damn it!"

Hanner walked out of the garage and down the street to Harold's house that settled itself in the middle of the block behind the Goshen. Hanner's pace was fast and swift. He climbed the front stoop of Harold's house effortlessly. He waited a second and then with one swift kick the front door buckled underneath Hanner's right foot. The noise of the front door collapsing wasn't enough to wake Harold from his drunken sleep.

Hanner made his way from the front of the house to the kitchen and found Harold passed out at the kitchen table.

CRASH! The table and its contents screamed as Hanner threw them aside. Now that the place Harold was leaning on was gone, Harold landed face-first on the kitchen floor. The thud was almost deafening as Harold's limp body landed. A stream of blood slowly trickled out of his nose and created a pool of warmth until the blood became one with the cold kitchen floor. Harold still did not wake up.

"Jesus, Harold," Hanner barked. "What the hell did you drink?" Hanner knelt to get a closer look at Harold and could notice the pool of blood moving ever so slightly with every breath Harold took. "You're still breathing."

Hanner walked over to the sink where Harold was soaking a large pan, and with one quick movement the pan was out of the sink. Dirty food water splashed all over the back of Harold's head. The cold water jarred Harold back to life. As he slowly got up, still fully buzzed beyond normalcy, he rubbed his eye and got a whiff of what was all over him. "What the hell?" Harold asked as he ran his hands through his hair that contained chunks of food.

"Harold! HAROLD!" Hanner yelled. "You have work to do."

"Work? I am not working," Harold replied as he slowly made it to his feet.

Hanner grabbed Harold and threw him up against the wall, with his right forearm landing on Harold throat. As Harold gasped for air, Hanner whispered in his ear, "No, Harold. You have work to do. And if you don't—oops, that evidence that pins you to the Drucker murders will suddenly reappear. Do I make myself clear?"

Harold's eyes were wide open and burning with redness. It was either from the lack of oxygen flowing to his head or the abundance of alcohol still flowing in his system. Harold blinked a couple times to acknowledge his defeat as Hanner slowly loosened his grip.

"Now, Harold, you have work to do at your shop and you will do as I say. We also will need Donny. So, you go take a shower, you stinky pig. I will meet you and Donny at your shop." Hanner spoke to Harold in a high voice with a grin that couldn't hide Hanner's dry, brown teeth.

"Yes, sir. I'll call Donny and, ah, we, well, we will meet you at the, the, ummm, garage. Okay?" stammered Harold back to Hanner as he slowly rubbed his now-aching neck.

"Good boy. See ya soon." Hanner smirked.

Harold made his way upstairs and started the shower. As the shower slowly warmed up, Harold made a dart for the phone and called Donny. As he dialed the phone, the house moaned as the warm water slowly rose up from the basement and brought life back to the cold pipes. The phone rang and rang at Donny's place without an answer. Harold hung up the phone and tried again.

"Do you know what time it is, motherfucker?" Donny yelled into the phone.

"Donny. Harold here. We have work to do. Hanner is demanding it again," Harold quickly said.

"More bodies?" Donny asked as he beat himself on the head.

"I don't know. Meet us at the garage in a half hour," Harold replied and made his way to the shower.

The water was hot, and the steam engulfed itself with Harold's stench. As the soapy water slowly rinsed Harold back to normal, the steam soon followed, and the stench of Harold was gone. Harold climbed out of the shower, dried himself off and found some trace of clothing.

The walk to the shop was not like most of Harold's walks to work. The sun wasn't shining, the sky wasn't blue, and it was not morning yet.

The moonlight was still glowing, and streets were empty. Harold's footsteps were the only indication that life existed at the moment.

"What the f….?" Harold asked as he noticed his shop door was kicked in like his front door. "Hanner. You know where my keys are. Did you have to kick in my door?"

Hanner looked at Harold and pointed to Callahan's car. Standing beside the cruiser was Donny. Standing there motionless waiting for some orders to be beckoned. Harold made his way to the car and said, "I'm guessing the body is in the trunk?—*Oouuff*," the wind exiting Harold's lungs said as Hanner's fist planted itself into his gut.

"Tsk, tsk, tsk," Hanner said as he waved his index finger back and forth, "No need to be a smartass now—is there?"

"Sorry," Harold said as he caught his breath.

"No issues here, boss," Donny chimed in.

"Good," Hanner replied to Harold and Donny. "We all are on the same page, then? Harold, take all items that hints this is a cop car off of it; radio, lights, all that shit and dispose of it. Donny, you help him. Then, Donny, take this thing and torch it at the same place you torched that other car. No one will find it there—ever. Got it?"

"Yes, boss," Donny said as he jumped towards the car to start stripping it.

"Got it," Harold mustered.

"Okay, then. Harold, I am going to take that car over there. Yes, that car, your baby and drive it home. You and Donny can pick it up when you're through here," Hanner said as he walked away from the guys and towards Harold's classic Chevy.

Hanner pressed the button at the rear of the shop and waited for the overhead door to open. Without saying another word, Hanner jumped into Harold's prize possession and drove away.

"Man," Donny said, "once he has his claws in you, there is no getting out."

Harold looked at Donny and nodded as he began to work. After a few minutes, Harold asked, "Beer?"

"Why the fuck not?" Donny replied.

"Hey, Donny," Harold said as he cracked Donny's beer, then his own, "where do you torch the cars?"

"The grave," Donny whispered.

Chapter | 32

It was still early in the morning and Harold and Donny were finishing up with Callahan's cruiser. Harold had the interior stripped of all the police items and Donny did the same to the outside of the car. Callahan's cruiser was ready to meet the same fate as its owner.

"Hey, Donny," Harold said, "drop me off at Hanner's so I can get my car. Sure, don't want him keeping it for too long. Next thing you know you'll be disposing of that one too."

"No problem," replied Donny. "Let's get this over with. I have to tell you, Harold, this is my last adventure with him. He can go fuck himself. I am getting out of town after this one."

Harold looked over at Donny as he started hooking the cruiser up to the tow truck that Harold had on hand. "You sure you want to do that?"

"Yes. I do," Donny declared as he walked toward the tow truck to pull the hydraulic lever that lifts the car up off the ground.

"Donny, you don't want to mess with Hanner," Harold said as the truck let out a wail as it began to lift the front end of the car off the ground.

"How is he going to know? Really?" Donny replied to Harold. "You know my brother Darrel? Don't you? He has some connections near Shreveport. I'm going to head down there as soon as possible."

Harold looked at Donny as a chill settled into the interior of the truck and whispered so the wind would not carry his voice, "He'll find you."

"Yeah, right. Find me? Highly doubt it," Donny belted as he started up the old tow truck and headed towards the hill.

Harold sat in the truck as Donny drove the old thing down the road. The truck's tires began to hum as Donny slowly picked up speed. The town was quiet. No one knew that anything had taken place in the town that night and as soon as the cruiser was at the grave. No one would know—ever.

"Hey look," Donny said as he pointed to the stack that was billowing smoke out of it. "Hanner."

Harold looked at Donny and nodded with acknowledgment. No words needed to be spoken to Donny at this point. The two of them knew that Hanner was behind the smoke.

Harold began to worry about Donny. He knew that Hanner would take revenge on him somehow. Either it was going to be on Donny himself or one of his brothers. You never know, Hanner might go after his sweet old mom.

Donny was the oldest of four brothers. He had it the roughest out of all of them all—roughest because he brought it all on himself. His mother raised him in a strict Catholic household and Donny bucked the system as soon as he was old enough to walk.

No one told Donny what to do. No one told Donny when to sit or stand, to eat or sleep, to pray to the Lord on Sunday or not. let alone his mother or the crotchety sisters that ruled the St. Mary's Catholic School. No one told Donny what to do. No one except Hanner.

Harold sat there wondering what Donny did to get Hanner's hooks into him, but it must have been something pretty bad. You don't cross Hanner and get away with it. Hanner must have something on Donny that no one else knows about.

"Hey, wait a minute," Harold barked at Donny as he missed the turn to Hanner's house, "Where are you going?"

"The grave."

"I don't want to go to the grave!" Harold exclaimed.

"Look. I want to get this car off the road. We'll drive up to the grave, drop the car, I'll torch it and we'll be on our way," Donny replied to Harold as he tried to calm him down.

Harold began to get nervous. The last time he was at the grave was to work on the star and he did not want to go through that again. Harold looked over at Donny and said, "Just drop me off before you go up the hill."

"No," Donny said.

"But, Donny," Harold stuttered, "I can't handle going to the grave."

"Tough shit."

"Come on, Donny. Drop me off before you go up," Harold begged.

"What is your problem? We are both in this up to our assholes, so just go with the flow," Donny spit out before he made the final turn toward the hill.

"The murders. Remember, the Drucker murders?" Harold whimpered.

"Oh," Donny came back with, "stop being such a girl."

"Donny. Please, Donny," Harold begged again.

"Then jump because we are going up," Donny spouted.

"Donny—"

"Look, I don't want to go up there either. There are only two things in this world that scare me. Hanner and the hill. I need you, Harold. Please? I need you." Donny spoke softly back to Harold as his tough guy image shed from its presence.

Harold looked at Donny and saw a side he had never seen before—fright.

"Okay," Harold said. "We go up, drop the car, and get the hell out of there."

"Thanks," Donny replied, "I am going to stop. Go lock the hubs in on your side."

Donny and Harold jumped out of the truck and locked the hubs in, so the old truck had a fighting chance to get up the side of the hill.

Donny jumped back into the truck and looked back up Stocker Hill and gunned the truck. The truck lurched forward and began to make the climb up Stocker Hill. The temperature slowly dropped more and more as the truck made its way up the side of the hill. A chill set into the cab. The gravel road whispered with every turn of the wheel while Donny and Harold hung on.

The road slowly lowered its pitch and the morning moonlight glistened off the green grass. Donny pulled the tow truck up next to the grave so that the cruiser was sitting adjacent to the hole. The large white rocks watched from a distance as Harold and Donny jumped from the truck.

"Hey, Harold," Donny said as they both made their way back towards the car, "unhook the chains and I'll lower the car down."

Harold moved as fast as he could as his nerves took over. He slowly began to dry heave until he could not hold back anymore. As Harold turned to throw up whatever was in his system, he noticed he was only a step from the grave and found himself staring down into the darkness.

The moonlight was not powerful enough to light the bottom of the grave and fear ripped through Harold's body. His dry heaves subsided, and fear helped guide him through the task at hand. Harold reached up and unhooked the rusty chains that helped hold the cruiser in its spot.

Donny jumped to the levers and slowly lowered the car to its final resting spot. As the car hit the ground Donny spoke up. "Harold, move the truck and I'll torch this thing."

Harold jumped into the driver's seat and fired up the tow truck. As he slowly pulled the truck away from the grave, he watched Donny walk around the car for a final inspection. Donny stopped near the passenger side of the cruiser and looked up at Harold to indicate all was good. As Donny reached into his pocket to get the lighter that would help begin the next set of events, he took one step back, one step down into the grave.

Harold looked up over the top of the steering wheel, thinking Donny had knelt down to torch the car. As Harold looked on, the moonlight got brighter, and Donny came running out from the back of the car. He was screaming with fear and was in a full off run towards the tow truck.

Harold sat still as he watched Donny run in terror. Donny jumped on the hood of the truck and slid across it on his way to the passenger side. He opened the door and leapt into the truck and planted himself next to Harold. Donny sat there for a second and in an incontrollable breath said, "I just fell into the grave."

"You did what?" Harold questioned.

"You heard me. I fell into the grave," Donny replied as his body began to shake.

"You okay?"

Donny looked over at Harold and began to scream, "Do I look okay to you? Do I? I can't do it Harold. I can't do it."

"Do what?"

"I can't torch the car. You have to do it?" Donny shot back with.

"No way. Hanner told you to do it. I'm not fucking doing it," Harold demanded.

"I can't, dude. That was the scariest thing I have ever experienced. I can't do it. When I touched the bottom of the grave, I felt it. I felt it. Please, Harold. Please," Donny said as he began to cry.

"Felt what?"

"Evil."

Harold looked at Donny and put his hand out for the lighter. Donny, grasping the lighter with all his might, slowly reached over to Harold's open hand and let the lighter fall from his fingers.

Harold, without skipping a beat, jumped out of the truck, and walked toward the car. The moonlight guided his way as he stepped on the glowing green grass. The white rocks looked on with curiosity as Harold approached the car.

A roar came over the valley as the once prominent police cruiser went up in flames and began to disappear from existence. Harold stood in awe as every flame that left the car took a part of the car with it. He stood and watched for minutes until there was no sign of the car left. No sign at all. The spot that once held the car was now empty and the green grass was rampant around the grave as if no one was ever there.

Chapter | 33

Rob and Reed walked toward the front of the shop. As they rounded the corner, they noticed the front door to Harold's shop was kicked off its hinges. The look on their faces went from pissed off men to frightened boys.

"Wonder what happened here?" Rob asked in general.

"Don't know," Reed said as his voice cracked in fear. "Should we go in?"

"You bet we are going in?"

"What if, what if someone, what if someone is still in there?" Reed asked, stammering.

"Then we will be in a bit of trouble," Rob barked as he began to get annoyed.

"We should call the guys first," Reed came back with.

Rob looked at Reed and threw his hands up in the air and slowly made his way to the front door. "Harold, you in there?" Rob yelled through the door. The shop responded with silence.

Reed slowly walked closer to Rob and looked through the door. There was no sign of any movement within the shop. Reed stood behind Rob and waited for Rob to make the next move. As Reed sat and waited for Rob, he got overly excited and yelled, "HAROLD, YOU IN THERE?"

"Jesus, Reed, that is my ear you yelled into," Rob growled as he gave Reed a push with one arm and rubbed his ear with his free hand.

"Sorry," Reed said as the shop responded with silence.

"Hello," Rob yelled back into the shop. The shop responded with silence.

"Ummm," Reed whispered back to Rob this time, "maybe we should go get the guys before we walk in there?"

"Look, Reed. I came here to talk to Harold and that is what I am going to do. If you were here or not, I came here to talk to him. If you want to be a puss and go, get the other guys, so be it," Rob said to Reed as he pointed his finger towards his face.

"Dude. Chill," Reed responded. "Let's go in, then."

The shop was quiet and cold. Even though the sun had been out and was flowing its warmth all over Walcott, Harold's garage was cold.

The boys' steps shuffled across the cold concrete floor as they looked around trying to figure out what was going on.

Reed's mind was racing. He became more frightened with every step that he and Rob took further and further into Harold's shop. Reed couldn't figure out what was worse, his mind racing or his heart beating in his chest with every step.

Boom, boom, boom, Reed's heart echoed throughout his body.

"I am getting a little nervous here," Rob said with every step.

"Me too. Actually, I am scared shitless right now."

Rob turned back towards Reed and acknowledged the fear that was now racing through his own body. "It is weird. There is usually some kind of sound coming from this place. Where's Harold?" Rob stated and questioned all at the same time.

Reed pulled on Rob's shirt as he was a few steps behind him and questioned, "You know what else is weird?"

"What?"

"This town. Where are all the people? No one is driving around; no one noticed that the door was kicked in. Where is everyone?" Reed asked.

"Yeah, I really didn't pay attention, but you're right. Weird," Rob said as Reed passed him and then turned back and looked at him.

Rob looked at Reed and then noticed something, noticed something in the background. As Rob looked past Reed, Reed noticed the blood rushing out of Rob's face. Within a second, Rob's knees buckled, and he was lying on the ground. Rob lay there frozen.

Reed stood over Rob and panic forced its way into Reed's existence. He knew something was wrong and whatever it was, it was behind him. Something that caused his friend to buckle with fear was right behind him. Reed's knees began to get weak as he slowly turned around. As his body turned ever so slowly, Reed lowered his head and closed his eyes. Scared of what he was going to see. As Reed came to a stop, he lifted his head and slowly opened his eyes. Fear was prevalent as he began to focus on what dropped his friend in his tracks.

"Oh my" was the only thing Reed could muster as he looked on at Donny's dead body hanging from the rafters of Harold's garage.

Chapter | 34

It was way past midmorning and Brad was itchy with questions. Harold's story spooked him. Spooked the guys and he knew it. Brad wanted to get the guys together and go over Harold's story. All Brad could do was wonder at this point about the story they heard.

As he began to get dressed for the day, he talked out loud to himself, "Was it true? Was it not? We need to get together."

His first call that morning was to Reed, but he wasn't home. His second call that morning was to Rob, and he was not home either. His last call that morning was to John, and he answered before the first ring was done yelling.

"Hello," John said into the phone.

"Brad here, buddy. Have you heard from Rob and Reed?"

"Nope. Why?"

"They're not home, and it is not like them not to shoot us a call," Brad replied into the phone.

"Yeah. You're right," John stated.

"Let's meet and then go find them. Half hour in the park." They agreed and then hung up the phones.

Brad made it to the park before John did and sat up against the half wall that divided the park into sections. As he waited for John to get there. His upper lip glistened with sweat, and he was now wishing he threw on some shorts instead of his typical jeans that he always wore.

John jumped out of the shower, threw on some clothes, and began the trek to the park. He strolled to the park like always. He was going to be late, and Brad would be annoyed, but he really didn't care. All he knew was that Harold's story got to him.

Brad looked up from his place on the wall and watched John from a distance making his way to the park. John never had any urgency in his steps and today was no different. John's stroll to the park ended when he finally made it to where Brad was parked.

"Glad you could make it," Brad sarcastically said.

"Uh-huh," John sarcastically responded.

Brad shook his head as he rubbed his ass which had fallen asleep against the wall. "I was wondering," he questioned, "you think those two went back to the garage?"

"Without us?"

"Yes. Without us," Brad snipped.

"No way in hell."

"Well, where did they go, then? I can see one of them not shooting us a call, but both of them. Fishy," Brad ended.

"Fishy," John responded as he acknowledged that Brad was onto something.

"Well, let's start with the Goshen and then the garage."

Brad and John made their way to the Goshen Dairy. The sun was shining, and the park was quiet. The entire town was quiet. John stuck his head into the Goshen and asked Amy if she had seen the guys. Amy shot back a shake of the head no and continued with her work behind the counter.

"Not here," John said to Brad as they began their walk to Harold's garage.

Out of the parking lot and down the street to Harold's place was their task at hand. As they got closer to the garage, Brad nudged John and pointed in the direction they were walking.

"Is that Reed?" John asked.

"Sure, looks like it," Brad replied, "Reed, what the hell is going on? What's with no phone call too?"

Reed looked up from his crouched position at the front of the garage and the fear jumped from his eyes into Brad's.

Brad looked at Reed as fear rushed in to take over that moment.

"Reed, you, okay?" John said.

"What happened? What happened to the door? Holy shit, is that Rob on the floor in there?" Brad blurted out.

John pushed Brad out of the way and ran to his friend's side who was lying on the floor of Harold's garage.

"No. Wait. Wait. WAIT!" Reed yelled. Brad looked at Reed and asked, "What is it?"

"For the love of God!" came roaring out of John's mouth and he turned and hurled his breakfast all over the place.

Brad looked at Reed and wanted some answers. "Reed, what the fuck is going on?"

Reed shook his head and curled back up into a ball at the front of the shop. He slowly looked up at Brad as tears began to well up in his eyes and said, "Donny, Donny is in there. Hanging from the rafters. Hanging from the rafters by his neck. He's dead. Dead."

Brad scrunched up his eyes, looked at Reed and made his way into the garage. He slowly inched his way farther and farther into the garage knowing he was going to see a dead body, see a person who he knew, to see Donny's dead body in Harold's garage. As he stepped over Rob, who was still out cold on the concrete floor, he slowly looked up at Donny hanging from his neck. Donny's silent body was hanging from the rafters.

Chapter | 35

The sun was trying to shimmer through the haze that floated above the valley. The haze was thin and light but had substance, enough substance to fight off the morning sun.

Hanner sat on his porch waiting for the sun to break. He slowly sipped his coffee and admired the haze of death that covered Walcott. With a slight grin, he took another sip of his coffee and watched Callahan float on by.

The sun got some life and started burning off the haze. The cool night air was long gone, and the morning was beginning to warm up. Hanner took the last sip of his coffee, sat his cup down on the porch and closed his eyes. As Hanner drifted away, his body began to twitch as he dreamed of that day on Stocker Hill years ago.

– – –

The sky was covered with a gray blanket with a slight mist in the air. The grass was green and slippery, Hanner could hardly keep his balance as he weaved his way through the woods toward the grave. The wind whispered to him as it flowed through the trees as he walked up to the grave.

The wind started to sprint faster, and faster past Hanner and the green grass flowed with every gust of air. Hanner looked down into the grave and opened his arms wide. He closed his eyes and spoke in a deep voice, "I'm here Father."

The wind picked up more speed and began to yell as it raced past Hanner's head. Yelling with all it's might, "lay with me, lay with me, lay with me…." Hanner closed his eyes in acceptance and turned his back to the grave. In one motion, he leaned back and fell into the grave.

Hiding in the woods when they saw Hanner making his way towards him were the Drucker twins—Brian and Doug.

Brian looked over at Doug as they watched Hanner from a distance, "What is Hanner doing?"

Doug replied, "Ummm, don't know."

"Let's get a closer look," Brian said.

"Get the fuck out of here," Doug barked.

"Come on," Brian barked back.

"Dude, we have our old man's crossbow, we are illegally hunting, we are on Stocker Hill where no one dares to go, and you want to take a closer look," Doug spouted off as he looked on towards the grave.

"Yep, that is exactly what I am saying."

"Okay but be careful, I don't want him to see us."

The Drucker twins slowly stood up from where they were hiding to make their way closer to the grave. Every step they took was precise and quiet. They knew the woods, they knew the hill, they knew Stocker Hill, but they stayed away from the grave.

Doug took one step closer to the grave. His right foot hitting a small tree branch that lay silently in the glowing green grass and it echoed as it snapped in two. Brian whipped his head around to look at Doug as Hanner yelled from the grave, "I know you're here boys."

Doug jumped as Hanner's voice bellowed from the grave, as he was falling backward his finger hit the trigger on the crossbow. The arrow raced off the end of the crossbow and impaled itself in the middle of Brian's chest. The blood spurted out of Brian's chest with every beat of his heart, as his body was grasping for life, he fell towards the ground; Hanner caught him and slowly laid him down.

Doug was stunned. He stood there motionless as he watched the life rush out of his brother eyes and streams of blood flowing from his chest. "I just killed my brother."

Hanner looked at Doug and said, "No Doug. I did." As he buried his knife into Doug's chest and watched the life leave his body.

"Complete, Father!" Hanner yelled out to the grave, "COMPLETE!"

Hanner looked at the twins whose dead bodies lay frozen in the middle of the grass. The wind began to slow down as Hanner's knife slowly cut into Doug's chest. With one quick grasp, Doug's heart was in Hanner's hand and on its way to the grave. As Hanner walked towards the grave he whispered, "This is for you, Father."

As the heart went into the darkness of the grave, the wind picked up and spoke out to Hanner, *"More."*

Hanner turned back towards the twins, with his knife in his hand; he lifted it up towards his lips and took a lick of the blood. As the blood became one with Hanner's tongue, he looked back at the grave and whispered, "Tasty."

Hanner made his way to Brian's body and pulled the impaled arrow out of his chest. He reached into his pocket and pulled out his lighter and lit the end of the arrow. As the arrow slowly began to smolder, then catch fire, he threw it towards the grave. The arrow went up in flames and began to disappear from existence. With every flash of the flame, it took a part of the arrow with it.

Hanner grabbed his knife and began to cut where the arrow once lived. His knife went deep into Brian's chest, and he pulled it down in an effortless motion, splitting him wide open. As with Doug, he reached into Brian's chest cavity for the heart and fed it to the grave.

Chapter | 36

Harold looked at Donny as he climbed back into the truck. Not saying a word, he slowly handed Donny's lighter back to him, and they both sat in silence. Silence in the truck that brought them to the grave.

"You know," Harold said, "I never wanted to come up here with you."

"I know."

"But you… you, Donny, wanted me to," Harold said back to Donny.

"Correct."

"And you knew what was going to happen," he angrily said.

"Partially."

"Partially?"

"Yes, partially."

"Oh please. Can you please explain to me what the fuck 'partially' means? Please…?" Harold shouted.

"I mean 'partially' that I knew what was going to happen with the car, but I did not expect you to light the car on fire."

Harold shouted at Donny in the small cab of the tow truck, "YOU ASKED ME TO!"

"Yeah, but that was not my plan," Donny replied ever so quietly.

"Fuck you, Donny. Fuck you."

"Sorry. Sorry, Harold," Donny replied.

"You've done this before?" Harold asked.

"Yep."

"What?" Harold asked.

"Yep."

"You can't leave it at 'yep,'" Harold stated.

"I have done this before; I've done this before for Hanner."

"Really?"

"Yep."

"Why?" Harold asked.

"Hanner has evidence of me on the Drucker murders. How? I do not know, but he does. And, with all the other shit I've done in this town, figured it was best to play along."

Harold looked on at Donny in awe. In awe that Hanner held the same bullshit over his head as he did over Donny's head.

"What?" Donny said as he looked back at Harold.

"It's a shame," replied Harold.

"Tell me about it."

Donny started up the truck and they made their way back down the side of Stocker Hill. As they hit the main pavement, the tires began to sing, and the sun started to show a sign of life. The wind blew gently, and Walcott began to wake up.

Donny and Harold drove towards Hanner's house so Harold could get his car back. The ride was short with no conversation. Only the tires were doing the talking on this trip.

Donny took the turn and headed up Hanner's driveway. The tires stopped singing and began to bark with every movement with the gravel.

"Look," Harold whispered, pointing.

"Damn it," Donny growled under his breath as both of them discovered Hanner sitting on his front porch.

"Just drop me off and leave and I'll get my car and go," Harold said to Donny while patting his shoulder.

"It's not like he doesn't want details. He always wants details. Plus…." Donny replied.

"Plus, plus what?" Harold asked.

Donny looked back at Harold and stated, "Plus, he does not want any witnesses and you are a witness."

"Holy shit, Donny. Holy shit," Harold now growled.

"Yep."

"And you can take all your 'yeps' and shove them right up your…." Harold barked while not finishing the last part of his sentence.

Donny and Harold jumped out of the truck and made their way towards Hanner. Donny hit the steps first and Harold followed. With every step they made, Hanner's steps creaked with pain.

"What's he doing here?" Hanner asked.

"He brought me to get my car?" Harold replied.

"I was not talking to you," Hanner said as he raised his voice.

"I brought him to get his car. Just like Harold said," Donny said.

"Did you both go and torch the car?" Hanner asked as evil began to rise in his voice.

"Yes! No!" Donny and Harold said in unison.

"Well," Hanner asked, "is it yes, or is it no?"

"No," they both replied.

Hanner slowly got up from his spot and walked across the porch to meet Donny and Harold. Like two little boys getting in trouble from their father, the two of them slowly backed up and were now standing on the steps. With each step backwards, the steps creaked with fear and Hanner's footsteps echoed power.

"I guess we have a little problem here. Don't we?" Hanner asked. "I think we have a fib that is growing some legs. That fib is now becoming a lie." Hanner hesitated before resuming sternly, "And I hate lies."

"But, but Hanner—" Donny stumbled.

"Shhh…," Hanner breathed as he brought his finger up to his mouth.

Donny tilted his head down in shame and stuttered, "I can explain. I really can. I really can explain."

"Oh, Buck," Martha said from the front door, "I did not know we had company so early. Boys, would you like some coffee?"

Hanner shook his head no as Harold replied, "Yes ma'am, coffee, would be real good right now."

"Donny? What about you, Donny? Would you like coffee?" Martha asked politely.

"No, thank you. I'm good."

"Well, I'll bring you some anyways," Martha replied to Donny's comment.

"Darling," Hanner said, turning to his wife, "I guess I could use a refill. Sugar and cream too. Thank you."

Martha made an about-face from the door and strolled back into the kitchen where she had a fresh pot of coffee brewing. The breeze from the back of the house was carrying the coffee aroma out onto the front porch for the guys to smell.

"Sure, smells good," Donny said as he took a big whiff.

"You just got saved by the bell," Hanner said back to Donny as he gritted his teeth.

"Yes, sir."

"So, Hanner, we have a problem here. No, no. Let me correct that. We have a big problem here," Harold said as he stared down Hanner.

Without a pause, Hanner reached up and bitched slapped Harold across his face. "You show a little respect… HAROLD," Hanner finished.

Donny looked on at Harold like he was nuts. He could not believe that Harold would talk back to Hanner like that, let alone disrespect him in front of another person.

Donny whispered under his breath, "Are you crazy?"

Harold shook his head in denial and looked back at Donny and then onto Hanner. The slap from Hanner brought Harold back from whatever world he was in and now he was overcome with fear. As Harold looked on at Hanner, he slowly lowered his head and apologized for his misdoing.

The hallway announced that Martha was on her way back to the porch with a tray of coffee. "Here you go, boys," she said in her sweet voice as the aroma of the coffee got stronger.

"Here, Martha, let me get the door for you," Harold said as he reached for the door and opened it.

"Oh, Harold, you are always so nice," Martha said to Harold.

"Thank you, ma'am."

"You are very welcome, Harold."

The three men stood on the porch and reached for their coffees. All of them taking a sip of the freshly brewed coffee and nodding to Martha how good it was. Martha stood there for a moment and as the uncomfortable silence set in, she said, "Well, well. I'll let you men go back to your business. If you need anything, just shout."

"Thank you, honey," Hanner said.

Harold and Donny both spoke up with a thank-you and then slowly took a couple steps away from Hanner.

"Now, let's get back to business. Donny, you were saying," Hanner prompted.

Donny started to stammer after he took a sip of his coffee to kill a moment of time, "Well, you see, I needed Harold's help with the car and I could not do it myself and Harold helped with the car because, well, you know, I needed help."

"Have you ever needed help, Donny?" Hanner asked.

"No, sir."

Hanner barked back, "No, sir. Correct. Harold, he is correct. He never needed help before and now he does. Harold, can you explain this to me since Donny is just digging himself a bigger and bigger hole."

Harold stood there in silence.

"Harold. I asked you a question."

Harold stood there in silence.

"Oh, I see. Mr. Bigman can't talk anymore," Hanner barked as anger began to take over. "Let me see. Let me see here. Maybe. Just maybe. We all should make a trip back to the grave."

Donny started to whimper, "Please. Oh, please. Not that. I messed up. I did. It won't happen again. I promise."

Harold looked at Donny whimpering and his lower lip started to quiver with fear, "Hanner, it was my idea. I wanted to go with Donny. Don't be mad at him. It was my fault."

"DON'T LIE TO ME!" Hanner yelled as he forgot where he was standing.

Martha rushed to the front porch from the kitchen as fast as her legs could carry her. "You called, dear?" she asked.

"No, no, darling. We are good. Just a little debate about good and evil. We're just talking. Go back to the kitchen," Hanner gently said to his wife.

Martha looked on with fear as she knew something was brewing on the front porch. She said okay and made her way back into the kitchen.

Hanner's anger was growing, and Donny and Harold could see it in his eyes. His once crystal-clear eyes were now flaming red along with his pupils dilated with anger.

"Tell me the truth and tell it to me now," Hanner whispered to the guys.

"I wanted Harold to join me. He didn't want to, but I forced him. I begged him. It is my fault he went to the grave," Donny confessed.

"Good. Don't you feel better now?" Hanner asked. "Donny, you can go. Harold, you stay for a moment."

Donny let out a big sigh as relief rushed over his body. Without saying a word, Donny turned and made his way off the creakily porch towards the tow truck.

"Oh, Donny?" Hanner asked. "What's this about you wanting to leave Walcott?"

Donny stopped dead in his tracks. The relief he felt a moment ago was now gone. Gone and replaced with panic. As he slowly turned to look back at Hanner, Donny's bladder gave way, and its remanence ran down his leg. Without finishing his turn, Donny spoke up. "Sorry, sir. I don't know what you're talking about." Donny then finished his walk to the truck.

Harold stood there in disbelief and stared at Hanner. *How could he know that?* Harold thought to himself as the breeze that was silenced picked up and began to blow.

"Oh, Donny," Hanner barked again, "Harold will meet you at the garage."

Donny looked at Hanner from the driver's seat of the truck and acknowledged him with a movement of his head. Donny started the truck and slowly maneuvered the truck down the gravel driveway onto the road. As the truck pulled away, the engine roared as Donny pushed the truck to leave Hanner's grasp.

"I am?" Harold asked.

"Yes."

"Why?"

"Because."

"Because why?" Harold asked again.

"Because we have a little problem. You saw things you were not supposed to see. Now, I have two of you to worry about. The only way to solve this problem is one of you need to go?"

"Well, you said it yourself, Donny shouldn't leave Walcott," Harold briefly said. "Maybe you should let him go."

"Not what I meant. One of you needs to die. To die," Hanner gritted.

"Die. Why die? I won't say a word. I promise. I promise. Me and Donny, we are hush, hush. Guaranteed."

Hanner sat down and motioned to Harold to sit next to him on the porch. Harold sat down next to Hanner and Hanner patted Harold's knee. "I know you won't say anything Harold. I know. A few things, though. I need you and I need your garage. So, at this moment, you are safe. The other thing, the Drucker murders—you don't want to go away for that one. Do you? One more thing; so, I don't forget, you know how things slip my mind at my age, you are going to kill Donny."

Chapter | 37

It was another beautiful day in Walcott. The cool evening had dissipated and left behind silence. The town was motionless underneath the sun that covered the town with warmth. The usual movement that went along with Walcott on a daily basis was absent. The sun shined down on an eerie silence.

Donny pulled the truck up to the front of the garage and jumped out to open the overhead door. The once present front door laid shattered on the floor and Donny walked through it without a beat. He knew the door lost its battle with Hanner's foot and he was praying to God that he did not suffer the wrath of Hanner.

He rounded the corner and pressed the green button that sat still waiting to be used. He pressed the button and the overhead door started to rise. He walked through it and made his way back into the truck. As he fired up the truck, the engine made a commotion throughout the town, Donny noticed that there was not a single person in sight. He looked around as the truck rippled its engine noise in the motionless town.

"Wow," Donny said as he slowly pulled the truck into the garage, "this is kind of spooky. Where is everyone?"

Harold jumped into his car that Hanner took from his shop. The car, a '57 Chevy, was Harold's prize possession. The car was a carbon copy of his father's first ever new car. His father loved that Chevy as Harold loves his.

As Harold sat in his car for a moment, he looked at Hanner who was still sitting on the front porch of his house. Martha had joined him by this point and the two of them sat there like an old, happily married couple. As Martha reached for her coffee, she leaned forward in front of her husband. Hanner made eye contact with Harold and whispered with his lips, *"You know what you have to do."*

A chill ran down Harold's back and his emotions started to run wild. He started up his prized vehicle and tried to get his composure as he waved back to Martha who gingerly was waving goodbye to him. The car tried to move under the direction of Harold's right foot. The tires on the Chevy said no. They grasped the gravel driveway with all their might. Fear was running through the car, through Harold—both hesitant of what needed to be done.

The engine began to roar as Harold fought harder and harder with his foot. The tires would not let go. Hanner looked on from the porch and rose to his feet. With one big stomp, his foot hit the wooden porch, a ripple ran through the ground and forced the tires to let go. Harold's foot was planted on the accelerator and the tires let loose with a wail as the engine roared with anger. The car bucked back and forth and slid onto the road sideways. The tires cried with smoke and yelled with a screech as the Chevy made its way to the road. The road to kill Donny.

As Harold blinked to clear his eyes of tears, the car arrived back at his garage. He did not remember the trip; the trip from Hanner's, past Lock 17, through the middle of town, to his garage—he did not remember. It was a blink of an eye. It was a blink, a second, a moment of time and now he was minutes away from killing a friend.

Donny looked out from inside the garage and could see Harold sitting in his car weeping with emotion. "I wonder what's up? Has to be Hanner, has to be."

Donny walked out of the garage and approached Harold and the car. The motor lost all its power as Donny placed his left hand on the car door and leaned down to talk to Harold. The car sputtered and died as Donny began to talk, "You okay, buddy? Did I miss something? You looked all messed up."

"I'm fine."

"No, Harold, you are not fine. What is it?"

"I'll be in, in a second."

Donny reached in through the window and grabbed the keys. With his right hand, he yanked open the driver's door and helped Harold out of the car. "Harold, talk to me."

The two men walked into the garage and Donny pushed a chair over to Harold to sit on. He found his own place to plant his ass and looked at Harold with a gaze.

"Dude, you are killing me. What is it?" Donny spit out, "Man, that was a close one. I thought Hanner was going to take me out."

Harold looked at Donny and his eyes began to well with water. As Harold lowered his head, the tears splashed from his face onto the concrete floor and echoed, *"die, die, die…."*

Donny looked at Harold and his eyes went wide. His mind began to race as a thought rushed into his head. He sat there for a moment and stared at Harold who was still looking down at the floor.

"I'm sorry, Donny," Harold said.

"It's okay, Harold. I know what you have to do. Go ahead and do it. I can't run. We both know that. And, if you don't do it, your life is in danger and so is the rest of my family."

"I can't, Donny. I can't."

"You must," Donny said as he walked over to Harold who was in an uncontrollable ball of emotions.

"Donny."

"Stand up, Harold. I am ready to die."

"No. NO!"

"Harold, do what you have to do." Donny said as a turned around and kneeled on the floor with his back to Harold.

"I'm so sorry Donny."

"It's okay Harold."

Harold walked over to the wall and grabbed the control pad for the ceiling winch. He pressed the down button, and the cable began to lower itself with the hook on the end of it leading the way. A small clank echoed through the shop as the hook hit the floor. Harold grabbed the hook and looped it back around and attached it to the greasy cable that ran back up towards the ceiling. Harold began to cry as he slid the loop over Donny's awaiting neck. He slowly pulled the cable upward and the hook closed its grip. The cable became tight causing Donny's face to slowly become red.

"Do it, Harold. Do it," Donny whispered with his last breath of air.

Harold pressed the button and the cable grabbed Donny with all its might and began to squeeze. Slowly the cable rose into the air as Donny's body began to twitch with every moment of lift. Twitching as it rose in the air until the cable found its resting spot at the ceiling. After a couple more efforts to grab ahold of any life it could, Donny's body gave up its fight as his face turned blue.

"Harold, you in there?" Rob yelled through the front door of the garage.

Chapter | 38

Time stood still as voices rushed in through the shop. Harold stood in a dead stare at Donny's hanging body as more voices echoed by. "Harold are you there?" bounced off the walls, bounced of Donny, bounced off the floor and ceiling. Harold stood there contemplating what to do.

Footsteps started to inch closer and closer to Harold as he stood looking at his friend's dead body. With every step, Harold drifted further and further into his own world, a world of silence, stillness, death, and then, with a snap of the finger, Harold heard, *"RUN!"*

Before the voices realized there was someone else in the room beside the hanging corpse, Harold was out the back door and in full flight home. Home to safety.

Walcott was silent. Harold's footsteps were the only conversation taking place in town. The eerie silence didn't detour Harold from his goal, the safety of the walls of his home. As he rounded the corner towards his house, the simmering sun shining in his eyes, he stopped. He stopped his flee, his flee to safety.

Harold stood in the middle of his street looking at his house. Sitting there quietly in front of his house was Hanner's squad car. Any hope Harold had was gone and he slowly made his way to his house. Finishing his flight in a dull shuffle.

The only thing stopping Harold from entering his house was the flight of stairs that rose up to his front porch. With every stride, the steps creaked with age as Harold made his way up to the porch. Fear had become a common occurrence for Harold, and entering his house through his broken door was no exception. He knew what lay waiting for him—Hanner.

"Welcome home, Harold!" Hanner yelled from the kitchen. "Aren't you glad I told you to run?"

"Great. F'ing great," Harold whispered underneath his breath.

"I heard that."

"Yes, sir," Harold replied to Hanner, "be right there."

Harold stopped at the little bathroom that lived quietly between the front of the house and the kitchen. Harold's worn hands turned the handle to the sink and the water slowly rushed out of the faucet into his awaiting hands as the pipes let the house know they were working. The cold water splashed onto Harold's face with every lift of his hands. Each splash of water, Harold gained more and more composure and was ready to face Hanner again.

"We have a problem," Harold said as he exited the bathroom on his way to face Hanner.

"What's the problem?"

"The boys, they're at the garage. They're finding Donny's body as we speak," Harold said to Hanner.

"No. We do not have a problem, Harold," Hanner replied. "You have a problem. You have a dead body in your shop."

"Come on, Hanner," Harold begged, "don't do this to me. I have done everything that you've asked."

"I wonder if we have another homicide on our hands," Hanner stated.

"Hanner. Please. Please don't, please don't…." Harold began to cry out before finishing his sentence.

Hanner looked on at Harold as he began to cry. As the tears began to flow from Harold's eyes, Hanner said, "Calm down. Calm down, you incompetent fuck. It's not a homicide—it will be a suicide. Donny. Well, Donny thought it would be best to leave this world."

"You are a sick man. Sick, sick man!" Harold bellowed out.

"Yes I am. Yes I am…," Hanner followed with a smirk.

"How can you smile at a time like this?" Harold asked with pure disgust on this face.

Hanner smacked Harold across his face with an open hand and reached for his throat. As he slowly squeezed his hand, which was now fully engulfing Harold's neck, he pulled him closer to him and whispered, "because I can."

The grip was released from Harold's neck, and he dropped to his knees onto his oak floor. The floor that was still covered with remnants of the front door that was shattered by Hanner's foot. Harold slowly coughed and spit as his forehead was now butted up against the cool floor. He reached for his neck to ease the pain as he tried to regain the air he had just lost. With a deep breath, he slowly rose to his feet, Harold spoke out, "Yes, sir. I am sorry. Sorry, sir."

Hanner reached up and slapped Harold across the face again and barked, "Get your shit together, Harold."

"Yes, sir," he replied as he began to rub his face.

"Okay, Harold. There are a few things you need to remember. Are you listening?"

"Yes, Hanner, please go ahead."

Hanner leaned up against the hallway wall and began to pick at his fingernails. "The most important thing you need to get through your head is that the corpse that is hanging in your garage, well, it saved your life. If it wasn't Donny—it was going to be you. Are you following what I am telling you?"

"Yes. Completely. I got it," Harold replied as he stood in his hallway being lectured by evil.

Hanner continued, "See, I only have room for a few people in my life and lucky for you, you are one of them. Now, get your ass over to the garage, act like you know nothing, get all emotional and call me about Donny. Better yet, call Becky at the office and she'll dispatch me out there. The boys won't know the difference and you'll be cleared of any wrongdoing. Act it up good, though, get those emotions going and maybe you can throw in a few tears too."

"I won't be acting," Harold whispered back to Hanner as he stared him down in the hallway.

With a flick of the wrist, Hanner's hand was planted back across Harold's face again while he commanded, "It better be convincing!"

Chapter | 39

Walcott was still silent as noon approached. The heat from the sun was flowing over the empty streets. No signs of life existed in Walcott at this moment. Birds weren't in flight, wind was calm, clouds were gone—no signs of life except the boys.

Brad got a small, damp cloth and was patting Rob's face. Rob's pale face accepted the cool cloth, and his eyes began to move and slightly opened. As the light in the room entered the small slits his eyes were peeking through, Rob asked, "What happened? Where am I?"

"You're in Harold's garage. You fainted," Brad replied as he helped Rob get in a sitting position.

"Fainted?"

"Yes. Fainted," Brad replied.

"From what? How long have I been out?" Rob questioned as his hand held the cool cloth close to his face.

Brad looked Rob in the eyes and pulled the cloth from his hands to get his attention, "I don't know how long you've been out, but we need to get you up and outside. John and Reed are out front, and you need to join them."

"Okay. Okay, Brad. Help me up."

"Okay, Rob, but I want you to get up and walk straight outside. Straight outside and no looking around," Brad commanded.

"Brad. I know. I won't look at Donny again. I'll stand up and go straight outside," Rob said as he slowly rose to his feet.

"You remember what happened now?" Brad asked.

"Yes. Yes, I do. Let's go outside; let's go outside now!"

Brad helped Rob to his feet and began to escort him outside. As Rob began to drag his feet out of the garage, his curiosity got the best of him, and he had to peek back at Donny's body. With a slight turn of the head while leaning back to see over Brad's shoulder, Rob caught a glimpse of Donny. The glimpse turned into a stare, and Donny's blue face shot Rob a smile. Donny shot his head around in fear – scared Donny was staring at him.

"Oh my God!" Rob yelled as his knees buckled under his weight again.

Brad caught Rob before he hit the floor completely and pulled him up to help him finish his walk out of the garage. "You looked? Didn't you? You fucking looked."

"I, I di… I did…," Rob stammered.

"Why would you do that?"

"Donny smiled at me, Brad. Donny smiled at me!" cried Rob.

"Please," Brad said. "You're imagining things."

"He smiled, he totally smiled, I swear!" Rob yelled.

Brad helped Rob sit down next to John and Reed against the front wall of the garage. John had evidence of vomit on his clothes and Reed had his head buried in his hands. The sun had a full blast stare on the boys and the smell of death was in the air. The stagnant air slowly rolled out of the garage across the boys' noses.

Reed lifted his head, "What are we going to do?"

Rob was in no shape to answer; he just sat there with his quivering lip, repeating, "He smiled, he smiled, he smiled…."

John just shrugged his shoulders and looked up at Brad who was standing over the other boys. Brad rubbed his face a little and ran his hands through his damp hair. "I'll tell you what we are going to do. We're going to call Hanner. We're going call him now."

"Yes. Call Hanner," Reed said.

John followed with, "Do it."

Rob just sat there and cried.

– – –

Harold walked out of his house and watched Hanner climb into his squad car. As he peered at Hanner who was now sitting behind the wheel of the car, Hanner motioned to Harold to approach. Harold's mind wandered with thoughts, but all he knew was he was going to keep his mouth shut so Hanner could not hear any whisper that might flow off his lips.

The sun fought Harold with every step as he made his way to Hanner's driver's side window. As Hanner glanced up from his seat in the car, he spoke softly, "Watch this."

Hanner lifted his left arm up in the air and stared at Harold with his gleaming red eyes. With his hand held high, he snapped his fingers and a rush of cool, deathly air rushed through the streets of Walcott. The beating sun disappeared, and dark storm clouds rolled in. As Hanner pulled away, he said, "I learned that from my father."

The clouds in the sky began to bark with thunder and began to throw lighting across the heavens. The people of Walcott came alive, and the streets bellowed with traffic. Harold stood speechless again as the wind blew across his face.

Beep, beeeeep! The horn shouted. "Get out of the street, Harold," yelled the driver.

Harold snapped too and began his jog back to the garage.

— — —

Brad was about to make his way back into the garage to call Hanner as a rush of cool air blew across his face. The sound of thunder echoed throughout Walcott and lightning began to flash.

"WTF?" Brad blurted out.

Reed looked up and stood up as fast as he could. "I didn't see this rolling in."

John sat against the wall and pointed—pointed at the people and cars that were now showing life in Walcott.

"WTF?" Brad repeated.

Reed shrugged his shoulders. "Beats the hell out of me. Go call Hanner."

"Boys, boys…," Harold yelled from a distance. "Boys, what's going on?" He finished as he began to jog towards the boys who were gathered in front of his garage.

The boys looked over and watched Harold run up to them. "What's going on?" Harold asked as he leaned over to catch his breath, "I'm too old to run anymore."

"Harold, we have a problem. Correction, you have a major problem," Brad stated.

"What problem? Hey, what the hell happened to my door? Who kicked in my door? Guys, I'm asking, who kicked in my door?"

"The door is not the problem. The problem is in the shop," Reed pointed out.

"No, the door is a problem. What? My shop? What's wrong with my shop?" Harold demanded.

Brad looked around at the other guys and then straight at Harold.

"Brad, what's going on here?" Harold asked as he watched Brad look around and then back at him.

"It's Donny, Harold!" Brad shouted.

"Donny? What about Donny?"

"He's in your shop and it's not good."

Harold tilted his head and asked, "What do you mean not good? Is he drunk again? What an asshole. I am sick of him sneaking into my shop and stealing my beer."

"It's not it at all. He's dead," stated Brad as he pointed towards the back of the shop. "He's hanging in there. He's dead."

"Dead... dead? What? Dead? What do you mean? Donny's dead?" Harold asked frantically as he darted into the shop.

"WAIT!" yelled the boys, but it was too late. Harold had already started to rush into the garage. Harold's mind raced with ever step. His sweaty head dripped with perspiration as his dry lips whispered, "please believe me, please believe me, Hanner's going to kill me, please believe me."

The boys all stood at the front of the garage waiting to hear a sound from Harold. The sounds of a man finding his dead friend.

Harold approached Donny's hanging, still body and looked at him with his eyes wide open. With no sound coming out of his mouth, he opened his mouth and stared at Donny—stared at Donny's blue face. As Harold stared on, Donny's face cracked a smile and whispered, "scream...."

As the boys stood in silence at the front of the shop, a screech echoed out of the shop, a bloodcurdling screech. A screech that would wake the dead. The people on the street stopped and looked towards the garage.

"Ummm," Brad began to speak, "I think he found Donny."

Harold rushed out of the garage screaming in fear. As he approached the boys, he collapsed onto the concrete sidewalk and landed face-first. The thud of his head hitting the sidewalk knocked Harold out as blood began to ooze out of his mouth and nose.

"Call Hanner and an ambulance!" yelled one of the boys.

"On it!" shouted Brad as he rushed back into the garage to find a phone.

As blood oozed out of Harold's face and Donny's dead body hung in the garage, the town's people began to gather around the front of the shop wondering what all the commotion was.

Chapter | 40

The window in the room threw off a glare and made the red blinking light the only indication that Jack was still alive. With every beat of his heart, the machines attached to him monitored his life. The morning was just starting to bloom as the sun started its climb to the sky.

The morning nurse walked into the room where Jack lay and checked his vitals. Jack's breathing was normal, and his color was starting to return. The few days before were filled with trauma and everyone on the floor knew Jack was lucky to be alive.

"We have a fighter here," the doctor said to the nurse as he walked into the room.

"We sure do, sir," the nurse replied.

"We sure couldn't let a good man like this leave this world too soon," the doctor went on to say. "Please keep an eye on him and let me know if anything peculiar comes up."

He finished up in the room where Jack lay and took a quick look at his chart. As the doctor began to walk out of the room, the nurse spoke up. "Excuse me, sir, I mean, Doctor, ummm, I was wondering?"

"Yes," the doctor replied as he stood in the doorway holding up the doorjamb, "you have a question?"

"Yes, Doctor, I do," the nurse began to ask. "Is it true that Jack died on the table?"

"Jack died three times. At the house, on the way to the hospital, and on the table with my hand in his chest. Like I said, we have a fighter here," the doctor said with authority.

"Thank you, Doctor," the nurse replied.

The doctor stood in the doorway and looked back at the nurse whose head was now hanging low and asked, "Why do you ask?"

"Well, I ah, well you see, he and I, ummm, went out on a date and I was hoping for a second one," the nurse spit out.

The doctor walked over to the nurse and reached for her face. With his left hand on her face while looking down at her, he whispered, "Don't worry, Donna. He'll be awake and able to ask you out very soon."

Donna started to cry and replied in a happy, but whimpering voice, "Thank you, Doctor."

– – –

Martha looked up and noticed the sunlight peeking through the morning blinds. Her eyes blinked as she began to get used to the morning light. Martha reached up to rub her eyes and turned her head to look at the clock that sat on Buck's side of the bed.

"Oh my," Martha said, "I can't see a thing without my glasses."

Martha rolled her body over in the bed and let her feet hit the floor. With one good push, she lifted herself up and walked to her dresser for her glasses. She lifted her glasses to her head and the once-blurry room became crystal clear to her eyes. With a slow turn, Martha glanced back to the clock. The red blur was now announcing it was 9:00 a.m.

"Nine o'clock," Martha blurted out. "Nine o'clock? Buck was supposed to wake me at seven. I want to go see Jack."

Martha did everything in her power to get rolling for the day. Her normal casual pace of getting ready that morning was changed to frantic movements. Martha laid out her clothes for the day and made her way to the bathroom to get ready for her visit. Her visit to Jack.

As Martha drew her bath, a tear rolled down her swollen cheek. Martha's tear was the first of many as she began to cry harder and harder. "Please Lord," she whimpered, "please help me find the strength to visit Jack. To stand up strong for him, to show Jack that I am sorry for what I have done, please help me find the strength. Please help me. Please help Jack."

Martha got her composure and finished getting ready. She had a long drive up to Dover to see Jack and wanted to get going as soon as she could.

Martha's mind was starting to race as she hustled to get out of the house. Half of her thoughts were to call her husband and yell at him; the others were to leave it alone.

Martha made her way out of the house towards the barn to her greenish gray Dodge Dart. The car hardly saw the sunlight anymore, but it was good enough for what Martha used it for. As she slowly pulled the squeaking door open on her car and made her way into the driver's seat, her mind raced, and she spoke to the Lord once more. "Why wouldn't Buck wake me up to see Jack? What is he hiding from me?"

Chapter | 41

The sheriff's office was buzzing that morning. Several of the local towns needed help that day and the office was short of patrols. All the deputies were out on calls helping where they could.

The Deputy Sheriff in charge walked into the office that morning to a bushel full of chaos. Jenny, the dispatcher in charge of the shift, yelled over the deputy, "Where have you been and where is Callahan?"

Jackson, the deputy in charge, stopped in his tracks and looked around at all the commotion and threw up his hands. "You know this is my late-start day and what do you mean where's Callahan?"

"Callahan. You remember Callahan? Our boss. He has not shown up at all today and the shit is hitting the fan!" Jenny yelled out before answering the next call. "County Sheriff's Department, how can I help you?"

Jackson waited for Jenny to get of the call before speaking up again. "Are you sure Callahan hasn't checked in?"

"I'm sure, dumbass," Jenny blurted out. "County Sheriff's Department, how can I help you?"

Jackson rolled his eyes and waited for Jenny to get off another call. As Jackson stood near the dispatch desk, he thought of Callahan and where he could be. Jenny finished her call and shot Jackson a look as if to ask, *"you're still here?"*

"Okay, Jenny, simmer down a little and let's go through this. Who was on dispatch last night?" Jackson asked.

"I think it was Margaret," she replied.

"You think?" Jackson questioned.

"It was Margaret," she said.

"On the log, what was the last interaction with Callahan?" Jackson inquired.

Jenny fumbled around with the computer log while mumbling, "Hold on, hold on a second, hold on…."

Jacksons patience wore thin, and he finally blurted out, "Come on, damn it."

"Don't yell at me," Jenny replied with a squeal, "I'm looking."

"Well?"

"Wait. Here we go. According to the log, he ended his interview at the firehouse around 6 o'clock and then he was heading out to Buck Hanner's place to interview the wife, Martha."

Jackson followed with a question after Jenny finished, "Anything else?"

"Yes," Jenny replied, "according to the log, around eight o'clock, Margaret says Callahan checked in, but it was staticky."

"Where is Margaret now?"

"At home. Why?" Jenny questioned.

Jackson sat for a moment and replied, "Because Callahan has been coming to this office for years and he has never broken his routine. Never. Get Margaret in here."

"Okay," Jenny said, trembling.

Jackson made his way to Callahan's office to check for any signs that he had been there since yesterday. As he walked into his office, a chill ran up his spine. Jackson could see Callahan's pickup truck through the window of the office. The same truck that Callahan drove to work every day of the week. It did not matter what time he got off for the day, Callahan loved that truck, and he was going to drive it home.

The deputy quickly exited Callahan's office and yelled to Jenny, "Forget Margaret. Call Callahan's house and talk to his wife. I'm heading to Hanner's place to check it out. I'll check in with you later."

Jenny yelled back with acknowledgment before answering the phone again, "County Sheriff's Department, how can I help you?"

Chapter | 42

The sun was at high noon when Martha pulled up to the hospital. She found the closest parking spot to the main entrance of the hospital as she could because her legs did not like long walks anymore. As she shut down her car for the moment, she looked up into the sky and spoke to the Lord again, "Please give me strength Lord, please give me strength."

Martha made her way into the hospital to find a single lady watching over the courtesy desk. She timidly approached the desk and spoke to the woman. "Excuse me, miss, I need to know what room I can find Jack Johansson?"

"Let me check for you," the woman replied. "I see here, ma'am, Jack is in the ICU and is not allowed any visitors unless they are immediate family."

Martha lowered her head and slowly began to cry. The tears rolled down her cheek and then landed on the counter. Before Martha could get her composure, the lady behind the desk spoke up. "Ahh ma'am, don't cry. Is that Jack your grandson?"

Martha put up her hand, asking for a minute as the tears still flowed out of her eyes. The lady behind the desk took that as a yes, and replied, "Okay ma'am, you go to the end of this hallway, and you'll see a set of elevators on your left. Take the elevators up to the sixth floor and when you get off the elevators, the ICU will be straight ahead."

Martha's voice cracked as she replied, "Thank you."

"Did you get all of that, ma'am?" the lady asked Martha as Martha began to walk away.

"Yes, dear," Martha gently remarked as she made her way down the hallway.

Martha did not want to let on that she was not Jack's grandmother. Her walk was brisk, as brisk as Martha could muster. She got to the elevators and pushed the up button.

Ding. The elevator moaned that it was ready as it opened its doors to welcome all passengers in.

Martha boarded the elevator for the ride up to the sixth floor. As every floor blinked by, Martha's heart began to beat harder and harder—second floor, beat, third floor, beat beat, fourth, fifth—her heart was racing and then the light came on. Sixth floor and *Ding!*

Martha's legs were now wobbly as her heart raced in anticipation. Martha made her way into the hallway before the elevator doors shut and she had to take another ride. She walked gently over to the closest bench in the hallway and thoughts of what she was going to say to Jack flashed aggressively across her mind. "Breathe Martha breathe," she said to herself.

Martha looked down the hallway and she could see the glass doors that separated the ICU from the rest of the hospital. Her legs still weak and wobbly, Martha collected her strength and got up from the bench. Step by step she walked toward the ICU doors. Her mind racing, her heart beating, her eyes watering, and then her vision started to get blurry. She began to rub her eyes as her sight went narrow. Martha dropped to her knees and face-planted in the middle of the hospital hallway.

"Holy shit!" yelled the doctor who was watching her through the ICU doors. "That lady just went down. Nurse, follow me."

The doctor and nurse rushed to Martha's side. The doctor knelt on one side of her and the nurse on the other side. The doctor felt for a pulse and found nothing. Felt again and found nothing again. There was no pulse. There was no sign of life. Martha was gone. Martha was dead.

Chapter | 43

The shop had a damp air of death around it as Brad rushed into the office to call for help. Donny's lifeless body was hanging in the shop and Harold was out cold in the front with blood oozing from his face. Brad's composure was running low as he picked up the old office phone from its cradle.

Beep, beep, beep, the phone replied as Brad pressed 9-1-1.

"Walcott emergency," a voice said from the other end of the phone.

"Becky, is that you?" Brad asked.

"Yes, it is," she came back with. "Who is this?"

"It's Brad. Brad Sm—" Brad did not finish answering before Becky jumped in again.

"I know who you are Brad, why are you calling the station over 9-1-1? What happened?"

"We have an emergency. Donny, Donny is, Donny is dead, and we need an ambulance, an ambulance, an ambulance for Harold. Hurt. He is hurt. Harold is—" Brad spoke frantically, barely getting the words out.

"Hold on a second," Becky replied. "Did you say Donny is dead and Harold is hurt?"

"Yes."

"What happened?"

"Don't know."

"Okay, you hang tight. I'll call Hanner and get an ambulance out there right away. You stay calm, Brad," Becky finished before dispatching Hanner and an ambulance.

Brad rushed out of the shop and announced to the crowd that Hanner was on his way and the ambulance would be there shortly.

The crowd of Walcott people stood from a distance watching the boys. They could not gather the strength, the will, to move closer. They appeared content to watch from a distance and stand there in unison, stand in silence, not moving any closer.

Brad approached Harold who was now being attended to by Reed. Reed rolled Harold over and was trying to wipe the blood off Harold's face, but with every swipe of the hand, more blood oozed out. Out of the cut the concrete aggressively added to Harold's face.

Rob was still trying to gather his wits as tears slowly subsided from his eyes. John stood over Brad and Reed as they dealt with Harold. A slight breeze rushed past John's face that caught his attention to look up. As his eyes made contact with the crowd, he noticed that the people he saw were almost faceless. They had a face, but he could not make them out. At a quick glance he saw them, but a full-on stare, he saw nothing.

John looked around and hesitated as he spoke to the guys, "Ummm, guys, is it me or is something wrong with those people."

Reed barked from his kneeling position, "Kind of busy here."

Brad followed, "Yeah John. Busy here."

Rob walked from where he was planted and walked out of his emotions. He had his composure back and was ready to face the day. The day without Donny. As he walked up next to John and saw the distant crowd, he whispered, "WTF. They have no fucking faces, but do they?"

The whisper in Rob's voice caught the attention of Reed and Brad and they both stood up at the same time as Brad commented, "Looks evil."

"Fucking evil," Reed followed as a shiver raced through his body. "Where's Hanner when you need him?"

— — —

A rush of anger raced through Hanner as the clock on his squad car struck noon. The sun was shining now as he gripped the steering wheel tightly. His burly hands went white as his grip strengthened. As his anger grew, Hanner had only one place to go.

Taking a left at the crossroad, Hanner headed towards the Hill. Toward Stocker Hill, the one place where he felt whole. The trip to the Hill was swift as Hanner's patrol car easily took the road. Mile after mile the car devoured the blacktop with vengeance until it arrived at the base of the Hill.

Hanner looked up at the gravel road that led up the side of the Hill. With a push of the throttle, Hanner's car was sitting on the road next to the green plateau. He exited the car as his body became engulfed with anger. The large gray rocks cowered in his presence as Hanner walked toward the grave. Every step towards the grave, his anger grew until he reached the edge of it and yelled, "WHY MARTHA?"

The wind whispered by Hanner's face and slowly became brisker. With every gust of wind, Hanner's face felt pain, the next gust of wind dropped Hanner to his knees. He was now kneeling on the edge of the grave. Hanner lowered his head and spoke into the darkness, "I understand." The wind stopped immediately, and he rose to his feet.

Hanner looked into the grave as his eyes became red with power. A silhouette of the grave glistened in his eyes. Hanner slowly reached his hand up into the air and with the snap of his finger it was done.

Chapter | 44

Hanner's squad car sat in silence next to the plateau. The eerie feeling of helplessness was in the air as Hanner stood still next to the grave. The air was cool and damp and all was silent.

The speaker in Hanner's car started to crackle, "Buck, you there? Come in Buck. Buck, you there?"

Hanner looked up from the grave as his red eyes faded out and his natural look became present again. The gray cowering rocks stood at attention again as Hanner made his way back to his car.

"Buck, it's Becky, we have a problem. You there?" Becky's voice bellowed out of the speaker.

Hanner jumped into his squad car and picked up the mic on the radio, "Here, Becky, what's going on?"

Hanner new exactly what was going on and had to gain back his poise. He had to be the town's local authority while knowing it was his snap that ended his wife's life. If there were any signs of the real Hanner left, the light on that life was extinguished when Martha left this world. There was no Buck Hanner anymore.

"Buck, I got a call from one of the boys. He says Harold is hurt and Donny is dead," Becky frantically explained to Hanner.

"Donny is dead?" Hanner replied.

"Yes. That is what he said," Becky came back with.

"On my way," Hanner said back into the mic as he started the cruiser up.

"I called an ambulance too," Becky said.

"I told you. I'm on my way!" Hanner yelled back before pulling away from the grave.

Hanner put the accelerator to the floor. The tires spun with vigor while churning up ruts in the plateau's grass. The car lurched from the grass and before he could blink his eyes, the car was at the bottom of Stocker Hill. The tracks left behind from the squad car were deep and dark. The tracks were the only sign that anyone was near the grave that day.

The wind began to pick up as Hanner faded away. A gust of wind flowed through the valley and up to the plateau. The green plateau began to move in the wind and with every gust the tracks slowly faded away until there was nothing.

Becky had an uneasy feeling in her belly. "Buck does not yell at me like that," she said out loud before picking up the mic again. "They're at Harold's garage."

Hanner's car started the journey to the garage. As the trees blurred by, Hanner picked up the mic and gently, with authority, squeezed the button on the mic and said, "I KNOW!"

"Yes, sir," Becky replied as she thought to herself, *how does he know where to go?*

– – –

The boys could hear two sets of sirens off in the distance.

Brad said, "Here they come. Must be Hanner and the ambulance."

The other boys nodded in acknowledgment while Reed was still attending to Harold. The faceless crowd was still watching from a distance as the boys tried not to stare. As the sirens got louder and closer, the faceless crowd became restless and started to appear normal. Their faceless faces started to become recognizable as eyes, ears, and noses all appeared.

"Holy shit, holy shit!" Rob said, "did you see that?"

Brad looked up and stared at the crowd. "No. What happened?"

"They have faces now."

John stood quiet for a moment and stammered, "Their faces just appeared. They went from nothing at all to looking at us with real eyes."

Brad stared into the crowd and began to make out the faces, "Son of a bitch, you're right. I know those people. Look, it's Miss Vasquez who runs the bakery and James that barber and look. Look. It's Dory. Dory is watching us too."

Reed stood up from Harold and looked over at Dory. Dory's face had no emotions whatsoever. He just stood there. "That's not like Dory. Dory would be over here, over here in the mix of things."

The sirens on Hanner's squad were loud and piercing as he pulled up to the garage. The boys covered their ears as the sirens echoed around them. The piercing sound suddenly stopped, and silence engulfed the boys. Hanner stepped out of his car and looked over at the crowd. Throwing his hand up in the air, he snapped his finger and the crowd suddenly disappeared.

"Whoa," Hanner said as he walked toward the boys and noticed Harold laying on the ground, "what happened to him?"

Brad did not say a word but pointed to the garage. Hanner nodded his head in acknowledgment as he turned to the other boys and asked, "You all okay?"

"Yes," John said, "except the crowd of people is kind of freaking me out."

Hanner stopped in his tracks and questioned, "What crowd?"

Rob pointed to across the street and yelled, "That crowd."

Reed stammered, "W-what crowd? They're gone."

John could not find the words and became emotional while the rest of the boys' faces went blank. Brad finally blurted out, "Oh, what the hell is going on here?"

"You sure you guys are, okay?" Hanner asked before making his way into the garage.

The ambulance's sirens screamed the entire way as it pulled up to the garage. Before the ambulance stopped, the sirens went from a full wail to a silent whisper. Two paramedics jumped out of the rig—Alex and Ray.

"What's going on, boys?" Ray asked as he made his way to Harold.

Alex went to the back of the rig and grabbed the bag of supplies. He rushed back to Harold to help Ray and noticed Hanner's car. As he kneeled next to Harold, he pulled out the smelling salt and whispered to Ray, "Did you notice who's here?"

Ray nodded as he cracked the smelling salt and waved it under Harold's nose. Harold began to flail and cough as he came to. "What happened?"

"We don't know. We just got here," Alex replied.

Harold coughed a couple times and sat up on the concrete. Ray grabbed some gauze and began attending to Harold's wound. Alex grabbed Harold's right arm and started an IV. The two paramedics worked in unison attending to Harold's needs as the boys waited in anticipation for Hanner to exit the garage.

"Boys, what happened?" Harold asked as he pushed Ray's hands away from his face.

Alex jumped in as he went back to working on Harold's gash, "Harold, we're here to help you. Let us get you situated before you start worrying about how you got here."

The boys looked on at Harold and then back to the garage. Seconds ticked by and no word from Hanner. The boys stood there waiting.

Chapter | 45

The hospital went quiet as Martha's body lay in the hallway. The only sounds that could be heard were the short breaths of the doctor and nurse who watched Martha die.

Martha's dead body lay in the middle of the hallway, and no one knew who she was at that moment in time. She died alone on her way to see Jack, to make her peace with him and ask the Lord for forgiveness in the presence of the person she hurt. That would not happen; that would not happen because of a snap of her husband's fingers.

"Nurse, do we know who this woman is?" the doctor asked as they both were still kneeling next to Martha in the hallway.

"No, Doctor," the nurse replied. "I've never seen her before."

"Okay then, poor lady, dying like that. Okay, let's get a gurney and call security ASAP," the doctor told the nurse as they both rose to their feet.

"Yes, Doctor," the nurse replied as she motioned to the few other nurses that were still standing behind the glass doors in the ICU.

The doctor rolled Martha over and looked into her eyes. With one motion of his hand, the doctor ran his hand down Martha's forehead, closing her eyes forever.

"Doctor, Doctor, security is on their way," one of the on-call nurses yelled out to the doctor.

The doctor stood still with his hand resting on Martha's face. His hand started to tremor as it lay on her face. The doctor's pink skin became white and clammy as his mind rushed with answers. Sitting there still, the doctor finally spoke. "She's cold. How can she be cold? She just passed. How can this be?"

"What, Doctor?" the nurse asked, standing close to him.

"Ummm," the doctor stammered, "ummm, nothing nurse. Ahhh, what did you say?"

"That security is on its way," she replied. "You okay, Doctor? You don't look so well."

"Yes, nurse. I'm okay," the doctor replied. "Excuse me, sir." One of the attendings on duty spoke up. "We need to get this lady on the gurney."

"Okay," the doctor replied. "After we find out who she is, I want to talk to the pathologist on call."

"Doctor," a nurse jumped in, "we can't send her to the pathologist without permission from the coroner."

"I know, nurse. Just do as I say!" the doctor shouted.

The two attending doctors on call reached down and grabbed Martha's body. One of the doctors was at her feet while the other doctor was at her hands.

The one doctor bent down towards Martha's feet and directed the other doctor, "on the count of three, we'll pick her up and put her on the gurney."

"Okay," the other attending replied, "let me get a grip of her hands first, then you count down."

The doctor bent down towards Martha's hands and positioned himself to get ready to lift. Once kneeling, the doctor reached for Martha's hands and took them into his own hands. Gripping Martha's hands, the doctor hesitated, shook with fear, and threw Martha's hands down.

"What's wrong?" someone asked from the sideline.

"She's cold."

"Cold?"

"Yes, she's cold. How can that be?" the doctor finished up with as he walked away to get his composure.

"Enough of this!" the doctor in charge yelled out. "Pick this woman up and take her downstairs. We will figure out what happened to her later. The last thing we need is for people to start traveling through this hallway and find a corpse on the floor. And where the fuck is security?"

"Yes, sir," one of the other doctors yelled.

"On his way," replied the nurse.

"Have security meet me downstairs in the autopsy room," the doctor ordered as a group of doctors and nurses lifted Martha's body onto the gurney.

The doctor in charge walked away from the crowd of nurses and doctors and made his way to the elevator. Pushing the down button, he looked up and began to watch the lights above the door light up until the sixth-floor light was lit. The elevator doors opened, and the doctor stepped into the elevator for his trip down to the morgue.

"Why is she cold? Why is she cold?" the doctor kept repeating as the elevator made its way to the basement.

As the doors opened, security was waiting for the doctor and so was the pathologist in charge.

"Frank," the doctor said to the head of security, "thanks for meeting me. We have a body coming down and I need you to check her purse to see who she is."

"Sam," the pathologist in charge said to the doctor, "you okay? You don't look so good."

"No, no I am not. I have never felt anything like this before. This is not sitting with me very well," Michael, the doctor, told the pathologist.

"What is wrong?"

"The corpse, the lady who died, she's cold," Michael finished with.

"Cold. We see cold stiffs all the time."

Michael looked over at the pathologist just as Martha's body was arriving in the elevator. As the elevator doors opened, Michael said, "Not a minute after the person died."

"What?"

"Yes. She died in front of us. We watched it. I checked for a pulse. Nothing. Then I rolled her over and she was cold. She was fucking cold," Michael said with urgency.

"You must have been mistaken. It takes hours for a body to cool down."

"Check for yourself."

The nurse rolled Martha's body out of the elevator into the hallway. Without saying a word, the nurse turned around and caught the next elevator up, up away from the basement, from the morgue, from Martha's cold body.

The pathologist walked over to Martha's body on the gurney. He picked up Martha's purse and tossed it to Frank. Frank immediately searched for any identification he could find to let them know who this dead woman was. Sam pulled the sheet back that was covering Martha's body and reached for her hand. Sam's warm hand touched Martha's hand and he instantly dropped it. Then he questioned, "How long has she been dead?"

"Ten minutes or so, fifteen at the max," Michael replied.

"Impossible," Sam stuttered.

"Got it," Frank said from the sidelines. "Her name is Martha Hanner. She lives in Walcott. If I am correct. She's the wife of the sheriff over there."

Sam looked over at Frank and said, "Don't call the husband yet. I want to check something out first."

Frank nodded with understanding and made his way down the hallway, before he got out of sight, he yelled, "Call me when you need me."

"Michael, push her in here. I want to check a few things out before we get anyone else involved in this," Sam directed.

"That's exactly what I was thinking. Let's draw some blood first and see if we find anything peculiar there," Michael followed.

Sam and Michael each grabbed a side of Martha's gurney and wheeled her into the main room. The room was lined with several stainless-steel tables, sinks, and carts with shiny tools on them.

Sam walked away from the gurney towards the back wall to grab a vial to take some blood samples. Along the way, he picked up a fresh needle and a few other devices.

Michael reached over to Martha's arm and positioned it for taking blood while speaking to Sam, "Let's take some blood first and then check her core temperature."

"Okay," Sam replied as he took an alcohol swab and cleaned Martha's arm where he was going to draw some blood. He attached the needle to the vial and went for Martha's vein in her arm. The needle slowly entered Martha's arm. Sam sat there for a moment and waited for some blood to exit Martha's body. Eventually, Sam spoke, "Michael, there's no blood coming out."

Michael replied, "What do you mean no blood?"

"Exactly what I said." Sam looked at Michael. "There's no blood. There should be blood and there is none."

"Are you sure?"

"Yes. There is no blood in this woman."

Chapter | 46

Midafternoon had set in, and Ray and Alex had an IV in Harold's arm and got the gash that was created under control. The smelling salt brought Harold's mind to full awareness and his mind raced with thoughts of pushing the button. Pushing the button that raised Donny to his death.

"Okay, you two stop fussing with me and get this tube out of my arm. What the hell is going on here?" Harold blurted out to Ray and Alex.

Alex looked at Ray and asked, "You taking this one?"

Ray nodded and began to speak to Harold, "Harold, you might have a concussion, you were knocked out, you need to go the hospital to get checked out. Plus, you might need stitches for that gash."

"I'm not going anywhere," Harold responded, "give me something for this headache and get me up. And get this fucking tube out of my arm."

"Harold. Please let's check you out. If all is well, you'll be back here in a few hours." Ray pleaded with Harold.

"No. Tube out now or I will rip it out," Harold stated as he gritted his yellow teeth.

"You heard him, boys," Hanner's voice echoed from the garage.

Hanner walked to the edge of the garage so he could see out. He shot a look at Ray and Alex that made them go white.

Alex whispered, "Same look he gave us before."

Ray replied, "Yes, sir. Harold, we just need you to sign this form stating you're refusing treatment."

"He's not signing anything!" Hanner bellowed from inside the garage as he walked out of sight again.

Ray pulled the IV from Harold's arm as the boys helped Harold stay stable on his legs. He put a piece of gauze where the IV was located and taped it down. Ray looked at Alex and motioned for them to leave the premises.

Alex looked at Harold before he walked away and stated, "Harold, you're making a mistake. You should really go to the hospital. If you need any help—please call us again."

Ray loaded up the rig with the equipment as Alex fired up the ambulance. The diesel engine in the ambulance purred to a tick as Alex waited for Ray to jump in the passenger seat. The door slowly opened, and Ray peeked his head into the ambulance. Looking at Alex, Ray stated, "We never went into the garage, there is supposed to be another victim."

"I know. Get in the rig," Alex responded.

Ray crawled into the rig and threw his hands up in the air while asking, "What are we going to do?"

"We're going to get out of here and call Callahan," Alex angrily stated as he dropped the ambulance into drive and pulled away from garage.

"Good idea. Let's get away from here. Hanner gives me the creeps," Ray responded as he picked up the mic to call into dispatch. "We're done here," Ray said as he pushed the button on the mic so it would accept his words, "patient refused treatment. Would not sign the consent form. We are leaving the premises and need to speak to Sheriff Callahan."

A voice came back over the speaker, "Roger that. Will note the logbook. You said Callahan?"

"Yes," Ray replied, "we need to talk to Sheriff Callahan."

"Got it," the voice responded. "I'll get him on the line. Hold on please."

Alex and Ray were well away from the garage by now and headed out of town. The ambulance billowing black smoke out of its tailpipe as it made its way down the blacktop.

"Come on!" yelled Ray as he smacked the dashboard.

Alex looked over at Ray and asked, "What's your problem?"

"I want Callahan on the line now."

"Give her a second. She's working on it."

"Whatever," Ray responded as he looked out the passenger window to see Stocker Hill towering in the background. As Ray gazed out the window, he mentioned to Alex, "Is it me or does the Hill look bigger?"

"Don't be silly," Alex responded.

Ray looked back at Alex as the voice crackled from the speaker, "You there?"

"We're here," Ray said into the mic.

"The sheriff's department said Callahan's gone missing. They're out looking for him now."

"Did you say missing?"

"Affirmative. He has not checked in since yesterday," the dispatcher finished before going silent.

"What the fuck is going on?" Ray blurted out to Alex.

Alex looked over at Ray as the speaker crackled again.

"What was that?" Alex asked.

"Don't know," Ray replied. "Kind of sounded like someone snapped their fingers."

"Weird," Alex responded.

"What are we going to do now?" Ray asked.

Alex's face went blank as he drove the ambulance down the road. Ray looked on from the passenger side as Alex's face went into full distress. A sense of panic was now overwhelming Alex as the ambulance began to speed up.

"Damn, Alex, what's wrong. Hey, hey man, slow down," Ray stumbled through as he gripped the door with all his strength.

Alex looked back at Ray and spoke in fear. "I, umm I can't stop it. I can't stop the truck. I have no control."

"What do you mean you have no control?" Ray shouted back.

"I have no…. Oh God—"

Chapter | 47

Harold stood in front of his garage with Rob and John close by just in case he needed some support. Reed stood away watching Harold's every move as Brad inched his way towards the garage door. Hanner had been in the garage for a while now and the curiosity was eating at the boys.

Brad finally had enough and walked to the edge of the garage and yelled in, "Hello. Hello Hanner?"

"What?" Hanner yelled back.

"What are you doing?" Brad replied.

"Examining the crime scene."

"Crime scene?"

Hanner's voice raised an octave, "Yes. Crime scene. I am an officer of the law, and we have a dead body on the scene. Stay out and don't go anywhere!"

Brad threw up his hands and backed away from the garage. He walked back towards the guys and picked up a bucket Harold had sitting against the wall. With a flip of his hands, Brad turned the bucket over and placed it in front of Harold. "Sit down. We're going to be here awhile."

Harold looked at Brad, "What is that supposed to mean?"

"Well," Brad replied, "Hanner said he is investigating a crime scene, and we need to stay here."

"Crime scene?" the other boys said in unison as Harold looked around in disgust.

"Yep. That is what he said. Crime scene," Brad replied to all of them. Brad walked over to the front of the garage, threw his back up against the wall and slid down it until he was sitting on the concrete.

"This is bullshit," Harold said as he grabbed the bucket and returned it to the place Brad found it. With a big sigh of disgust, Harold sat on the bucket with his back against the wall. The wall was cool to the feel and Harold enjoyed the sensation the wall gave him.

"I don't know about you guys, but I think it's a suicide," Reed stated.

"Who made you a medical examiner?" John bounced back with.

Reed looked over at Rob and shot him a look as he lowered his head and said, "I'm just saying."

"Why would Donny off himself?" Brad asked.

Reed responded, "I don't know."

"Donny was the toughest son of a bitch I knew. No way he off's himself, no way in hell." Brad's voice became irritated as he talked.

"What are you trying to say Brad?" Harold asked.

Brad sat in a moment of frustration before answering Harold, "I'm just saying that Donny is not the type of dude to off himself. It doesn't make sense at all. I think someone took him out."

Harold stood up as the bucket he was sitting on fell over on its side and began to rock back and forth, "You saying I killed Donny? Is that what you're saying Brad? My garage, so I killed him? If it is, we are going to have a big f'ing problem."

"Dude," Brad replied, "relax. I didn't say that. I'm saying Donny wasn't the cleanest guy in Walcott; he ruffled a lot of feathers. I think his lifestyle caught up to him. That's all I'm saying."

Reed walked over to the bucket and picked it up and placed it back at its home. Walking over to Harold, Reed motioned to Harold to sit down and patted him on his back at the same time. Turning around towards Brad, Reed opened his hands flat and motioned to Brad to relax.

As the afternoon ticked away and the sun started to make its journey down, the boys sat waiting for Hanner to appear from inside of the garage. Harold's head was now buried in his arms as his damp, greasy hair stuck up in all directions and the bucket was the only thing keeping him upright.

John, sitting in silence, finally spoke up. "What about Donny's mom. Someone needs to tell her. Who is going to tell her?"

"I'll tell her!" Hanner shouted from inside the garage. "I'll tell her."

The boys were startled by Hanner's powerful voice. Harold slowly lifted his head up from his arms and looked around to see what was happening.

"All of you," Hanner shouted, "get in here. NOW!"

"I don't want to go in there, I don't want to go in there, I don't want to go in there," Rob kept repeating to himself.

Harold made his way into the garage as the boys waited for Rob to get his wits together. Brad walked up to Rob and looked him in the eyes. "It's okay, buddy. I will be by your side the entire time. Just don't look. Okay? Look away."

Hanner shouted again, "What's taking so long? Get in here."

The boys turned back towards Rob and motioned that it was time to walk back into the garage. The damp garage brought the boys' senses to attention as they journeyed back to where Donny was hanging.

As they turned the corner expecting to see Donny hanging from the rafters, they found Hanner and Harold standing over Donny's body which was now lying on the ground under a tarp. Rob's body was overcome with a sense of relief knowing he didn't have to view Donny's body one more time.

"I did a little investigating," Hanner said, "and I think this is a suicide."

"Why do you think that?" Harold asked.

"Well, there are grease marks on the control pad and grease on Donny's hands. I think he put the cable around his neck and pressed the up button. Pressed the up button to take his own life."

The boys stood over Donny's body and looked on in disbelief. The damp garage was the last place Donny took a breath and the boys knew it. The last place they wanted to be right now was in Harold's garage.

"Harold," Hanner said to break the silence, "I need to go get the hearse. Watch over Donny until I get back. Boys, you are free to go."

The boys nodded their heads in acknowledgment as they stared at a tarp on the floor.

"One more thing, no mentioning this to anyone until I can go out to see Donny's mother," Hanner finished as he exited the garage.

The boys looked up from the tarp, then back to Harold. As silence captured the air, the boys looked around until Brad finally spoke up. "Not tell anyone? Donny commits suicide and we can't tell anyone. How am I supposed to go home and not tell anyone what happened here? What we saw today."

Harold found his way back to his favorite chair and sat down. His dried, bloody face was staring at the boys until he spoke up in a crackly voice, "stay here boys. Let's wait for Hanner to get back and we'll go home then. Let's just wait together."

The boys agreed as they all found a place to sit and relax. The room was silent as Donny lay quietly underneath the tarp on the floor.

Chapter | 48

The sunlight of the day was dimming with every passing second. Hanner's patrol car was making its way out to Donny's house before heading into town to get the hearse.

Hanner talked to himself as he drove out of town towards Donny's mom's house. "Okay. I've had a few busy days; turning Gail off, Jack getting shot by Martha, dropping Callahan from existence, taking out dumbass Donny, my Martha, and lastly, the two pain in the ass's Ray and Alex—a couple of pricks. Man, Stan sure is hungry... I mean—the Hill sure is hungry."

Hanner's throat started to tighten up and sweat began to roll down his forehead. The patrol car began to pick up speed down the deserted country road. The heat within the car slowly began to rise as Hanner began clutching his neck with both hands. His face was a bright red, and his uniform was getting drenched with the sweat that was being forced out of his body. The cab was now engulfed with Hanner's body odor as the patrol car moved faster and faster down the road. Hanner managed a whisper into the air as he rode helplessly within the car. "I understand. I'll never mention your name again. I underst—please stop, please...."

Within a second, Hanner's car came to a halt in the middle of the country road and the windows opened to let the cool air rush in.

Hanner held his neck as he gasped for a big breath of air. The cool air rushed into his lungs as he leaned his head back while taking in every breath. His body slowly cooled down and the sweat dissipated from his brow. As Hanner got his composure after his little scolding, he realized his squad car was sitting in front of Donny's house with Donny's mother, Joni, standing in the front window.

Hanner sat in his car in the middle of the country road. The sun was setting, and his gray car was becoming part of the night. Joni, sick of watching Hanner from her window, stepped out onto her front porch, and yelled out to Hanner, "What's the problem now? What did Donny do?"

Hearing Donny's mother yell at him through his windows, Hanner dropped his car into reverse and backed up so he could get his car up the gravel driveway that he drove by. The gravel driveway crackled underneath Hanner's squad car as it made its way up the drive to meet Joni. Hanner parked the car and got out of it.

Joni made her way towards the front of the old gray porch and threw her arms into a fold while saying, "Okay. What did he do this time?"

Hanner stepped closer to the front porch while staring at Joni.

Donny's mother had no filter as she shouted out, "Holy shit, Hanner. You look like you just crawled out a dead cow's ass. What wrong with you?"

Hanner looked down and realized he was drenched with sweat. He wiped down his forehead with the hanky he had in his pocket and tried to fix his disheveled hair. Looking back up at Joni who was now towering over Hanner from the porch, "Joni, we have a problem with Donny."

"No shit, Hanner!" Joni bellowed back. "We always have a problem with Donny when you show up at my home. What did the little prick do now?"

"Well, Joni—" Hanner began to say before being interrupted.

"Last time you were here, you arrested Donny for running dope for that asshole down in Port. Is that what he did again? If I remember correctly, I gave you that shotgun you always liked and a little piece of ass to let him off. Is that what you're looking for again, Hanner? You want another piece of ass to let my son go? Speak up, Hanner. Speak. I can't hear you!"

Without wasting a second, Hanner's old self came back to life and evil was now present. "No, Joni. I'll pass. If I remember correctly, the gun didn't work, and it took me a week to wash the smell off."

"Asshole! Why are you here?" Joni asked as she shot Hanner the finger.

"Donny is dead."

"What did you say?"

"I said, Donny is dead," Hanner repeated.

"What? How?"

"He offed himself at Harold's garage. Hung himself by the rafters. He was all blue and shit."

"Where is he now?"

Hanner turned his back to Joni as he walked back to his car, "I'm getting the hearse now and going to pick him up. He's lying in Harold's garage under a tarp. I bet he is ice cold now—kind of like you, Joni."

"You're an asshole, Hanner!"

"Thanks, Joni. I'll prep the body; let me know what you want to do with your loser son." Hanner shouted and waved goodbye as he jumped into his squad car and headed towards the mortuary.

Joni sat down on the decrepit steps that led up to the porch and watched Hanner drive away. Thoughts of her son entered her mind as she sat there. A tear rolled down her cheek as the night finally set in.

Chapter | 49

Donny's body lay in the place where Hanner had left it, under a greasy tarp on the floor of the garage. The damp floor of Harold's garage was drawing out whatever warmth that was left in Donny's body. As Donny lay dead on the floor, the boys began to talk. Talking about the day, talking to Harold who was sitting still in his chair.

"Boys, get me a beer," Harold said as he picked the dry blood from his face.

"Harold," Reed responded, "you're grossing me out picking that blood from your face. Can you go wash up? Please?"

"Fuck off, Reed."

John walked over to the fridge and grabbed a handful of beers. He began to toss a beer to all the boys and gave one to Harold. In unison the cracking of the cans echoed through the shop.

Brad cracked a joke, "Do you think Donny wants one?"

"Nice. Real nice Brad," Rob said, disgusted.

Harold stood up from his chair and walked over to where Brad was standing. Harold reached up to scratch his left shoulder and within a second, planted the back of his hand across Brad's face. As Brad's head thrashed to the side from the impact, Harold barked, "Have respect for the dead! Have respect for my friend!"

Brad took some time to get his poise back as his cheek stung from the force. The boys stood in awe as Harold returned to his seat and sat down. Brad, still reeling from what had just happened, finally spoke up to break the silence. "Sorry, Harold. I was just trying to make light of the situation. No disrespect. Really. No disrespect at all. I'm sorry."

Harold nodded his head but did not mention anything and did not apologize for what he had done.

"Harold, you have to admit, this is really weird," Reed said.

"Yeah, Harold," John jumped in, "we're sitting here drinking beer again, and there is a dead person six feet away from us."

"Yeah, Harold," Brad stepped in, still comprehending what had just happened to him, "What the fuck are we doing?"

Harold let out a big sigh before talking. "Listen, boys. We are going to sit here, all of us, together until Hanner gets back. We are not going to mention any of this to anyone until we are allowed to. The best way to accomplish that is we stick together, shut our mouths, and wait. Do I make myself clear?"

The boys nodded their heads in acknowledgement as Rob put as much distance between himself and Donny's body as he possibly could.

"Boys, what are you doing here anyways?" Harold asked. "You were here yesterday and now you're back today. What's up with that? And, which one of you boys puked all over my garage floor?"

John slowly reached up his hand, admitting he was the one who tossed his breakfast all over the shop this morning when they discovered Donny.

The rest of the boys didn't muster up much conversation until Rob barked out, "You know, Harold; I thought you were going to be honest with us yesterday and tell us about the grave, but you're a liar. A big fat liar."

"I don't know what you are talking about."

"Yeah," Brad replied too.

"What are you talking about?" John asked.

Rob sat there with his beer in his hand before replying, "Harold left something out of the story yesterday."

Harold asked, "What? What did I leave out?"

"Yeah, Rob, what did Harold leave out?" John curiously said as Brad and Reed stared on.

"Let me tell you, Harold. Let me tell you who you left out of the conversation. Brad, John, Reed—Harold forgot to tell us that there were five of them that went to the grave. Five of them—not four of them."

"What? What's up with that Harold?" one of the boys spoke out.

"Yeah, Harold, what's up with that?" John jumped in and said as Reed sat there drinking his beer.

"Reed, no comment from you. Aren't you curious too?" Harold asked directly to Reed.

Reed responded, "Harold, I know there were five of you. I know you left things out of the story. I want to know why?"

Brad shot up from his seat, "What are you two talking about and why do you know this?"

"I had a talk with my dad last night. He told me a little. I know there were five of them; I don't know the whole story, though—just that there were five of them," Reed finished.

Rob stood up and tossed his empty beer into the garbage. As he sat back down and replied, "Harold forgot to mention that my dad was with them on their little adventure. My dad was the fifth guy. Isn't that correct Harold?"

Harold rubbed his head and placed his face in his hands as he divulged a spew of obscenities, "Shit, damn, fuck…."

Brad barked from the sideline, "Start talking, Harold. Start talking now."

"Okay, Rob," Harold began, "you want to know what happened. You want to know about your father?"

"Yes, I do."

"Your father was a coward that day. Him and Dory hiding behind the trees, watching from a distance, too scared to come near the grave. That's what happened that day."

"So, he did not go near the grave. So what. Why keep him out of the story?" Rob asked.

"Because your dad went back to the grave without us, he went back alone. He went to prove something to himself. To prove something to us. To prove he was brave. Something? I don't know."

"Let me get this correct; my dad went back to the grave all by himself?" Rob asked.

"Yes."

"Why? Why would he do that?"

"I already told you why."

"Yes, you did, but what caused him to go back? What was it?"

"All of us gave Dory and your dad a lot of shit for staying away from the grave. Even Bill gave them shit. After that, he had to prove something. I really do not know what was going through your dad's head at the time. We were just messing with him—he took it to heart."

"So, you're saying, my dad went back because his friends were being a bunch of assholes? Is that what you're saying?" Rob asked as his temperature started to rise.

"Basically."

"What happened after that?" questioned Rob.

"It changed him."

"How?"

"It just did. It changed him. It changed all of us to some extent. Can we stop talking about this now? I've told you everything I know."

"No!" Rob bellowed. "We are not done talking about this."

Harold stood up and kicked his chair away from where it was parked and yelled, "The grave killed him! The Hill killed him, something killed him. That's what happened. The grave killed your father!"

Rob was now standing and yelling back at Harold, "My father took his own life."

"Exactly," Harold shouted back, "and the grave caused him to do it. The grave killed your father!"

Chapter | 50

Early evening set in as Hanner pulled up to the mortuary. He needed to get the hearse to pick up Donny's body from Harold's garage. The ride back to the morgue was swift with lots of thoughts. His mind was racing with death, and he had a lot to deal with. Donny and the two dead paramedics.

"Damn," Hanner said as his cell phone rang again, "I'm not answering you."

Hanner unlocked the door to the mortuary and made his way to the office to get the keys to the hearse. As he grabbed the keys off the hook, the phone rang out in urgency, *Ring, ring, ring!*

"Damn it," Hanner beckoned. "Damn it."

The phone rang louder, *RING, RING, RING!*

"What the—" Hanner said before picking up the phone, "Hello."

"Hello," the voice said from the other end of the phone, "is this Buck Hanner?"

"Yes, it is," Hanner replied.

"Is this Mr. Hanner who is married to Martha Hanner?" the voice questioned.

"Yes, it is. Can you tell me what this is about?" Hanner questioned back.

"Well, sir, this is Central Dover Hospital, it is about your wife, Martha. We have been trying to get ahold of you. It is very important that you come to the hospital as soon as possible."

"What's wrong?"

"It's your wife, sir. She is not doing very well, and it is very important that you come to the hospital as soon as possible," the voice replied.

Hanner rolled his eyes as the voice spoke to him over the phone, "what's wrong with my wife?"

"Sir, we do not like to discuss these things over the phone. Please come to the hospital as soon as possible." The voice finished.

The frustration in Hanner's voice peaked at this point, "My wife is dead. I know. If you know who I am, you know what I do for a living. Get her body ready for transport and I'll pick her up later."

"Sir, sir, how do you—?" was the last thing the phone said before Hanner slammed it down on the desk.

Hanner, being annoyed now, bolted from the mortuary, and headed for the hearse so he could head back to the shop and pick up Donny's body. As he was about to open the door to the hearse, his cell phone chimed alerting him he had voice messages.

"Damn it!"

Hanner grabbed his cell phone, flipped it open and pressed the key to get his messages. "Fuck!" he yelled before his phone began to speak.

"*You have four unheard messages, to continue press one,*" the phone said.

"Damn it. One for Christ's sake."

"*First unheard message: 'Mr. Hanner, this is Central Dover—'*"

"Delete!" Hanner yelled as he pressed the number four.

"*Second unheard message, 'Buck Hanner, this is about your wife Martha, please call Central—'*"

"Delete, damn it."

"*Third unheard message, 'This is Central—'*"

"Delete again, asshole!" Hanner bellowed.

"*Fourth unheard message, 'Sheriff Hanner, this is Deputy Jackson from the County Sheriff's Department, it is important you call our dispatch. We are looking for County Sheriff Richard Callahan; his last known whereabouts was your home location. I am on my way out to investigate, please contact the County Sheriff's Department dispatch for my location.'*" The phone message finished.

"Damn. Another hassle to deal with." Hanner thought out loud before finally jumping into the hearse and heading towards the shop.

The hearse drove itself quickly through the streets of Walcott as Hanner sat mindlessly waiting to arrive back at the shop. In an effortless turn, the hearse was parked in front of Harold's shop waiting for the body. Hanner jumped out of the hearse and walked into the garage.

"I'm back!" he shouted.

"Great," Brad whispered as the rest of the guys stood up from where they had parked themselves.

"Can we go now?" Reed asked.

"Do we still have to be quiet about this?" Rob followed.

"Yes, you can go," Hanner said, "and no you do not have to be quiet. I already spoke to Joni about her son's death."

Harold stood in silence as the boys began to walk out of the shop.

"Hold on, boys," Hanner said. "Harold, I need to speak with you."

"What?" Harold asked.

"Please step over here, Harold," Hanner replied.

The boys stopped in their tracks and waited for Hanner to get done speaking to Harold.

Harold walked closer to Hanner and asked, "Yes, sir?"

"That's better, Harold. You are getting it. Show me some respect and you'll receive some respect," Hanner followed.

"Yes, sir," Harold said again.

"We have a little mess that needs to be picked up and you are now, let me say that again, NOW the guy to clean it up."

"Mess. What mess do I have to pick up, clean up, whatever…?" Harold asked, annoyed.

Hanner replied with, "Tsk, tsk, Harold. Show some respect."

"Just get to the point, Hanner. For the love of God!" Harold followed.

Hanner reached up to scratch his neck as Harold began to slightly cough and whispered, "Don't bring God into the conversation and show some respect or I'll tighten the noose on your neck. Got it?"

Harold hands were up around his neck at this point and his head nodding with acceptance. "Got it." Harold mustered under his breath.

"There is an ambulance that needs to be picked up on the outskirts of town. You'll know how to get there. Get your tow truck and bring the ambulance to the morgue."

"Yes, sir." Harold coughed out.

"First, help me load Donny's body into the hearse."

"What about the boys?" asked Harold.

"Oh yeah, the boys," Hanner replied as he spun around to look at the boys who were standing at the edge of the garage waiting to leave. Hanner lifted his hands and spoke up, "Boys. You be careful out there. Don't do anything stupid. You can go now."

The boys looked at each other before leaving the garage. As the four boys walked away from the garage, Brad said, "Do something stupid? What does he mean about that?"

Hanner watched the boys walk away knowing they were going to be in trouble at some point in time. Hanner then walked over to the tarp that was hiding Donny, and with a big yank, he exposed his corpse.

"Strange," Hanner said.

Harold followed with, "What's strange?"

"I thought he would be bluer than that—being dead and all."

"Nice, Hanner. Real nice," Harold followed.

"Pick up his legs, I'll get him from this end, and we'll throw him into the hearse."

"No gurney?" asked Harold.

"No gurney. We'll just throw him into the back."

"Hanner, Donny was my friend. Can we show him a little respect?"

"Shut up, Harold. Grab his fucking legs. We have a ton of shit we have to do tonight."

"Goddamn it Hanner," Harold said as he grabbed Donny's legs and helped load his body into the hearse.

Donny's body was now on the floor of the hearse as Hanner shut the doors. As Hanner walked to the front of the hearse to head out, he barked a few last commands to Harold. "Go get the ambulance, meet me at the morgue, I'm running up to Central Dover Hospital to get Martha."

"Is Martha okay?" Harold asked.

"She's fine," Hanner responded as he pulled away from the garage.

Chapter | 51

The evening was in full bloom as the boys walked out of the garage. In unison, each boy walked with their head down and their feet shuffling across the blacktop alley. With each step, the boys walked toward the park, toward the place where they have always found peace.

"Park?" Brad asked.

Reed replied, "Sure."

"Why not? Nothing else to do at the moment. Sure, the hell don't want to go home," John said.

"Damn right we are going to the park. We are going to discuss this. Things are fucked up; that is for sure," Rob barked as the boys made the turn toward the park.

With each step, the boys got closer and closer to the park until they found themselves at the swings. The moon was high, and the breeze flowed as it did with most cool nights. The swings moved back and forth gently in the wind as the boys found a place to plant themselves for a bit.

Reed grabbed the closest swing and sat down. His feet pushed the gravel around as his hands held the swing's chains tightly; Reed's head hung low with his chin resting in his chest.

John did the same; he found a place on an adjacent swing and mimicked Reed's body language.

Brad leaned up against the wooded wall with his arms folded and his mind racing with thoughts.

Rob just stood in the middle of the boys with his head held low and slowly kicked the rocks out from underneath his feet as the moonlight engulfed the boys in a blue haze.

"Well?" Brad said, "What are we going to do now?"

"I'll tell you what we are going to do; we are going to find out what really happened to my father. We are going to find out why he went back to the grave. Why he killed himself? We are going to get some answers!" Rob finally shouted.

"Don't we know some of the answers already, Rob?" Reed said from the swing he was nestled in.

John replied, "Yeah, we know some of the answers."

"What answers do we know?" Rob followed.

"We know there were five of them. We know your dad went to the grave by himself. We know that everyone involved with that day is a tad off center now. And we know your dad killed himself because of the grave. That's what we know," Brad explained as he adjusted himself against the wall.

"My father killed himself because of the Army. Because of what happened to him in the war. That is why he killed himself," Rob explained.

Brad threw his hand up in the air and began to speak briskly. "Let's look at the facts; Hanner was there, Dory was there, Harold was there, Reed's dad was there, and your father. You can't tell me that any one of those guys is not off their rocker in some way. Something happened to them on the Hill and the only way to find out is to go to the grave ourselves."

"What?" Reed shouted.

John jumped up from his swing and yelled, "Are you nuts? Have you completely lost your mind?"

Rob stopped kicking the rocks for a second and replied, "Yes, that is what we must do."

"So, it's settled," Brad said, "we are going to visit the grave."

"This is a bad idea," Reed followed, "a very bad idea."

"It might be, but no one is going to give us the answers we want. At least, they are not going to give us the answer we want to hear," Brad explained.

"Exactly!" Rob shouted, "Exactly!"

"I'm with Reed," John spoke up from the swing that he was now sitting in again, "this is a bad idea.

The boys sat in the moonlight for a while as the breeze gently flew by. No more words were said. As time ticked away, each boy slowly got up and made their way home. Their lives changed forever.

Chapter | 52

The shop was now empty. The boys had left, Hanner was gone, and Donny was on his way to his final resting place. Harold stood in the middle of the garage and took in the silence. The silence overwhelmed him so much that he buried his head in his hands. He started to cry, cried with every muscle in his body, until the tears continually flowed from his bloodshot eyes. Cried about the day, cried about his friend Donny, and for the things he was about to do.

As the tears made their way down Harold's face, Harold dropped to his knees and spoke to God, "Please forgive me for what I am about to do. I know evil is present and I do not have the strength to fight it. Please give me the strength Lord, please help me," Harold finished up saying before he went to the office to get the keys to the tow truck, "Oh Lord…. I'm so sorry."

The truck waited in the dark night for Harold to arrive. The moonlight barely glistening over the top of the truck - just enough light for Harold to find the key. With a crack of the door handle, Harold yanked the old, rusted door to the cab of the truck. Cigarette butts and ashes lined the floor of the truck as a gush of musty air passed Harold's nose.

The key went effortlessly into the ignition, but the truck was hesitant to start. Harold turned the key while pushing in the clutch and giving the old truck some gas. *Rrrrr; grrrrr; pop, pop…*, the truck sputtered as Harold tried to start it.

"Come on, darling." Harold spoke gently to the truck. *Rrrr; grrrr; pop, pop…*, the truck replied again. "You can do it," Harold calmly said as he pulled the choke out and feathered the gas. *Pow, pow!* The truck finally barked to life.

With every press of the gas, the old truck would billow out a dark, dense cloud of blue smoke. Harold popped the clutch; him and the old truck headed away from his shop to the outskirts of town. Harold had no idea where he was going, but he just drove out of town.

Harold clutched the old steering wheel as pain slowly entered his body. The location where the IV had entered his arm was tender and he could feel the gash in his nose with every heartbeat. "Where am I going?" Harold asked as the reflection of Stocker Hill engulfed his rearview mirror. Harold drove the truck out of town, past the school and into the darkness.

With a click of his left foot, Harold turned on the bright lights to see better, but the lights were not needed. As he drove farther into the darkness, the moonlight was glistening and lighting the path— lighting the path to the ambulance.

Up over a slight hill and through a sweeping turn the truck drove. Drove briskly through the night air, through the moonlight, through the darkness of the night until the old headlights found what they were looking for. The ambulance. The ambulance lay silently at the end of the road.

Harold's eyes caught sight of the ambulance at the end of the headlights' reach. It lay at the end of the road in the long, trampled grass it destroyed on its way to its resting place. As Harold drove closer, the moonlight took over and the emergency stickers on the side of the rig glistened with life.

Harold's stomach was in full flip-flop mode as he gently pulled the tow truck up behind the ambulance. "Please don't find anything bad, please don't find anything bad, please don't…," Harold repeated as he brought the truck to a stop. With his left hand, Harold gripped the steering wheel until his knuckles were screaming white and with his right hand, Harold slowly reached for the key to bring the tow truck to silence. Harold continually gripped the steering wheel until he could find the courage to let it go.

"Here we go." Harold said as he reached down to pull the handle that would open the door allowing him to get closer to the unknown. To the unknown that was waiting for him inside the ambulance. Harold's first step out of the truck was drowned by the echo the creaky door sent racing through the valley. As Harold's foot hit the long-dried grass, his belly decided it did not want to play anymore as it forced Harold to vomit everything he had in him. With every retch, Harold's body forcibly heaved and bellowed its unhappiness into the night air.

Harold got control of his vomiting ways and wiped his face off with this shirt. The night air began to cool Harold's face as he tried to find the courage and strength to get closer to the ambulance. His spent body started to move slowly through the tall grass. His steps trampled the grass with every movement towards the ambulance. Harold looked up at the glistening moonlight as he made his way around the driver's side of the ambulance.

"Okay, Harold," he spoke into the night air, "we need to look into the truck. Don't be scared, you can do this."

The cool night air was filling Harold's lungs with every deep breath his body could handle. With one last breath, Harold arrived at the driver's door.

"This is where Alex sits, Alex always drives the rig, please Alex, don't be behind the door," Harold said as he reached for the door handle. With a slight yank, Harold opened the door and looked into the rig. His eye went wide open as his belly sank. Harold whipped his body around as he spewed vomit into the grass. His body yelled out again with every heave.

Harold reached up with his arm and wiped any residue of spew off his face again. As he threw his hands up and ran them through his sweaty brow, he turned back towards the rig to take another glance. Glance at what he found a second ago—a glance that found nothing.

"Jesus Christ," yelled Harold as he slammed his fist into the side of the truck, "there is nothing there. I got myself all worked up for nothing."

Harold took a couple big breaths and began the process of hooking up the ambulance to the tow truck.

"They must be hiking it back into town."

Chapter | 53

The cool, night air surrounded the hearse as Hanner pulled away from the garage on his way to Central Dover Hospital. The dark hearse blended into the night as the lights barely glistened onto the road. As usual, Hanner's driving was swift, without hesitation, as he guided the vehicle to pick up his wife.

The hospital stood north of Walcott off the main highway. It is the largest hospital around and serves as the main support for the surrounding towns. Its reputation is second to none and several hospitals send their most difficult cases to Dover for their expertise. The hospital was founded in the early 1900s by three brothers. Today, in remembrance of the brothers, the hospital has three main towers to house the patients and for all the doctors to perform their duties.

Hanner pulled around the back of the hospital near the morgue's entrance. The morgue is housed in the basement of the center tower, which is the largest of the towers. Hanner parked the hearse in the shadows of the tower. The tower reached up to the sky hiding the moonlight that shimmered throughout the hospital grounds.

The hearse lay quietly with Donny's cold body in the rear of the vehicle. Hanner walked throw the shadows towards the back-swinging doors of the hospital. He glanced around when he got into the rear hallway of the hospital, looking for the sign pointing to the morgue.

"Come on," he shouted, "where the fuck is the morgue? How many times have I been here?"

As Hanner's profanity resonated through the hallways of the hospital, a young nurse technician turned the corner and looked at Hanner with disgust. Hanner's uniform was a mess. Dirty and wrinkled, shoes all scuffed up and his badge was dark and dull.

"My I help you, sir?" the nurse asked as she looked Hanner up and down.

"Yeah, you can," Hanner barked in his normal tone, "where the fuck is the morgue?"

The nurse was taken aback by Hanner's gruff response before she responded, "Excuse me sir; there is no need for language like that in this establishment. We are here to serve the community and I am happy to help you. What are you looking for?"

Hanner's body became flush with rage and his now beet-red face said ever so gently, "I need to get to the morgue. What direction is it? It used to be around here somewhere. Please…."

"See? That was so much nicer, sir, and as a matter of fact, the morgue hasn't moved at all. Still in the same place it has always been," the nurse replied as her beautiful blue eyes squinted slightly with her large smile.

"Well, I forget. So, please, please point me in the right fucking direction!" Hanner yelled.

"Sir, please, no need for that," the nurse replied as she pointed down the long hallway, "See the sign above the doors. The morgue is down there, sir."

Hanner looked at the nurse and turned towards the doors of the morgue. His steps toward the morgue were strong and powerful as thoughts raced through his head, *You going to let her get away with talking to you like that?*

With every step, the rage brought his face to a boiling point, and it smoldered in red anger. He took two more steps and whipped around and started back from where he came from. His voice bellowing back down the hallway, "Excuse me, miss. Excuse me."

The nurse turned around and looked at Hanner briskly walking back towards her and her beautiful face with that nice smile turned into surprise as the muttered the words, "Yes, sir."

"One more thing before I go to the morgue," he replied.

"Yes, sir?" the nurse questioned as Hanner approached.

"You see, something has to change around here, and I think that change will begin with you!" Hanner yelled as his hand went for the nurse's neck.

The nurse reared away as she dropped to her knees trying to escape Hanner's grasp. Hanner's powerful hands dropped down in pursuit of the fleeing nurse and just got ahold of the nurse's ankle. With a slight yank, the nurse was violently pulled into Hanner's arms. Before she could yell, Hanner grabbed the nurse's neck and lifted her up off the ground. Her eyes now squinted as she fought for a breath. Her smile was gone, and her beauty quickly faded from her face. With one last breath before death raced into her body, she whispered, "Why?" Hanner threw the nurse's body into a nearby room and silently said, "Because."

After Hanner's minor pause during his morgue visit, he began a calm walk to the morgue. As he reached the doors, his left arm shot out briskly, Hanner's hand hit the door and it flew open letting him gain access to the morgue.

"Hello!" he yelled as he walked into the morgue.

Sitting behind the partition was Frank the security guard. "May I help you?" Frank questioned.

Hanner looked at the security guard and answered, "I am here to pick up a body."

Hanner was now calm after his little episode with the nurse and his chubby face was now back to its normal color.

"Okay," Frank replied, "what is your name and where are you from?"

"I'm Buck Hanner from Walcott. I am the sheriff of Walcott and the funeral director. I am here for a body."

"Oh…," replied Frank and he sat up in his seat, "we've been expecting you. Please wait one moment and I'll be right with you." Frank jumped up from the desk and rapidly walked to the backroom of the morgue to let the doctor, coroner, and pathologist know that Hanner was there.

"Excuse me, gentleman," Frank hollered as he entered the room. "He's here."

Stephen the coroner looked over at the other men and stated, "Well, Doc, you ready for this conversation?"

"I guess so," Michael replied. "Frank, please bring him back."

"What do you want me to do?" questioned Sam.

"Hang out and keep your mouth shut," the coroner and the doctor both replied.

Frank walked back towards the front room where Hanner was waiting. He opened the doors and motioned to Hanner, "Please follow me, sir."

Hanner walked into the backroom to find three men standing around Martha's body. Her body was covered with a white cloth and all the men had a puzzled look on their face. Sam, the pathologist, slowly walked away from the table and found himself gazing at the situation from afar.

"My name is Michael Hanratty. I am the doctor on call this evening and was there when your wife suddenly passed away. I am so sorry for your loss," Michael spoke in a soft, comforting voice as he reached out to shake Hanner's hand.

Hanner looked at the doctor's extended hand and looked back up at him without shaking it. "Thank you."

Michael, surprised with Hanner's reaction, gestured over to Stephen and stated, "This is Stephen, the local coroner."

"I know Stephen," Hanner replied.

"Okay," responded Michael, "and over here is Sam our pathologist."

Hanner looked over at Sam and then back to the other gentleman and stated, "I understand why the pathologist is here, but what is up with coroner, and you doctor, you being here?"

Michael looked at Hanner with a cringe on his face and wondered why Hanner did not show any emotions about his wife's death. He then began to speak. "You see, sir; I was there when your wife passed, and it happened abruptly. Very suspicious. It shocked us all. Shocked everyone involved. You see, we found that your wife has no blood in her. None at all. We would like to perform an autopsy on her to see what we can find out."

"No autopsy," Hanner replied.

"But, sir, this is critical we do an autopsy."

"No autopsy," Hanner replied again.

Sam jumped in and began where the doctor left off. "Mr. Hanner, your wife's death was highly unusual, and it would be for the better good for us to do an autopsy. To see what happened. To see if there was any foul play."

Hanner began to chuckle and grabbed his belly while he laughed. He slowly cupped his hands and began to laugh into them and whispered to himself, "Do you believe this shit?"

Sam, the doctor and the coroner all looked puzzled at Hanner. He is laughing at the situation with his wife's dead body not two feet away from him.

Stephen stood in disbelief as Hanner laughed into his hands. Before Hanner was done, Stephen raised his voice and said, "Excuse me. This is not a laughing matter."

Hanner in mid-laugh stopped laughing and looked over his hands and the men standing next to him. Rage began to boil within him, and he burst out, "This is a laughing matter and if you do not prep the body to move right now, my wife will not be the only carcass in the room on a steel table. Do I make myself clear?"

"Umm…," Stephen mumbled, "we need you to sign the release for your wife's body and you can go on your way."

"Get it now!" Hanner barked.

"I do not think that is a good idea," Sam jumped in and stated. "We need to investigate what happened."

Hanner shot the look of death to Sam as anxiety entered Sam's body. Fight or flee Sam's body was saying to him and his mind chose to flee. Sam looked over at the rest of the guys, threw up his hands and agreed to let the body go. Hanner signed the paperwork as Frank and Sam loaded the body into Hanner's hearse. Martha's visit to the hospital was now over.

Chapter | 54

Deputy Jackson's squad car made its way down the road toward
Walcott. The late afternoon day burned away quickly after Jackson left headquarters looking for Callahan. The sight of Callahan's
truck and Jenny stating Callahan had not been heard of since eight
last night resonated through his head.

Jackson knew of Buck Hanner through the law enforcement gossip that flowed throughout the industry. He knew that Hanner was a
stern, sloppy man who ran a tight ship and also had a kind side to him.

Walcott sat silently as Jackson's squad car rolled up into the center
of town. The squad car sat at the stop sign in the middle of town,
waiting for Jackson to make a decision on where to go. Go right to
headquarters or go left for Hanner's home. With anticipation the car
waited for Jackson's decision, waiting for what he was going to do,
waiting to follow protocol, or waiting to follow his gut.

Protocol it is. Jackson slammed the accelerator down and turned
the wheel right to head towards police headquarters, to follow protocol, out of respect for the badge, out of respect for the position of
being in law enforcement.

The squad car pulled up to Walcott's police station like it would to
any situation—with caution. Jackson turned off the car and exited the
vehicle. The door shut behind him and his heightened sense of emotion

took in the surroundings of Walcott. The police station stood in silence as it waited for someone to enter it. Jackson found it creepy as Walcott sat in silence and all he could hear were his own footsteps.

The door to the police station was inviting as Jackson opened it and entered without any trouble. Like the town, the police station was silent.

"Wow, this is creepy," stated Jackson. "I don't know what's worse, the silence in here or the silence out there."

Jackson looked around and looked for some signs of what was going on. Looked for some signs of Hanner. Looked for some signs of Callahan. Was Callahan here? Where did Callahan go? His gut was telling him he should have taken that left instead of taking that right.

Jackson quickly left the police station and ran towards his car. As he jumped into the squad car to head to Hanner's place, his hand was already on the mic calling Jenny, "Jen, can you hear me? Jen, you there?"

"I'm here," she replied through the speaker.

"No sign of Callahan or Hanner at the police station. I'm going to head towards Hanner's house," he responded.

"Okay," she answered. "I'm here if you need anything. Be careful."

Jackson threw the car into gear and did a U-turn in the middle of the road. He was not concerned with traffic since there was no movement in town that evening. The engine roared as his right foot was aggressive with the accelerator. Jackson came back to the intersection which became a blur as he raced through it and headed out of town.

As Jackson raced out of town towards Hanner's place, the speaker in his car spoke with Jenny's voice, "Jackson, come back, Jackson."

"Yes, Jenny."

"I spoke with Callahan's wife, no word from him since he left for work yesterday morning."

"Nothing?" Jackson questioned.

"Nothing. The wife did not think much of it because of all the commotion that was going on. Figured Callahan got caught up with work."

"Thanks for the info Jen," Jackson came back with.

"One more thing, Jackson."

"What's that?"

"She is totally freakin' out now. Worried about her husband," she finished.

"Great. Just great," Jackson blurted out as he switched his lights on so he could be more aggressive with his driving.

The lights of the squad car glistened with every rotation, white, then red, then blue until Jackson got to Hanner's house. The squad car simmered down after the lights were shut off and his foot jumped off the accelerator.

The car pulled onto the gravel driveway and a conversation began with the gravel and the tires with every rotation. The gravel spoke its mind, but the tires did not back down. The argument ended as the car came to a stop.

Jackson flipped the search light on to take a look at the premises. One push of the switch and the bright light screamed out of its socket and cast a heated glow over the farm. The animals scurried as the night disappeared while he moved the light back and forth to get a good look at the surroundings. First, he lit up the house and then the yard around it; flipped it over to the barn and gravel driveway then ending up back at the house. The house stood firmly in the spotlight's glare.

"Well, there are no signs of people here, but I better take a look," Jackson said before jumping back on the mic. "Jen, you there?"

"Go ahead, Jackson," she replied.

"I just got here. No signs of anyone. I am going to do a perimeter check and then check the house."

"Roger that," Jenny closed.

Jackson jumped out of his cruiser and grabbed his flashlight. The heavy, black flashlight lit up its surroundings the best it could after the spotlight just dominated the situation. Jackson threw the heavy flashlight up on his shoulder and canvased the entire area.

The barn stood alone as the flashlight lit up the door to the barn. The faded paint wasn't very welcoming, but he proceeded towards the barn and the large door that separated him and its contents. The large, rusted hinges stared back at Jackson as he flipped the latch over and pulled on the door. The hinges voiced their displeasure as he pulled open the door, but all they could do was creak and moan and do their job.

Jackson stood in the doorway and shined his light into the darkness that the barn provided. Around and around, he shined the light before making the initial step into the barn. The warm evening weather faded quickly as Jackson got farther and farther into the barn. The flashlight lit the area, but Jackson was engulfed in a cool darkness wherever his light didn't penetrate the night.

"Damn," Jackson murmured, "nothing in this hole. Nothing at all."

Off to the house Jackson went. The flashlight left the barn and made a path for Jackson in the dark night. His brisk walk towards the house came with caution. As Jackson got closer to the house, the night air became thicker to walk through. Thicker to breathe. A chill raced through his body to signal something evil. As the chills initiated chaos on his skin, he reached down and unbuckled the strap that held his 9mm handgun in place.

The porch was not inviting, but Jackson stepped up onto it anyways. His flashlight lighting the way. The house looked in shambles like its brother the barn. The paint was chipped and cracked. The screens and windows were dirty, and the porch squeaked with every step. Jackson shined his light in through the windows and lit up all the rooms he could see. No signs of Hanner. No signs of his life. A big empty house.

The front door clanked as Jackson beat on it. "Hanner, are you in there?"

The house answered with silence.

"Come on, Hanner," he yelled as his fist was hitting the front door.

The house answered again with silence.

Jackson whipped around as frustration overcame his body. His strong shoulder dipped a little as the flashlight rested on it. He began to think and remembered about the funeral home. "He must be there," he thought out loud.

The flashlight led the way as Jackson headed back to his squad car. As the light glistened the way, a flash caught Jackson's eye.

"What the....?" he hollered.

Jackson shined the light back over the area and the flash appeared again. A coppery flash just in front of his squad car. Jackson approached the area trying not to lose the location in the darkness. He walked close to the front of his car and began to kneel and shine his light over the area.

"Holy shit," Jackson spoke into the night.

A spent casing rested quietly on the gravel driveway.

"That's a weird place for you. How did you get there?" Jackson questioned as he grabbed his handkerchief and picked up the casing. Jackson held the casing between his fingers with the handkerchief and examined it a little closer. "Looks like it's from a 357."

He jumped back into his squad car and put the casing in the middle console. Instantly he picked up the mic and called for Jenny.

"I'm here, Jackson," she replied, "go ahead."

"I'm heading to the funeral home. Figure that's where Hanner is. No signs of life out here at the house."

"Roger that."

"Oh, please note I found a bullet casing on Hanner's driveway. I'll bring it in for evidence."

"Evidence?" Jenny questioned.

"Yes, for the disappearance of Callahan, County Sheriff Richard Callahan," Jackson finished as he heard Jenny gasp over the speaker.

Chapter | 55

The boys left the park how they found it—deserted. They all made their way home except for Reed. Reed had other ideas that evening. The moonlight's blue glow led Reed towards Krista's house, the only safe place he could think of at that time.

The rocks slowly moved out of the way as Reed shuffled his feet across the blacktop towards Krista's. The breeze was light and refreshing at the late hour and the moonlight actually had a warm, holding sense as Reed's mind wondered over the walk.

"I can't think straight right now," Reed whimpered into the night air as he missed the turn to Krista's house.

"For God's sake," he mumbled as he took a couple left turns and began the shuffle walk back towards Krista's again.

Krista's house was dark that evening. The front porch light put out a slight glow, but it couldn't fight off the moonlight that was washing over the house and yard, casting shadows as the air blew through the trees while the shadows danced gracefully. The windows were dark, but there was a slight sparkle coming out of the kitchen as the oven clock glistened its time into the room. Reed approached the house with caution. No need to wake up the household when all he wanted was a hug from his girl.

The bark cracked underneath Reed's feet as he stepped closer to Krista's window. The green bushes touched his leg and continued their movement as the wind picked up briefly. Reed got close to the window and started the conversation with a couple taps on the window.

Tap, tap, tap. The window spoke as Reed's nail made contact.

Within a second of the last tap, a small glimmer came out of the window as Krista turned on her desk lamp. She slowly adjusted herself, wiped the sleep out of her eyes and rubbed her face to get the blood flowing again.

Click, click. The window responded as Krista unlocked it before sliding it open.

"Boy, what in the world are you doing? It's late, Reed, and I am tired.

"Oh, honey, I needed to see you. I need my girl.

"Reed, what's wrong?

"Long night. A really long night. I'm so tired and confused."

"Reed," Krista said as concern rushed into her voice, "what happened? You're scaring me."

"Donny's dead."

"Donny, you mean Donny from Harold's garage? That Donny?" Krista questioned.

"Yep. He's gone," Reed cried as tears began to flow.

"Oh, Reed. Come in. Please come in," Krista invited.

Reed put his hands on the windowsill and pulled himself up into Krista's room. This visit was different than the other times Reed visited Krista. This visit was full of sorrow.

Reed sat on the bed right away and kicked off his shoes. Krista reached up and touched Reed's head as he collapsed backwards into the bed. His body was tired, and his mind was trying to process the day. "Hold me," he said as he picked his head up off the soft bed and looked Krista in her eyes.

"Sure, babe," she responded as she moved to the other side of the bed, but never stopped touching Reed in the process. She lay down next to Reed and pulled him closer into her loving body, holding him tight. "Tell me tomorrow, tell me tomorrow."

The moonlight slowly faded out of the night as Reed slept in Krista's arms.

– – –

The morning came in as every morning does; the birds chirping, the wind blowing off the Hill and the sunlight sneaking through Krista's blinds. The warmth of the sun patted Krista on her face until it hit her with enough force to jar open her eyes.

A moment passed until Krista got her wits. Reed was still sound asleep, and her nerves raced. *Should I wake him, should I wake him?*

"Babe," she said as she rubbed Reed's face, "babe, you need to wake up."

Krista rubbed Reed's face until movement started to happen in his body. A few facial expressions and Reed was awake. He brought his hand to his face as the emotions began to roar. Reed started sobbing. Started sobbing uncontrollable next to the woman he loved. He looked through his hands and the puddle of tears to see Krista's wonderful face.

"Oh, honey," he said ever so gently.

Krista, with tears in her eyes, placed Reed's face in her hands and pulled him closely to kiss him. The tenderness in her kiss helped Reed come to his senses. The love pulled him from where he was, and he was able to start the day.

"Are you ready to talk?" she asked.

"Yeah," Reed replied as he got his bearings.

Krista sat back on the bed as Reed stood next to the bed and let the emotions run. He went through all the details, Donny's death and Stocker Hill, Harold, and Hanner along with his dad and the grave.

"I've heard of the grave, but you stay away from it. That's what I have heard anyways," Krista responded.

"Well, we're going," Reed stated.

"Who is going?"

"Us. The guys. We are going," finished Reed.

Krista stood up next to Reed and angrily barked, "No, Reed. You are not going. You can't go. You and the guys are asking for a world of hurt if you start opening Pandora's Box."

A puzzled look flashed on Reed's face as he asked, "What are you talking about? Pandora's Box?"

"Jesus Christ, Reed, did you pay attention in school at all? Pandora's Box is evil. That evil needs to stay closed," Krista specified as her hands went to her hips and the sympathy raced off her face.

"Why didn't you just say that? You and your big words. Fuck!" Reed burst out in frustration.

The love rushed out of the room as Krista and Reed stood eye-to-eye looking at each other. A moment of silence turned into hours as the clock slowly ticked off time.

"Listen, Reed," Krista gritted through her teeth, "I love you; I love you with all my heart, but you and your friends are going down a path that could change everything. You said it yourself about your dad and Dory and whoever else was involved. It changed them and it will change all of you too."

Reed looked at Krista and reached up and pulled her closely. They kissed and Reed whispered, "Thank you for loving me."

Reed turned from Krista, pulled back the blinds and opened the window. In one big swoop, Reed was out the window and faced-planted on the ground with a big, *ooooffff*, racing from his lungs.

Krista looked out her window at Reed lying on the ground. He was now on his back and looking back at her. He lifted his hand and pointed at her, "We're going."

The last sound in that area was the window slamming shut.

Chapter | 56

The glow of the night air helped Harold as he finished hooking up the deserted ambulance and backed it out in the trampled grass where it was resting.

The old tow truck popped and moved as it started down the road towards the morgue. The chains bucked back-and-forth, and the ambulances springs squeaked from the pressure of being held in tow. The conversation continued as a stream of smoke exited the cracked window of the cab.

With each draw of breath, the cigarette that was planted in Harold's mouth would glow with excitement until his lungs could hold no more. A slight tilt of the head and a rush of smoke exited Harold's lungs though his nose and did all it could to get out of the cab.

In between each drag, Harold would think. The quick moment before the cigarette headed towards his mouth again was filled with sadness, anger, and a bit of relief. The relief that still filled his body when he found the ambulance empty.

"Thank you, Lord," Harold said as smoke billowed out of his mouth. "Thank you for not letting me find Alex and Ray dead in their office."

As Harold's nerves calmed slightly, he realized his half-hour truck ride to the morgue was a lot quicker than expected. The old tow truck pulled into town and headed towards the morgue.

"To be honest, God, I'm sure not looking forward to spending any more time with Hanner," Harold said as he rolled up to the morgue with the ambulance in tow.

Harold parked the long-connected vehicles on the side of the street directly in front of the morgue. The hearse was not anywhere in sight. Harold fired up another cigarette and sat in his truck waiting for Hanner to arrive.

– – –

Hanner raced from the hospital with the same vengeance he entered it. His hearse whistled through the night air as the air rushed across its bulky frame.

Martha's body lay quietly in the back of the hearse as her husband drove her to her next location. She didn't make any sounds or hardly moved at all during the trip. All she knew was the person driving the hearse wasn't the love of her life. That person was gone.

Hanner's aggressive driving made the usually long, sad trip into an emotionless event. No tears of sadness. No reminiscing of old times or happy moments. This was a brisk trip to solve problems.

The hearse's lights shined down the street as far as the eyes could see. They fought the brightness of the moon with all their might until their efforts were rewarded and Harold's truck was insight.

Hanner's eyes caught Harold sitting in his truck as he bellowed out, "Harold. Why do I end up with all these useless people?"

Harold watched the dark, glistening hearse come down the street and could see Hanner's creepy eyes watching him. The hearse cut through the night air, then vigorously pulled into the morgue's lot. The tires slipped through the loose gravel at the entrance of the parking lot. The tires held on to some of the gravel and threw them specifically at Harold's truck. *Ding, ding… Ping!* the old truck barked back.

"Asshole!" Harold spouted as he watched the dark vehicle disappear into the shadows on its way to the back of the building.

Hanner drove the hearse to the area of the building where the bodies of the deceased are brought. The hearse briskly backed up and waited for the next steps to be taken. The driver's door swung open, and Hanner's feet hit the ground before taking him to the back of the hearse.

"Come on Martha," Hanner said as he reached for the large, chrome handle that directs the large door what to do.

With a little yank, the large door gave way to Hanner's might as the moonlight lit up the bag that was housing Martha.

"Where is Harold? I swear the incompetence in this world is... FUCKING UNACCEPTABLE!" he yelled as he left the door.

Hanner walked around to the front of the building to find Harold sitting in his truck smoking.

"Damn it," Harold said as he reached for the door to leave his musty safe place.

"About time!"

Hanner turned around and headed towards his wife. Harold followed shortly behind Hanner until he caught up to him waiting at the hearse.

"Grab a handle and pull. The legs will drop to the ground, and we'll get Martha inside."

"Wait," yelled Harold, "you said that Martha was okay! What's going on Hanner? Martha is dead?"

"Martha is dead. What else do you need to know? She's dead." Hanner coldly responded.

"What the fuck Hanner," Harold murmured as tears began to flow from his sad eyes, "I've known her my entire life and all you can say is that she is dead. What happened?"

Harold was looking at Hanner as pure evil steadily flowed from Hanners eyes as a slight growl rolled from his tongue, "pick up the fucking gurney."

Harold grabbed a handle and pulled when the gurneys legs suddenly dropped to the ground. The wheels of the gurney barked as they hit the pavement getting ready for movement. Hanner led the gurney into the back of the morgue with Harold pushing. All three of them ended up in the freight elevator and prepared for the ride to the basement. Hanner pushed the basement button and a loud click echoed throughout until the doors opened to the lighted morgue. The wheels fought their way out of the elevator and over the metal edging that introduced the elevator to the basement floor.

Hanner led Martha to the closest empty table and locked the wheels on the gurney. He looked down at the body bag and began to mumble something.

Harold watched Hanner closely for a couple minutes. The mumbling continued and he was afraid to make a noise. He just sat there waiting for Hanner's next direction.

Another moment passed and Hanner came back to his wits and started to speak, "Umm…. Harold… can you grab the other end and help get Martha on the table?"

"Sure, Hanner, whatever you need," he gently replied.

"Okay. On three. One, two, three."

The two men lifted Hanner's wife up off the gurney onto the awaiting table.

"Please wait for me upstairs. I need to take care of a few things down here."

"Okay. Okay. You got it. I'll be upstairs waiting for you, but don't forget about Donny."

"What?" Hanner barked and then followed, "Yeah Donny."

Harold turned and headed towards the stairs. With a brisk walk to get away from the situation, he was up the stairs in a moment and left Hanner with his wife.

Chapter | 57

The moonlight shined through Suzy's window for John. He could just make out his beautiful girl's red hair on the pillow as the time on the clock was flashing 2:00 a.m. He thought for a moment and decided to let her be.

John wanted to wake up in Suzy's arms, but he knew that would be trouble. Their passion gets the best of them, and he had a busy day ahead. His walk back home was guided by the moon. With every step, his mind thought of Donny.

John arrived home to a quiet house. Everyone was asleep and the only thing to keep him company was Donny. His thoughts were out of control. He tried to find some comfort in whatever the fridge had to offer, but it was useless. Donny was his obsession, and he had no inclination of leaving his thoughts anytime soon.

His large bed engulfed the room and it tried to comfort John. He laid his head on the pillow and watched the dark sky through the little view the window was providing. With every passing minute, sleep was nowhere in sight. It was just John and Donny together in thought.

– – –

Brad left the rest of the boys and moseyed on home. The moonlight lit his walk as well, but Brad had no thoughts. He enjoyed the silence and the night breeze on his face. The last few days were too hectic for his liking and all he wanted was one of his dad's cold beers.

The trail Brad was walking on was about to end and with a few quick turns he'd be walking up to the estate. The estate was home to Brad. His dad did well with the coal mines and rewarded his family with a beautiful Victorian-style home. The steep pitched roof and textured shingles finished off the top of the house as its red bricks stood tall on the few acres the family owned.

Brad walked up the white steps and along the front of the house. The garage in the back of the house housed a small fridge that was always filled with beer. His dad's crappy beer, but it would be cold, and he needed it.

The garage door was beat up and warped and would let you know you were in a fight every time you went to open it. Brad was smarter than the door. He turned the knob, threw his shoulder into it and kicked the sill of the door all at the same time. *Pop!* the door barked as Brad easily walked through it.

The moonlight gave him enough light to find the fridge and find the thing he was craving. A beer. The cold beer was desperately waiting for Brad to pick it up. The outside of the can was moist and welcoming. His big hand reached for the beer as his other hand went for the top. *"Hello there!"* the beer said as Brad cracked open the top. The cold beer ran down Brad's throat after spending a brief second in his mouth.

"Damn," he said with joy, "that's good." With every sip, he would drift into thoughts. "I need another one," he said to himself as his thoughts changed into nightmares.

With another big swig, Brad was sick of seeing Donny's body hanging in the air.

Brad threw out the last of the beer and sighed, "I do not need these thoughts anymore."

Off to bed he went.

– – –

Rob arrived at his home. The trailer welcomed him with its moans and groans. The steps creaked and the door squealed as Rob pulled it open. His mom was nowhere in sight and all that was on Rob's mind now was the couch. He lay down on it as he kicked off his shoes.

The couch gladly greeted him as it sat all day without any friends. The divot where his ass always landed was as comfortable as always. Even though his ass was happy, his mind was not. It was full of thoughts. One second it was Donny and the next was his dad.

The moonlight was disappearing, and the morning was ready to set in. The thoughts of his dad and Donny had left with the last of the night as Rob fell asleep.

Chapter | 58

The moonlight shined down on the cruiser Jackson was driving. No luck out at Hanner's house, just the bullet casing he found. Jackson drove from Hanner's home and headed towards the funeral home.

"Jackson, you there?" Jenny questioned over the speaker.

"Yep," Jackson briefly replied.

"Where are you heading now? Thought I heard you say the funeral home," Jenny came back with. Jenny sat quiet for a moment before the follow up, "Why the funeral home?"

Jackson barked back, "Because Hanner is either at the funeral home or the station, since there is no crime spree going at the moment, figured he'd be at the funeral home."

"Sorry, Jackson," Jenny replied as her lower lip began to quiver. "I'm just worried about Callahan. And I'm worried about you. It's not like Callahan not to check in or anything. You be careful."

"Sorry I snapped, Jen. Everything will be okay. I'm sure Callahan is fine."

Jackson continued his drive towards the funeral home. His thoughts were on Callahan and what Jenny just said. He lied to her. He lied to Jenny since her voice was stumbling with emotion. She didn't need to know that he was worried too. Something was wrong with Callahan, and he needed to find out.

Walcott welcomed Jackson and his squad car back into town. Through the square he drove, and a couple turns later he was heading towards the funeral home.

"What do we have here?" Jackson questioned as the light from his car shined on an ambulance that was attached to a tow truck.

"I think this is Harold Addy's tow truck. What is it doing here?" Jackson drove his cruiser into the lot and parked it near the building. He jumped out of his car and instantly shined his flashlight on the truck with the ambulance in tow. The flashlight shined all over the combination of the two, inside the cab of the ambulance, then off to the tow truck and then vice versa.

Jackson thought for moment and, *Nothing strange with these things, just the location*. He headed towards the rear door of the funeral home when he thought of the bullet casing. Jackson changed direction and jumped back into his cruiser. He opened the middle console and carefully pulled out the bullet casing with his handkerchief. He rolled it up into a ball and shoved it in his pocket.

The funeral home waited for Jackson to enter it. The rear door was glowing in the night air and the silver handles were cold to the touch. Jackson pulled open the door and found himself in a little room.

"Decisions, decisions," he said to himself, "stay upstairs or head downstairs to the morgue?" With a couple steps Jackson stated, "The morgue it is."

He looked at the stairs and the elevator. With a quick decision, Jackson was on his way down the stairs. Each step echoed in the narrow staircase. The descent towards the morgue brought a temperature change. The closer to the morgue he got, the cooler things got.

The light shined through the little square window that was housed towards the top of the door. Luckily, Jackson had some height on him, and he could peer through the window. At first glance Jackson did not notice anything peculiar. He reached for the door handle and pushed down on the top lock. The door clicked opened, and the sound echoed all the way up the staircase and into the cool morgue.

"What the fuck?" Hanner blurted out.

Jackson walked through the open door and slightly around the corner. His eyes lit up, his ass clinched, and he froze when reaching for his gun.

Tap, tap! his forehead shouted as Hanner's revolver found the middle of Jackson's head.

"Boy, you sure are lucky you have a badge on your chest, or I would have split your head wide open."

"Yes, sir," Jackson stammered, "sorry for scaring you."

"You didn't scare me, boy."

"Sorry, Hanner," Jackson replied, "I didn't mean to come unannounced, but I am looking for Sheriff Callahan. Sheriff Richard Callahan."

"How do you know my name?"

"I met you once before with the sheriff."

"Where?"

"Before I answer any more questions, do you mind taking your gun away from my head? You're starting to make me nervous."

Click, the revolver stated as Hanner pulled back the hammer.

"Now, *that* sound should make you nervous," stated Hanner as he pulled the gun away from Jackson's head and re-holstered it in its leather home. "I asked you where?" finished Hanner.

"Callahan and I were around for the Drucker murders."

"Oh, that's right," Hanner said in a nice, condescending voice, "you were a new pissant officer at that time. You still seem pretty weak to me."

"Kiss my ass!"

"Wow, you have a little zip to you now. I take that back then. So, answer this. What are you doing here?"

"Callahan is missing."

"What's that have to do with me?"

"His last known location was your house. He's been missing ever since. Wondering if you know where he is?"

"Well, what was your name?" Hanner questioned.

"Sheriff Jackson."

"Well, Jackson, Callahan and I chatted after Jack got shot in my house. That is the extent of it. After the conversation, Callahan got in his car and pulled away. That was the last I saw of him."

Jackson stood there for a moment as *bullshit* raced through his mind and then he said, "Don't you find it kind of strange the last person he saw was you and then went missing?"

"No."

"You don't find that strange?"

"Not at all."

"Well, I do," Jackson said.

"I really do not care nor do I have the time for your questions, Jackson; I'm kind of in the middle of something."

"You'll need to find time. Also, I'll need to speak to your wife Martha too."

"Oh, my wife, Martha? You want to speak to my wife, Martha. Is that correct?" Hanner's somewhat nice demeanor started to switch gears.

"Yes, please," Jackson replied as he stared down Hanner's now-glossy gaze.

"Follow me." Hanner walked to the table where Martha lay to rest and pulled the sheet off her.

Jackson stammered, "Is that, umm… that, umm… Martha, I mean is that Martha?"

"Martha, can you take a moment to answer Sheriff Dipshit's questions?"

Jackson was taken aback and could not take his eyes off Martha. He tried to get his bearings, but the situation was overwhelming.

"Sorry, Hanner. I didn't mean any disrespect. I did, umm… I did not know she passed. I'm sorry for your loss."

"Get out of here, Jackson; I do not have time for this, time for you or any other idiot that would present themselves right now."

"Yes, sir," Jackson replied and headed towards the stairs. As he reached the last step in the room before heading up, he turned and asked, "What type of gun did you have resting on my forehead?"

Hanner stated, "A .357 Magnum."

Chapter | 59

The morning sun shined over Walcott like any other morning. Bright and crisp, becoming one with the breeze flowing through the valley. Stocker Hill stood back and enjoyed the sunlight that was given to it. The breeze flowed over its body and its tall, strong trees danced with every breath. Things were changing in Walcott and Stocker was standing by watching.

Reed raced home from Krista's that morning. His back hurt a little from the fall, but he had enough strength in him to make it home before the parents made their appearance.

The front door was locked, and Reed had to jiggle the key and lock ever so gently so as not to wake the Ps. The door released from its closed position, welcoming Reed home. At the bottom of the stairs, looking up at him with his sad, little eyes was Buster.

"Oh, Buster buddy," Reed said as he went to pick up Buster, "you look sad."

Buster cowered away from Reed when he tried to pick him up. "Come here, buddy," he said. "What's wrong. You mad at me?"

Buster allowed Reed to pick him up but looked away every time Reed tried to kiss him on his face. Buster was sad and Reed knew it.

Reed was flushed with sadness on how his buddy Buster was reacting. "Okay, buddy, we are going to cheer you up. Okay?" Busters little stump of a tail wagged briefly and then stopped moving. "First thing, we are going to get a treat; then we are going to go cuddle in bed. Sound good?"

Buster perked up as Reed carried him into the kitchen. There on the counter, Buster's round, wooden treat heaven. Buster heard the cap open when Reed reached for it and went bananas.

"That's the Buster I know; you just needed a little love," Reed said as he nuzzled his face up next to Buster's.

Buster returned the love with little licks to the tip of Reed's nose.

"Okay, Buster, let's go veg on the bed and get some winks."

Reed let Buster down and he raced up the stairs. Taking a hard right towards Reed's room, his little paws were going full blast and trying to get as much traction as they could to make the leap onto the bed.

Reed followed Buster at a slower pace. When he reached the room, Buster was already planted in the middle of the bed waiting for some company. Reed climbed next Buster in the bed and whispered into Buster's ear, "safe."

– – –

Brad awoke in a slight haze as the sunlight crept in through the blinds to touch his face. His eyes were crusty, and his mouth was dry. Brad buried his face in his hands and rubbed his face vigorously, anything he could do to knock the haze from his head. Brad had a plan for the day. Meet the guys and head up the Hill.

With a moment of hesitation, Brad pulled the covers off and headed for the shower. The old, cool floor felt refreshing on the bottom of his feet as he turned the shower on and cracked the window to let the steam out.

Before jumping in the shower, he looked in the mirror and watched his bloodshot eyes look back at him. His blue eyes that normally swim in a sea of white, were now drowning in rivers of red.

"Damn, Brad," he said back to the reflection he was not enjoying.
With a slight yank, Brad pulled the shower curtain back and
jumped into the warm, awaiting shower. The water berated his back
with an ever stream of warm drops. All Brad could do was enjoy every
second as the shower helped him get back to normal.

With his hair washed, body clean and his teeth brushed, Brad
doused himself with a manly scent and headed out of the house.
Through the front door, down the steps and off to Reed's house
he went.

— — —

Rob woke up on his couch as he normally did. The morning air
brought out the musty smell of the trailer and the scent rushed
through Rob's nostrils.

Not wanting to lay on the couch with his thoughts, Rob jumped
up quickly and headed for the shower. His mother was asleep in her
room; Rob's plan was to get clean and out the door before his mother
came back to life.

The shower trickled to full force before Rob jumped into the
small, stand-up shower that was a standard staple in most trailers. He
washed his body and hair and got out of the shower as soon as he
could. Even on high heat, the shower never really got up to temperature and the last thing that Rob wants is to wallow in a lukewarm
shower at best.

Rob was dressed and out the door before the rusty steps could
react to him leaving.

— — —

John awoke from his slight nap with trickles of sunlight running down his face. He left Suzy's in hopes of finding sleep in his bed, but that good night's sleep never came to visit.

John wished he was at Suzy's holding and kissing the woman he loves. Her beautiful red hair is a joy to wake-up next to, and he hoped someday that he could do that on a permanent basis.

After a few thoughts of the guys rushing into his head and the adventure that was waiting for him that day, John said goodbye to the bed and shot for the shower. The large, frosted door towered over John as he stepped through it into the shower. With all the options the shower offered, John loved the rain effect as the tall ceiling drenched him with warm water.

John got lost in thought, he looked down at his hands that were full of shampoo and couldn't remember if he washed his hair or not. With no recollection coming back to him, in a general pissed off voice, John stated, "What the!" And washed his hair again.

With pure frustration, John vigorously dried his body, threw on some deodorant, grabbed some clothes and was out the door headed towards the park.

Chapter | 60

Brad was on his way to Reed's in a slow, lumbering walk. The few pebbles that met his shoes leapt with every kick and launched them in all directions. They jumped and danced along with their small shadows in tow. With every roll and bounce, the pebbles tried for one last leap into the sunshine before finding their next resting place.

Brad's thoughts were on the adventure ahead as he made the final turn onto Reed's street. His shuffling walk was replaced with a brisk, purposeful walk to his destination. Up the walkway and a trot over the awaiting stairs, Brad found himself at Reed's front door. The smell of breakfast quickly entered his nostrils and as he did a big sniff, Brad rang the doorbell, announcing his presence.

Ding, dong! the doorbell yelled into Buster's ears, and he leapt off the bed and used Reed's face for traction.

"Ouch…!" Reed shouted as his face lit up in pain.

Reed's mother answered the door and welcomed Brad into the house. "Morning, Brad." she said.

Before Brad could get out, "Morning, ma'am," Buster was attacking his feet with vigor.

"Are you hungry?" she asked. "I am fixing up some breakfast now." She then followed with a motherly yell, "Reed, get down here and take care of Buster, and Brad is here!"

"Yes, ma'am. That would be great," Brad let out with excitement.

"I'll be right down," Reed yelled through his hands as he was still recovering from Buster's launch off his melon.

"You go ahead and have a seat at the table, Brad," Reed's mother stated. "I'm sure Reed will be down once he gets a whiff of what is brewing in the kitchen."

"Yes, ma'am," Brad responded as he headed into the kitchen.

Reed made his way down the stairs after he gained his composure and shook off the pain. With each step, the stairs creaked in response to his steps until they started to clap as his footsteps got faster, "Damn, Mom, smells good…."

"Reed Benjamin, don't you use that language in this house."

"Yes, ma'am," he followed with as he shot a smirk to Brad when he grabbed the chair to sit down.

"You boys dig in. Remember, take all you want, but eat all you take."

"Yes, ma'am," the boys said in unison.

"Where's Dad?" Reed asked.

"No clue, son. He left early in the morning to take care of something. I'm sure it's important… well, important in his eyes."

Reed devoured his food while Brad ate like a civilized human being. The fork and knife barked at every bite Reed was taking while Buster looked up from the floor waiting for a runaway slice of something wonderful.

"Great chow, Mom. Going to take a quick shower and then we can go, Brad," Reed said as he left the table.

Reed's mom rolled her eyes as she watched her son leave his dishes on the table and a half glass of milk still sitting there. As she grabbed for the dishes, she asked Brad, "So, Brad, what are the big plans today?"

Brad just shrugged his shoulders as he took the last bite of his breakfast.

"Oh, I see, you don't want mean old Mom to know what you two are up to today. I get it."

Brad shrugged his shoulders again and smiled ever so lightly.

Buster lay on the kitchen floor watching all the dishes go into the sink with no extra treats for him. The shower was echoing down from upstairs as Reed took time to make himself somewhat presentable for the day. A few minutes had passed, and the shower went silent. Brad sat at the kitchen table watching with Buster as they waited for Reed to make his appearance.

"Let's go and do this," Reed said, pouncing into the kitchen.

Brad was startled by Reed's entrance as he was lost in thoughts watching the dishes get cleaned.

"Do what?" Reed's mom asked, "and next time clean up after yourself."

"Nothing, Mom, yes, Mom," Reed responded as he signaled to Brad so they could leave the house.

Before Reed's mom could respond, Reed and Brad were out the door and all she heard was the door slamming goodbye.

Chapter | 61

The morgue stood still in the night. It was cold and damp and waited for the next move to be made. Hanner stood in silence with Martha as she lay there quietly as Jackson left the room. Harold sat in silence upstairs waiting to see what was supposed to happen next.

The upstairs of the morgue was as creepy as the basement in Harold's eyes. He waited in the stillness as he watched Jackson's patrol car drive away.

"Wonder what he wanted?" Harold said to himself.

"Callahan is missing!" Hanner blurted out as he entered the office Harold was sitting in.

Harold leapt from his seat and grabbed his chest, "Jesus Christ, Hanner, you scared the shit out of me."

Hanner returned with anger, "Yeah, ask me if I give a shit!"

"What do you mean Callahan is missing?"

"Oh, that Jackson asshole is saying Callahan is missing ever since he came to see me at my place."

The hairs on the back of Harold's neck stood in full attention as a pale rush of white hit his face, "Missing after seeing you? That's strange."

"Oh, I bet he's off with some whore and too busy to call in," Hanner replied.

"Yeah, yeah, that's it," Harold replied, while he thought to himself, *bet Hanner offed him.*

Hanner swung around towards Harold and looked him dead in his eyes. Harold was clammy by now and his eyes opened to full capacity. Fear raced through every inch of Harold's body as Hanner stated, "If I offed Callahan, no one would ever know, would they?"

Hanner walked out of the office and yelled back at Harold, "get out of here, take the ambulance to the grave and dispose of it. This is why I chose you over Donny. No mistakes. Do I make myself clear?"

"Yes, sir," Harold stated as he headed towards the door. In a faint voice, Harold could hear Hanner talking to himself, "That man better toe the line or he'll end up on the slab like Callahan did."

Harold rushed to his truck as tears ran down his face with every movement he made. He knew at that point that Alex and Ray were gone and that he better follow orders, or he would be next.

The truck started without hesitation as Harold grabbed the wheel, released the clutch and got the truck moving with the ambulance in tow. The ambulance bucked on down the road behind Harold's truck. The Chevy was pulling the ambulance effortlessly, until it arrived at the base of the Hill and the gravel road entrance.

"Oh man," Harold stated, "this is going to be a tough one carrying all this weight."

The truck cracked with hesitation when Harold pressed in the parking brake. He jumped out of the cab as the truck idled quietly waiting for his next move. Harold checked that the towing chains were still securely connected and locked in front hubs to engage the four-wheel drive system.

Harold groaned as he jumped back into the truck. With his left hand he pulled the lever to disengage the parking brake while with his right hand he pulled the lever to engage the four-wheel drive. The gears grinded in hesitation then finally popped into place. With a couple revs of the engine, Harold released the clutch and started the climb up Stocker Hill.

"Please, buddy, you can do it," Harold begged as the truck's front tires hit the initial grade in the gravel road.

The road was dark and hazy while the gravel glistened with moisture. The truck's front tires began to dig into the gravel while the rear tires pushed with all their might. The road talked back to the tires with a gentle chat and made the drive easy.

"Weird," Harold said as the truck made a graceful journey up the side of the Hill. "The last time you fought me the whole way up."

The green plateau stood waiting for Harold's arrival. The dark sky opened to bring attention to the grave. There it sat, inviting Harold to it, waiting in the light for him to arrive.

As Harold pulled in as much oxygen as he could, he guided the truck to the grave and allowed the ambulance to stop perfectly next to it. Without thinking about it and trying to stop his nerves from failing him, Harold unhooked the ambulance and dropped the front end down until the hardworking black tires were sitting on the plush green carpet.

The ambulance now sat alone next to the grave as Harold pulled his truck away from the area. In his left pocket lived his cigarettes and matches. *Crack!* The match barked as Harold struck it with force to fire it up. Harold's dried, coarse lips held the cigarette up while the little flame crackled to bring it to life. With one big suck, the cigarette was dancing with light as the smoke slowly billowed from Harold's nostrils.

"Oh, Lord, please guide me," Harold whispered as he began the walk to the ambulance.

The driver's side window was already down on the ambulance and was waiting for Harold's next move. The two empty seats stood at attention in the front of the ambulance, waiting for Alex and Ray to arrive. Harold crept closer to the open window as a subtle, cool breeze rushed past his face. The lit cigarette danced with excitement as the breeze fueled the glow. With a flick of his fingers, the red, glowing cigarette flipped through the air and landed on the floor of the ambulance.

Harold walked away from the ambulance and whispered, "I don't like this," and then he turned back to watch the show.

Whoosh! yelled the ambulance as the front cab went up in flames.

"Here we go," Harold said as he found himself sitting on the white rocks away from the grave.

The green grass started to glow as the flames from the ambulance began to dance into the air. With every dance, the flames began to disappear into the grave. Harold sat in awe, watching each flame disappear into the grave and bringing a part of the ambulance with every flicker. Slowly, the ambulance started to disappear, starting with the cab.

A faint sound started coming from the burning ambulance, "Help, help us, please!"

"What was that?" Harold stood up and shouted, "Hello?"

Faintly, "Help, help, help us, please help us!"

Harold ran from the rocks towards the ambulance. With every step the faint sounds got louder, "Help us, help, please, Lord!"

Confusion overwhelmed Harold as he started searching for the voices. Running back and forth next to the ambulance as the voices rushed out. The heat started pushing Harold with every step.

"Hello, anyone there?" he shouted.

"In here!" a voice yelled as a pounding noise echoed from the back of the ambulance.

"Oh my God, no…!" Harold yelled as he was forced away from the ambulance as the flames became fierce.

"Save us Harold!" Alex yelled while pounding on the back doors.

Harold made eye contact with Alex and tried to move closer to the back doors to get him out of the ever-disappearing ambulance.

His feet were stuck in location, being held there with a might he could not overcome.

"Ray is gone, please save me!" Alex yelled.

Harold started to cry as he stood powerless to move, powerless to help, powerless to make a difference. The tears blurred his vision as the eye contact with Alex disappeared as screams of agony raced from Alex's mouth.

The green grass caught Harold as he fell, "I killed them."

Chapter | 62

The County Sheriff's Department stood alone in the valley—trapped between Walcott and South Port. Standing alone, watching over the county, watching over several counties, watching over Walcott.

The front door swung open as Jackson yanked on it furiously. It had no fight in it; it knew Jackson was pissed.

"Have you heard from Callahan?" shouted Jackson to Katie.

Katie took over for Jenny at dispatch. "Haven't seen or heard from him, sir."

Katie was a timid, shy girl with beautiful brown hair and warm glow about her.

"That's just great!" Jackson shouted.

"What do you want me to do?" Katie asked.

"We need to send a message to law enforcement around, but with one stipulation."

Katie looked at Jackson. "And what is that?"

"We can't let Hanner of Walcott know we are doing this."

Katie responded with a delay, "So, we can't send this out with our regular communications. I have to call each station individually?"

"Yes."

"But that will, that will—" That is all Katie got out before Jackson interrupted her.

"Yes, I know, that's a lot of calls, but we need to do this, we need to find Callahan and I think Hanner has to do with a big part of his disappearance."

"Yes, sir," she responded.

"Also," Jackson chimed in with one last comment, "call Rodney and get him out of bed early, we need all hands-on-deck."

"Yes, sir."

Rodney is the other deputy that works under Callahan and takes most of his orders from Jackson.

"One more thing," Jackson barked.

Katie replied in a frustrated voice, "For crying out loud."

"Simmer down, this is about Callahan, when does the lab open? I need to get this bullet casing checked out."

"I do not know for sure," she responded as guilt swept over her for her response, "but I will check and let you know."

"Thanks," Jackson replied as he made his way to the back of the station.

Katie sighed a breath of frustration and rubbed her hands through her thick hair before starting the task. Katie's first call was to the FBI forensic site located in Cook County.

"Hey, Elizabeth," Katie spun her frustration around into her happy voice, "I have a bullet casing here we need analyzed. Going to be sending it over by messenger. Can you put this as a priority? Deputy Jackson has this as an urgent request."

"Sure thing, Katie. We'll get this going as soon as we get the evidence," Elizabeth promptly responded.

"Thanks, hon."

Katie swung her chair around from the large welcoming desk to grab her list of county sheriff department contacts.

"Hey!" Katie barked over to conference system, "how many counties out do you want us to call?"

"Out past Morrison County," Jackson replied.

This time Katie's sigh got larger; her hands tugged at her hair as she guided them through it. Strands of brown hair ending up on the floor behind her chair.

Chapter | 63

The bright, crisp morning had Bill wide awake as he drove his old Ford down the road. With every turn, Bill could feel the Hill watching him, wondering what he was doing. Remembering. It has been years since the two of them have chatted.

The old Ford slowed down near a little home near Lock 17. Bill sat in the front seat for a moment, but knew he needed to get moving. He slowly opened the old door, put his feet on the ground, and headed for the front door of the home.

The home sat off the road a tad and was well kept. The white paint stood proudly for a little place and the shingles covered the roof with strength. The welcome mat was old, but clean and waited daily for friends to visit.

"Damn," Bill said as he walked up towards the groomed house, "Dory keeps this place nice."

With a flick of the wrist and his steel toed boots standing firmly on the welcome mat, Bill knocked on the small glass window that surrounded the front door.

Knock, knock, knock, his knuckles commanded the windows to shout.

Bill stood on the mat that seemed like another lifetime before his impatience's took hold.

"Come on, Dory," he blurted before making the windows shout again. *Knock, knock, knock!*

The inside of the house was as pristine as the outside. The fine wood floors gave no hint that Dory was on his way to see who was rapping on his window.

The disturbing noise interrupted the daily peace he enjoyed when he wasn't working at the bar.

Click, click, the two locks whispered as Dory unlocked the front door before opening it.

"Bill? What are you doing here?"

"We have a problem; one that we knew might jump up and bite us someday," Bill replied.

"What problem?" Dory questioned.

"The boys."

Dory's head dropped and his eyes looked down at his feet while they twitched with sadness. Dory always prayed that this day would not happen, especially to people he cared for.

"I understand," he said. "Now what?"

"We need to go see Harold; I think the boys have been talking to him," Bill responded.

"Okay. Give me a minute and I'll be right out."

Dory headed back to his bedroom to get a clean T-shirt, a standard hunting hat and his boots. He stopped in the bathroom and splashed fresh water on his face. Took a shot of mouthwash and a quick spray of deodorant.

The once pristine house became deadly silent as the man who took care of it slowly walked out the door. As the two men walked to the car, Bill asked in a curious way, "Dory, why don't you have a dog or two? They're great company."

Dory looked at Bill over the top of the car before climbing in, "I can't see anything else die."

Bill nodded, lowered his head and climbed into the seat next to Dory. The car carrying Bill and Dory left Dory's house in silence. The road to be traveled is the road no one ever wanted to happen. Bill, Dory, Harold, and Hanner knew sooner or later someone would be knocking on the door to the past.

Bill and Dory sat quietly as the car took them through the town to Harold's garage. The morning was nice, and Harold's garage stood like it was any other day. It knew what was to come, it knew the past and if it could, it would have left Walcott years ago.

"Ready to do this?" Bill asked.

"Yep."

"That is not a confident *yep*."

"Well. Bill, we have not all sat together in years, and this is not how I wanted to visit my old friend," Dory wearily replied.

"I understand, but this is my boy we're talking about, this is about Rob and his father."

Dory looked over at Bill. "His father, Rob's father, we can't even say his name anymore?"

"You know what I mean," Bill stammered, "let's find Harold."

The two men slowly climbed out of the car and lumbered their way to the front door of the garage. Dory reached for the door and expected it to open, but the door had others plans as Dory's face planted on the locked door.

"Ugh," Dory barked as he reached up to rub his face.

"That's strange. The door is never locked at this time in the morning. Harold is always here."

As Dory finished rubbing his face back into its natural state, he replied, "You got that right. This is strange. Let's check the back."

The two old friends made their way to the back of the garage and found it in the same state as the front, locked.

As they walked back to Bill's car, Bill stated with frustration, "Let's head to his house and if he is not there, we'll regroup and figure something out."

Dory nodded in agreement as they climbed into the car and headed towards their old friend's house.

Chapter | 64

Central Park sat around like every other morning in Walcott—waiting for visitors. The morning was nice, the air was fresh, and the park was setting the scene for a great day.

Rob strolled around the corner thinking about the past events. His stroll was a lonely one, especially the more he thought of his father, his lonely mother, and the pain his father must have gone through.

"I'm sorry, Father, for calling you a coward, I am so sorry," Rob cried as he slowly got closer to the park.

A crisp breeze shot over the top of the park that sent chills over the rocks, swings, and surrounding trees. The park looked past the chilly breeze to see Rob making his way to it while off in the distance Brad was on his way too. Brad split from Reed at some point, and they found their way to the park on different journeys.

Rob arrived at the park and planted himself in the usual location that the boys would always congregate to. He sat there with his head down, arms crossed as his mind raced through what was to come.

Brad's arrival was far more jovial. His trip there was more of excitement than of remorse or sadness. He knew that there were answers to be had; he was all in on what lays ahead.

"What's up, Robbie be rottin'?" Brad joked as he entered the edge of the park and saw Rob sitting there.

Rob stood in silence and did not make any attempt to acknowledge that Brad had arrived.

Brad made his way over to where Rob was standing in sorrow and pulled him into his arms. Brad held on tight until Rob slowly went limp and launched into a full body weep. With every breath that Rob pulled in, he slowly started to grip Brad tighter and tighter. Every weep, every breath, Rob let out his sorrows while gaining his strength.

"There you go, bud," Brad gently said. "You needed that."

As he reached up and wiped his tears, Rob replied, "Thanks so much. I can't tell you how much that helped."

"No problem," Brad followed as he punched Rob in the arm.

Another crisp breeze took a shot over the top of the park as both Reed and John got closer. They were in sight of the park, walking on different paths, different strides, but the same thoughts were flying through their heads.

Reed was the first to arrive, ahead of John by a few steps and Rob's swollen eyes caught his attention. "You okay, buddy?"

Rob nodded without any comment, signaling he was okay.

John arrived last and walked up to each of his friends and shook their hands. Looking each in their eyes, sending an indication that "I am here, I am ready."

The boys stood around their normal meeting place with only a few words being said. The breeze stayed cool and crisp as the park was showing its sadness on the events that were going to take place.

Brad finally blurted out, "Okay. Enough of this standing around in uncertainty. What's the plan?"

"The plan?" John questioned. "You tell us. This started with you?"

"Started with me? Hell you say?"

John looked at Brad through his squinted eyes. "The plan to meet. The plan to go to the grave. The plan to climb Stocker. *That plan.*"

"Oh yeah. That plan. Well, let's get to it," Brad stated as he turned and looked up at the Hill.

Reed walked up next to Brad and whispered to him so the others could not hear him, "You sure about this? This could cause a lot of trouble."

"Yes. Yes, I am sure. Can you imagine us sitting around, hanging out together with this big question hanging over us? Over us all the time and we ignore it? Can you imagine that?"

Reed looked up at the Hill, turned his chubby body around to look at the other guys and whispered back, "That's a life I could not handle."

Reed and Brad headed back to John and Rob to map out the day. As the leader he was, Brad took control of the situation.

"Listen, guys. Listen closely. We learned a lot the past few days, we saw a lot the past few days; now we have this knowledge that none of us ever really wanted. But we have it. We need to close the book."

"Close the book," Reed said in a quiet but forceful tone.

John and Rob looked at each other and back at Brad. With nods of their heads, they agreed on the situation, the past, and what was about to happen.

Brad pounded his chest with his fist. A motion of power and confidence spoke out in leadership. "Let's climb this fucking Hill, let's find this grave, let's get some answers, and close this chapter of our lives. We need to go back to our lives before we opened Pandora's Box!"

Reed looked up at Brad. "Pandora's Box?"

Brad looked back at Reed while squelching his eyebrows closely, "Greek mythology, motherfucker."

"Oh. Kind of over the top—don't you think?" Reed said, smirking as he looked at the other guys.

A slight calmness came over the guys after some Greek mythology jokes, the perfect time for some levity. The cool breeze evaporated, and the park gave its approval to the boys it ever so enjoyed.

The boys turned and headed out of the park towards the garage, towards the entrance of the Hill.

"Umm," Rob coughed while pulling on Brad's sleeve.

Brad turned and looked over to Rob. Pointing with his eyes, Rob signaled for Brad to look in the general direction of Harold's garage. There on the path in front of them was Reed's father, Bill, and Dory getting out of an old Ford. Brad looked back at Rob and John, who saw the same thing as they did; shaking his head with disapproval while he mouthed, *"Reed does not need to see that."*

Without hesitation, Brad spoke up. "I am sick of the garage. Let's head the back way, enjoy the weather before we make the hike up the Hill."

Reed looked up from his walk and followed Brad's lead. The boys took a quick right, cut through the Rizors' backyard and into the alley. From the alley they found the next road that took them to the Hill. While walking past the houses they have always known—no one spoke. Not even a peep.

Chapter | 65

The morning light started to tap on the small, slotted windows that stood watch over the morgue. They were letting enough light in to notice, but not enough to take control of the room.

Hanner looked down at Martha and felt a warmth of love and affection. His mind jumped back and forth between memories of their life together. Happy and sad memories, the life of good and evil. The life that was present before evil was born with the Drucker murders.

Hanner, knowing that this time of love and warmth would be short-lived; he made a rash decision. He slowly knelt towards Martha's ear and whispered, "Ashes to ashes, dust to dust. Sorry, my love. It's the only way. I know this is not what you wanted. I love you."

Hanner turned and walked away from his wife while heading towards the crematorium.

Opening the operation panel, Hanner fired up the oven where Martha was to lay at rest.

Martha lay in waiting as the oven came up to temperature. Hanner watched the gauge knowing once the oven was at temp, his time with Martha would be over. A memory that he does not know if he will ever have control of again.

The oven shouted as the greenlight lit up the room stating it was ready for the task at hand. Hanner, by this time, had Martha laying gently on the loading gurney. Her hands were crossed, her hair was combed while her jewelry was shining at attention. With the door open, Hanner slid his wife in the awaiting oven and closed the door. Martha's life was over as the flames engulfed a wonderful woman and sent her up the chimney to be with her family along with her friends who were waiting in the distance for her to arrive.

Hanner walked from the oven as it took care of what needed to be done, walked past the tables, past the elevator and up the stairs away from the morgue. Hanner arrived at the top of the stairs and peaked out the window as the morning sunlight hit the hearse— "Donny!"

Making his way to his office to callout to Harold, Hanner stopped and made a fresh batch of coffee. As the coffee began to brew and the aroma became one with the room, Hanner picked up the mic and with the caring individual still in charge, called out to Harold, "Harold, you there? Come back, buddy."

Hanner sat back for a moment and enjoyed the aroma of the coffee. After a few more seconds, he reached out again, "Come back, Harold. You out there? I need you, buddy. I know you're upset. Come back."

The wave of Hanner's voice went out for all to hear as he headed to get that cup of coffee. The pot was hot while the cup was waiting for the black gold to be poured into its soul. Hanner took a big whiff and sipped ever so gently on the edge of the cup. The coffee overwhelmed his mouth with flavor and gave him a nudge to pick up the mic again.

"Harold, buddy. You out there?"

Hanner sat and waited for a response while he finished his cup of coffee. The coffee was gone, which made the cup sad. Hanner walked out the back of the premises. Once he reached the back of the hearse, he opened the door. Reaching in to uncover Donny's body, a rush of wickedness impaled him, and any love or compassion left his body without a trace.

"Alright, Donny, it looks like it's just you and me" he said as he tugged at Donny's legs and pulled him out of the hearse.

Donny's head bounced off the bumper to the half-pathed parking lot below him.

"That might have hurt if you weren't so dead right now."

It's true. Compassion was gone. Hanner pulled the body through the slight gravel, through the doors and onto the elevator. Donny's body pulled pebbles of gravel with him while his head bounced over any uneven terrain thrown its way. His head bounced over the door partition, bounced over the gap entering the elevator and stopped on the elevator floor.

The elevator guided Hanner and Donny down to the morgue which will be home for Donny until his wake and burial. Hanner pulled at Donny again and his body slid along the basement floor without anything fighting its way. With a swoop of strength, Hanner picked up the body and threw Donny on the waiting table.

As Donny lay there immobile, Hanner prepared the body to be embalmed and began the embalming process. Hanner watched Donny as any color he had left his body; disappearing as the fluid was being pumped into him.

Chapter | 66

.

Katie let out her trademark sigh as she worked her way down the list of counties to call. The evening sky currently has no personality, initiating the boredom that overcame the room.

"Call all the counties," Katie snipped as she crossed another department off the list.

Katie adjusted her headset before, making another call. *Click, click, click,* the buttons bounced back at Katie's fingers as she was dialing the next county.

"Good evening, Arapaho Police Department, this is Diana; how can I help you?"

"Hey, Diana," Katie said, perking up after hearing Diana was working, "this is Katie over at the County Sheriff Department."

"Hey, Katie, what's up, girl?"

"I need you to do something for me. We have not seen or heard from Sheriff Callahan. We last heard from him when he went out to see Sheriff Hanner," Katie said to Diana.

"Ugh," Diana replied, "that Buck Hanner sure is a gem."

"That's what I am finding out. Actually, that is what this call is for. We are having issues with him and want to know if anyone from your department has seen Sheriff Callahan?"

Diana replied, "I'll get on the radio and get a message out to the guys."

"No!" barked Katie. "Sorry, but no. We don't want him to be able to hear over the radio we're looking for Callahan."

"Okay. I will put a note into all the lockers about Callahan and have them contact me directly if they know anything."

"Thanks, so much, Diana. We are all so worried about Callahan. We think Buck has something to do with him being missing," replied Katie.

"Considerate it done, Katie," Diana finished with.

Katie sat with a little more confidence than before her call to Arapaho. Diana is a sweet lady and always brings a smile to everyone's face.

As Katie sat there collecting her thoughts, the door to the station flung open letting Rodney the deputy walk in.

"Hey, Katie." Rodney said, "you want to tell me what all the hub-bub is? I'm feeling like a secret agent."

Katie shot up from her seat and pointed her finger right at Rodney's face. "Show a little respect, you child!"

"What? What I do?" Rodney questioned.

"You know exactly what you did."

Rodney stood there dumbfounded. He looked at Katie as she stared him down. Looked at the clock on the wall, looked at his watch and shrugged his shoulders.

"See you're doing it again," Katie barked again.

"Well. Katie. I was told to come in and no one has told me why. So, please tell me why I am here?" Rodney followed.

Katie looked at Rodney as her anger and frustration with him left her face. "You don't know anything about what's going on?"

"Not a clue."

"Callahan is missing. Sheriff Callahan is missing. Sheriff Richard Callahan is missing," Katie finished as tears rolled down her cheeks.

"Sheriff Callahan is missing? What do you mean missing?"

Katie held back her tears and got Rodney up to speed on what was going on. The reason for the secrecy, Sheriff Hanner and what Deputy Jackson's plan was.

"Did you say Sheriff Hanner? Buck Hanner from Walcott?" Rodney replied.

"Yep."

Rodney stood for a moment collecting his thoughts after everything that Katie told him. He looked around, then hung his head down low. As his body took in a big breath of air followed by a slow exhale, Rodney said, "That Buck Hanner is bad news. Bad news, I tell you. Does Jenny know what's going on?"

Katie replied to Rodney as her eyes began to well up and her lips quivered with every word. "She's the one who first noticed Callahan was missing. She called Jackson in."

"Got it," Rodney replied as he headed towards his locker to get a few things. "Please let Jackson know I am here and will catch up with him shortly."

Chapter | 67

Harold's garage stood in a cold silence as Bill and Dory drove away in the old Ford. The old Ford let out a screaming bellow from the exhaust and a blue haze shot out matching the color of the car.

The garage watched as the car drove off looking for Harold. Harold was struggling and the garage stood scared and alone, missing the one constant person in its life.

"You think Harold's at home?" Dory asked.

Bill looked over at Dory after checking his speed as they drove past the square. "Don't know, Dory, just don't know."

"Years and years Harold is a constant at the garage. Anytime, any day, any moment. Where is he?"

"Dory, I do not know, but I am hoping he is at home. We'll find out soon enough," replied Bill in a worried voice.

The old Ford floated down the road to Harold's house. Every bump and rock, every crack and pothole the car encountered, the sound echoed through the car of silence. Bill and Dory stopped talking. They were waiting for the car to get them to Harold's house.

The house that Harold lived in wasn't really a house. It was a couple of trailers he pieced together over the years that sprawled across the little land that he had. The large gravel driveway helped guests find his home, which was located towards the back of his property.

The old car arrived at the drive and slowly made a turn from the bumpy, noisy road to a slight chatter of the gravel under its tires. Bill and Dory still sat quietly in their locations as the car moved up the driveway. With a slight slide, the car came to a rest in front of Harold's home, in front of the main door to his sprawling trailer estate.

A slight howl came from the side of the trailer as Bill and Dory exited that car.

"What the hell was that?" asked Bill.

"Harold's dog, I think."

Sure enough, Harold's dog came galloping around the corner looking to see who was visiting.

Dory looked at the floppy-eared dog and gave him a good petting on his head. "I forget your name dog."

"Duck is his name, no not Duck, I think it's Luck or something like that… I really don't give a shit, Dory!"

"Just a question, Bill."

Bill approached the trailer door and gave it a rap while waiting for a response. Dory found himself leaning against the car and spending time with the floppy-eared dog without a name.

Bam, bam! Bill's fist shouted as he pounded on the door, and then he waited again, peeking through the windows.

Dory spoke up. "I'm going around to the back to see if I see anything.

Bill nodded and had another conversation with the front door with his fist.

"Come on you floppy-eared mother, let's go see what we can find." Dory motioned to the dog to follow him on his little adventure to the back of the trailer.

The back of the trailer was cold and isolated, the sun was shining on the front that left a cool loneliness in the rear. Dory approached the back door and noticed the dog bowls were empty—no food or water for the pup.

Dory picked up the water bowl and took it to the outside faucet to get the dog some fresh water. The pipes hissed as the water trickled out into the bowl. The floppy-eared dog drank up the water like he had just walked across the desert. Dory watched in disbelief and filled up the bowl again, "Sorry, pup, I have no food for you, but this should help."

The back door stood cold as it watched Dory approach. It was waiting for the same beating the front door was going through. Dory lifted his fist and rapped away on the back door like Bill did to the front. He waited. A moment went by, and he rapped again. Waited again. This went on for a few more tries before he and the dog made their way back to Bill.

Bill sat leaning against the trunk of the old Ford as he waited for Dory and Floppy-Ears to make their way back to the front.

"Any luck?" Bill asked.

"Nope," replied Dory as he shrugged his shoulders, "no clue where he could be."

"The bar?"

"What bar?"

"Lock 17?"

"Dumbass, I own Lock 17. Don't you think I would know if he was there or not?"

"Is he there?"

"I have no clue."

Bill looked at Dory, Dory looked at Bill, and at the same moment said, "Let's go to the bar."

Floppy-Ears sat and watched the two men talk back and forth. He sat and watched them get into the car. He sat and watched them drive away. He sat and cried, he was alone again.

Chapter | 68

The warmth of the sheriff's station kept Katie comfortable as she finished up all her calls to the surrounding counties. Callahan was missing and everyone that needed to know—knew.

"Now we wait," she said to herself as she let out her signature sigh and played with her hair. She watched the phone and flipped through her magazine, did some filing, and waited. She had hours to go in her shift and she was worried about Callahan.

"Hey!" bolted Rodney.

"Jesus Christ, Rodney, you scared the living daylights out of me."

"Oh. Sorry. Ummm, anyways, have you heard from Jackson?"

"No. No, I have not," she bolted back. "Okay. Hey. I'm going out to check things out."

"Check things out?" Katie asked.

"Yeah. Police work shit. You wouldn't understand," Rodney followed with a smirk on his face.

Katie shot up her middle finger to let Rodney know what she was thinking as he walked out the front door.

– – –

Rodney jumped into his squad car with a light giggle in the air. He loved messing with people and Katie's reaction was priceless.

He started the car and picked up the mic, "Yo Jackson, you out there?"

He sat for a moment listening, dropped the car into drive and pulled away from the station and picked up the mic again, "Yo, yo Jackson. You out there? Comeback?"

The cruiser drove Rodney around the small streets of Walcott for a bit and no response from Jackson. The car drove past the square, past Goshen Dairy and down around Lock 17. No response from Jackson.

"Jackson, you out there?"

"I'm here."

"Where?"

"Sitting at the basin."

"Heading your way," Rodney said before hanging up the mic.

The cruiser did a hard turn around as Rodney hammered the gas down. The car ate up the road as he guided it through the streets, past the square again, and out to the basin, out to the entrance, out to the entrance to Stocker Hill.

Jackson sat in his patrol car with the windows down puffing on a cigarette. The cool air coming off the Hill felt good as he took several drags on the cigarette. The noise of Rodney's cruiser started off quietly, but as it got closer, Jackson could hear it gobbling up the road.

Rodney looked up from the steering wheel as he approached the basin. Off in the distance sat Jackson in his car. Sitting alone. As he got closer, he finally laid off hammering the gas and slowly rolled his cruiser up to Jackson. Their open windows met. Both men staring at each other while Jackson took another drag.

"I thought you quit?" Rodney asked.

"I did."

"What's with lighting up old smoking again?"

"Callahan."

"Callahan?"

"Yeah, Callahan."

"So, this is serious, then?"

Jackson took one last drag and launched the bud of the cigarette onto the entrance of the Hill. The bud slowly went from a glowing red tip to a dark dead object.

"Yeah, Rodney, this is serious. Callahan is missing. The last known location was Buck Hanner's place and I found a spent casing on the driveway. Didn't Katie mention something?"

Rodney's normal smartass nature disappeared; he didn't take Katie's explanation very seriously. His police training kicked in, "What size casing did you find?"

"Looks like it's from a .357."

"Where is it now?"

"Being analyzed," Jackson followed as he reached for another cigarette.

"Analyzed? Hard to analyze a bullet casing without a gun."

Jackson flicked opened his once-retired lighter and fired it up to add life to the awaiting cigarette. With a big drag and a long exhale, the cigarette jumped to life and smoke flew out of his mouth while he talked, "I understand that, but I needed to get them going on it."

Rodney nodded with acknowledgment, "You know who cares a .357?"

"Yes, I do—Buck Hanner."

"That old school prick always carries that snub-nosed pistol," Rodney replied in disgust as he followed with, "Now what?"

"I have no idea at the moment. Waiting to hear if any other of the counties have seen Callahan."

"Let's go visit Hanner!" shouted Rodney.

"Did that already."

"And?"

Jackson took another drag and replied, "Same old Hanner prick. Gave me nothing. Think I jarred him, though."

"How?"

"Mentioning to him that I found a spent .357 casing on his driveway."

"Really?"

"Really."

The two officers sat in silence as Jackson smoked and Rodney watched the smoke flow from his nostrils as he began to talk again, "I'm going to check in with Katie and see if anything came up. Please cruise around the surrounding counties and see if anything stirs up some suspicion."

"Got it. I'll be in touch."

They nodded, started their cars, and went their separate ways.

Chapter | 69

Stocker Hill stood tall that day. Shuttering the wind, blocking the sun, having total control of the valley. It watched over Walcott and saw the boys strolling its way. It knew something was a brewing, but what? The Hill did not know that morning.

The boys made it to the basin as they had done before. They looked up at the Hill with different thoughts than ever before. No mischief on this trip, no throwing rocks or breaking branches, no searching for mud to throw at the beehives or disturbing some critter's home—this was a serious trip.

"Well, boys," Brad said with confidence, "here we are. This trip is different this time. No stopping halfway up."

"We've never climbed to the top before," Rob kind of whimpered.

John walked in front of the other boys and looked up the steep path, "we'll be fine."

"Yeah. We'll be fine. We have each other. We'll be fine," Reed followed.

The boys took a moment to get their senses and take in the surroundings. The entrance to the path was wide and open, then tapered down to a single-file path. With one large breath and a very large exhale, Brad started up the path. John followed then Rob. Reed took control of the back of the line, and they walked in sequence up the Hill.

Stocker Hill was not happy. It sensed trouble in its future and had a feeling that the boys were going to stir something up that they shouldn't. It couldn't stop them from making the climb, but it could make it far more difficult.

The boys made it to where the trail started to narrow; the brush started to let the boys know it was there and going to harass them the entire walk up. With every step, each boy experienced a branch that was trying to tell them to turn around. Go home, go be safe. The boys were not listening.

Reed, from the back of the line yelled up to Brad, "Slow down up there. My legs can only go so fast."

"Dude, not my fault you have to take twice as many steps as me," Brad followed.

With a sympathetic moan, "Come on, boys. Slow down a little. What's the rush?"

John and Brad eased their strides as Reed slowly caught up.

"Thank you," he blurted.

John asked, "How long is it to the plateau we usually stop at?"

"Guessing," Brad wondered, "guess another fifteen minutes. Kind of fast compared to us messing around like previous trips."

The Hill watched as the boys made themselves up the side battling the branches all the way. It could tell they were on a mission and hoped the mission was going to end at the lower plateau. The lower plateau was high enough for most people to adventure to. It was a good hike, easy to get to and welcoming.

"Here we go." Reed let out a breath. "Time to rest."

Reed planted his ass on a large log that most people used as a resting place.

"Hey, remember this?" Brad asked, pointing to something on the log.

Rob followed with a perk in his voice, "Yeah, our initials. Took us forever to carve those."

John nodded his head in agreement, and Reed followed with, "Hours. Took us hours."

"Man," John replied, "how long ago was that?"

Reed threw his arms up acknowledging he had no clue while Brad searched for an answer.

"Three years ago."

"Really?" someone said.

Rob spoke again. "Three years ago. I remember it like it was yesterday."

Reed asked, puzzled, "Yesterday?"

Rob sat back on the log admiring the carving and followed with his heart, "Guys. I remember all the good times with you. That was one of them."

A quick smile jumped all over the boys' faces after Rob said that. They all sat on the log, catching their breath, remembering the good times they had always had.

At that moment, the Hill spoke. Not very loud or aggressive, not powerful, or dismissive, but a stern voice that shot a message across the bow.

"Something just changed," Reed said.

"Yeah," John replied.

Rob stood up from the log and spouted, "Yeah. Kind of creepy."

Brad stood up and walked away from the boys before turning around, "What are you talking about? Everything is okay."

The boys all were standing now and looking around, looking over the valley and up the Hill.

"Okay. I felt it too," Brad finally admitted as a chill ran across his arms and his hair stood at attention.

"I guess it means we're on the right track," Reed said with hesitation.

Stocker Hill was pissed. It knew now the boys weren't stopping at the plateau. It knew that this visit was far more than a bunch of kids messing around. The lower plateau was a safe place the Hill would let people visit—the boys had different plans this day.

Chapter | 70

The morgue was enjoying its evening as Donny lay on the stainless-steel table. His body empty of any resemblance of itself and was now filled with chemicals. Chemicals that allowed pathetic people to look over an empty vessel to say goodbye and cry.

The room was slightly lightened and cool. Donny's body mimicked the room's temperature. The morgue was ever so happy as the furnace was cooling down from its latest firing, waiting for the fresh corpse that lay in its presence. The morgue liked death and wanted more.

Hanner was enjoying a few last sips of coffee when he felt a shift in the air. Something was up and he did not like the feeling that was rushing into his body. The last time this happened, a bullet had to be put into Callahan.

"I need to solve this. I need to solve this now," he said as he whipped his coffee cup into the awaiting sink.

A brisk breeze shot across Hanner's face, *"yes you do!"*

Hanner left his office and headed towards his squad car. The car jumped to life as he sat behind the wheel. He reached over to the glove box to get what was inside of it—a box of bullets.

The gun that once lived actively on his waist was flipped opened and loaded with fresh shells. Hanner reached into his belt and pulled out two quick load cylinders. The cylinders sat for years without ever being used. They relished that they had a chance to participate. He loaded the cylinders then returned them back to their homes.

The car was waiting for directions from Hanner as Hanner messed around with his gun. The gun was put back into place—the car and Hanner were on the move.

The car ripped through town, past Ethel's place on its way out to the County Sheriff Station. Hanner had a feeling that that was the place that was causing all the ruckus in the air. "Another fucking problem to solve!" he spurted out as he mashed the gas, which caused his cruiser to roar with excitement.

As Hanner raced off, the morgue could sense the tension in the air and was waiting for another body to arrive to keep itself comfortable. It didn't know Hanner's plan, but it was hoping it included death, bodies, some embalming sauce, and maybe a fire or two.

Hanner began to slow down his cruiser while flicking off the lights then stopping a few hundred yards away for the station. Hanner sat and peered at it to see if he could see any movement at the station. He sat, watched, and waited. Tension was in the air and the breeze kept reminding him.

Hanner opened the car door and placed his feet on the uneasy ground. The car door closed effortlessly without a sound. The breeze went away, the cruiser was quiet, and it was all hush hush from the crowd on his waist.

His steps toward the station were forceful and quick. No sneaking up or hiding behind anything, he was on a mission to solve a problem, and nothing was going to get in his way.

As he approached the front of the station, he gazed through the window and saw a lone woman fussing around. He watched her get up from her place then headed down the hall while messing with her clothes.

A cool breeze was constant now and lowered the temp in the surrounding area. Hanner waited for the right time. As he stood there as the breeze spoke— *"it's time."*

"It's time," Hanner repeated. "It is time to solve another problem."

Hanner opened the front door that gave normal people a fuss, but to Hanner's touch, it opened with vigor and hit the wall behind it. He entered the building and stood waiting. Waiting for her to return.

– – –

Katie sat in the warm station as several sighs and thoughts of hating men flowed through her head.

"You know," she sighed out loud, "that Rodney really gets under my skin!"

"UGH!" she followed up with a scream.

The station sat there and let her have a little temper tantrum. It knew she did work hard and was worried about Callahan.

Time kept passing and there was no word from Rodney or Jackson. The evening was starting to pass time quickly and silence became the norm.

"I'm so bored," she said as she grabbed her blue zip-up sweatshirt. "What's with the chill?"

The station's furnace kicked in and tried its hardest to get the chill out of the air. The furnace was in full force, but the chill would not leave the room.

Katie got up from her safe place and made her way back in the hallway to the thermostat. She glanced at it as a subtle wave of confusion came across her being.

Katie pulled her zipper up a tad more, "Strange, at that temp, I should not have the chills."

A slight noise came from the front door of the station that caught Katie's attention. As she walked back up the hallway to the front of the station, she normally called home, she noticed a figure standing there.

"Who's there? Buck Hanner?" Katie said as the color rushed from her face. She knew he was the one causing all the problems in the valley.

"That's right."

"What do you want Mr. Hanner?"

"Mr. Hanner, now that's funny," Hanner replied, "I heard you were sending messages out there about me. Is that true?"

"How did you hear about that? I was just doing what I was told to do. You know, following orders."

Hanner tapped his foot slightly to capture her attention as he slowly unsnapped his revolvers holster, "Who told to do that?"

"Mr. Hanner, I mean, Hanner, umm Buck Hanner, sir," Katie stammered, "just doing my job."

"Who?" he yelled with a force that knocked the chill out of the room.

"Please," she whimpered, "please no."

Hanner tapped his foot along with placing his hand on the revolver. He pulled the .357 Magnum up in the air before Katie could even blink. The bullet left Hanner's revolver then split Katie in two. She fell to the floor with a large, end-of-life thud. The revolver went back to its home. The rest of the bullets on his belt were jumping for joy.

Blood was everywhere. Hanner reached his arm up to his face and gave it a little cleaning. His mind was not clear yet. He looked around and headed to the back of the station to the kitchen.

Finding a cup of coffee to accompany him as he waited. Waiting for his next problem to be solved.

Chapter | 71

Lock 17 smelled musty and alone that afternoon. The normal patrons inside drink cheap beer while playing the same ten songs they grew up on. Each of them telling each other how great they were.

With the same old music playing, the musty smell of beer wallowed in the air. For some reason the mood changed instantly; the beer tasted better, the songs were snapper, and the stories got better. Dory and Bill walked into the bar; the good old bullshit was about to fly.

"Drinks are on the house!" yelled Bill.

"Fuck off," replied Dory as he signaled to his sister for a couple of the classics. Dory smiled, "Hey, sis."

"Hi, Bill," Dory's sister said. "Usual?"

"Please."

Dory looked over at Bill as his sister slid an ice cold PBR over to him, "PBR? Seriously? I thought you were higher class than that?"

"Dory," Bill replied as he finished his first sip of beer, feeling it go all the way down to his belly, "if I was high class, I'd be sitting at the other side of the bar with those fine gentlemen." Bill sat for a moment then finished with, smirk and all, "But I'm here by you."

"Good one!" barked out the sis as she walked to the other end to tell the town losers what just happened.

Dory sat for a moment, then another moment, and then said, "I have no good comeback." He smiled as a took a swing.

Dory and Bill sat chatting about nothing in particular. Chatting about life, catching up on things and saying they needed to do this more often.

Dory's sister got bored with the bums on the other side of the bar and threw some money in the jukebox. She played some tunes that made the afternoon go by quicker.

"So," she said, "been a tad bit since you two sat here together. What's up with that?"

Bill got quiet and looked straight on.

Dory looked at his sis and said, "Harold."

"Oh no. Guessing you two need another?"

In unison the two men nodded and sat quietly. Dory's sister knew there was going to be some major sorrow if she didn't step in and take control of the situation.

"I got a surprise for you two bums," she said as she reached far into the cooler, "it's going to be very tasty."

Sis pulled two beers out of the cooler and wiped them off with the bar rag. She walked over to the two men as they watched her every step, she turned her back on them as she opened up the beers.

Click. Beer one spoke.

Beer two did not sit in silence either, *Click*.

She turned around and placed two cold Old Milwaukee's Best on the bar in front of the two men.

"Old Milwaukee?"

"That's right, you two assholes. You have one beer to wallow in your sorrow about your old friend Harold, then you're going to get off your pity pot and start having a good time. Do I make myself clear?" she said.

"Well, goddamn."

Bill followed with, "Exactly."

"Let's get this over with," Dory replied as both men downed the beers so fast that they were trying not to taste it.

Bill slammed his hand down on the bar and yelled, "I win! Better call Katherine. Daddy is going to get drunk!"

"Drinks on the house!" yelled the losers on the other side of the bar.

"One round, guys, one round!" shouted Dory.

Dory's sister smiled and started handing out chips, "One chip, one drink." When Dory wasn't looking, she slid a handful down to the bums and watched them giggle like little boys.

The Lock 17 bar made a few men smile that day, just like old times. Dory got up from his seat and made his famous burgers for everyone. While Bill listened to all the bullshit that was slinging. As far as Harold went... well, he would have to wait for his friends to find him another day.

Chapter | 72

The Hill was upset. It shot a warning to the boys, which they did not listen to, they did not budge and worst of all—they did not stop. The Hill's total control of the valley had been shuttered and its mood began to turn to anger.

The boys had left the lower plateau behind and continued in single file up the side of Stocker Hill. Stocker's dismay with the boys was starting to show with every step they took. It tightened up its grip so that the boys felt very uncomfortable as they moved up the trail.

"What's up with this?" Rob spouted as another brush smacked into him.

Reed had his arms up blocking every swipe the brush threw at him, "No shit. I'm getting my ass kicked back here."

Brad let out a yowl, "Enough complaining. Walk!"

John followed in stride and didn't complain as he, too, was getting walloped with every step. Stocker was annoyed at this time but figured what's the point as the boys fought on.

The trail started to lessen, and the brush went back to behaving. The boy's irritation started to fade and Reed's steps from the back of the line got more aggressive. He started to walk stride-for-stride with his friends.

With each step, Stocker Hill turned into a welcoming neighbor. It stopped blocking the sun and let the warm breeze flow. The eeriness that once surrounded the boys was gone and a kindness started to infiltrate their every move.

"Man," yelled Reed from the back, "I feel fantastic."

"Me too," The once-silent John replied.

Brad was leading the crew and chimed in, "That spooky feeling is gone, and I feel like I could run up this Hill in one giant step."

Stocker Hill had the boys right where he wanted them. The fight from before was now surrounding the boys with love and affection. Making them comfortable and weak. Weak being the main objective.

The boys challenged on, no complaining, no hesitation, no stopping. The trail started to slowly fade off and the next steps they took were onto a gravel road. The road welcomed the boys allowing them to fan out to start to walk side-by-side.

"What's that?" one of the boys asked.

"I think that is the tip of the star," another replied.

"That star. We're going to see the star up close?"

The chatter between the boys stopped and they continued down the gravel road. The road began to flatten while curving slightly to the right. A green, wet plateau lay to the right side of the gravel road up a bit. Up ahead, on the plateau was something the boys were not expecting.

Chapter | 73

The grave slowly glowed in happiness under the moonlight that the Hill provided. It was full of pleasure after being fed the ambulance with a wonderful surprise enclosed—the tasty Ray and Alex. It relished that Alex's heart was pounding with every nibble and the warm blood flowed effortlessly.

The green grass held Harold in comfort as he lay motionless, staring at the edge of the grave. The grass was soft and supple, comforting and loving, a far change from when it wouldn't let Harold save Alex from the burning ambulance.

Harold's eyes began to well with tears as the thoughts of evil he had seen rushed through his mind. He wanted the bad memories gone and needed help. Harold found the strength to lift himself to a kneeling position and prayed to God.

Harold began to speak to the sky as every word of Psalm 23 flowed from his broken heart, "The Lord is my shepherd; I shall not want. He maketh me to lie down in green pastures: he leadeth me beside the still waters. He restoreth my soul: he leadeth me in the paths of righteousness for his name's sake."

Harold sat on his knees waiting from some kind of sign from God, a sign of hope, a sign of the direction he shall go.

Harold stood up after more disappointment came his way.

He looked around to see the moonlight shining in happiness, the grave glistening with joy and the green plateau standing up with its chest out.

"Lie me down in green pastures," Harold cried out, "that's a load of bullshit. God where are you? Where are you now? All there is, is evil around here and you allow it!"

Harold continued to yell and curse everything around him. Yelling at Alex and Ray, Donny for dying, Hanner and Stocker Hill. His yells echoed through the trees, skimming across the plateau, down the gravel road, and dissipated over the town of Walcott.

"Fuck this!" was Harold's last roar as he jumped into his old faithful truck and exited Stocker Hill. The gravel shot from his tires as he accelerated downhill onto the blacktop, racing through the center of town and out past Ethel's house.

The Chevy truck found itself at home. The once-angry man cursing God and everyone was back to being beaten down. Harold poured himself out of his truck to the loving panting of his old floppy-eared companion. Harold petted the head of his friend, signaling him to follow him into the house.

The kitchen table presented itself with a slight layer of grime. Harold's keys plopped down into the middle of the table and eventually slid to a stop. Harold grabbed Floppy-Ears's bowl, loaded it with food, then gave him a fresh bowl of water.

Floppy-Ears lost interest in Harold at this point as he was famished. After his belly was full and his thirst quenched, he felt his eyes begin to get a tad heavy with every step. Floppy-Ears lifted his hefty paws and made a mighty jump onto the awaiting couch.

While his faithful dog was eating, Harold made his way upstairs to his guest room. In the corner of the room was a large rusty cabinet that once lived side by side with other cabinets at his repair shop. At some point in its rusty life, the cabinet got a promotion and made its way to Harold's extra room.

The cabinet door opened with excitement when Harold pulled on it; Harold didn't visit the cabinet often and when he did, it was a real treat. The cabinet waited in anticipation, waiting to see what Harold pulled out from its belly. The cabinet felt Harold reach around a bit, heard some clanking and lots of shuffling of things. As Harold pulled items from the cabinet, he closed the door and pushed it tightly closed.

Harold held his double-barrel shotgun in one hand and fed his pockets with a bunch of shotgun shells. The Browning double-barrel shotgun shined as the little light that was in the room landed on its barrels. The barrels that wanted some shells.

The cabinet whimpered once it saw the shotgun in Harold's hand. Nothing good ever came from having that gun out.

Chapter | 74

Jackson took one last drag of his latest cigarette as he watched Rodney drive away in his mirrors while the basin slowly disappeared from site.

With his window down, the air warmed a little since leaving the Hill as the evening sky slowly pulled the haze of smoke out of his car. Jackson's cruiser blazed its way back to the station to check in with Katie.

As Jackson entered the town square, he took a hard right and headed west out of town. On the edge of town was a little gas station that serviced everyone in town with gas, cigarettes, and the best slushies next to Goshen Dairy.

Jackson pulled the squad car into the station as the clerk inside turned on the pump that Jackson landed at. The car welcomed its first meal of the day as Jackson started pumping the fine fuel into its belly.

The car was famished and so was Jackson. As the squad car filled up, Jackson entered the little station for a day-old pizza puff and a blue slushy. "Hey, make sure you don't tell those fine folks over at the Goshen that I like your slushies better or there will be hell to pay."

"Hell to pay?" asked the clerk. "Where did you learn that from?"

"Yes. Hell to pay. Meaning I'll whoop your ass."

The clerk did one of those fake laughs and followed with a gentle reply, "Yeah. Right."

"Yeah, kinda of a stupid joke. I'll work on it for next time."

Jackson grabbed his pizza puff, the slushy and headed out the door. Before the door closed, Jackson heard the clerk say, "Hello, is this Goshen Dairy? Jackson just bought another one of my slushies."

Jackson started to laugh as he turned around to glance at the clerk. The clerk, holding up his hand like a telephone, smiled and winked at Jackson as he strolled back to his car.

"Well," Jackson said to his car, "that was funny. Way better than hell to pay."

A large click from the pump notified Jackson that the pump was done. The car had a full belly and didn't want to start on Jackson's initial try. It was way too tied to start working again. On the next try, the car gave up and started. Jackson pulled the running car off to the side of the parking lot so he could enjoy his meal.

Jackson talked to himself while devouring his meal. "Take a bite then a sip of slushy. Every bite gets a sip. Every sip gets a bite and so on until the last bite coincides with the last sip. My timing is impeccable. Finishing everything at the same time. Weird."

With a slight belch, Jackson jumped out of the running car and headed towards the garbage to discard his mess. "Time to go see Katie," he said into the air as he climbed back into his patrol car.

His car felt invigorated as it gobbled up the blacktop back to the station. Up towards the outskirts of town and eventually landing at the station. Jackson jumped out of his car and slowly walked towards the front of the station. He let out one of his signature belches as a little spit up entered his mouth.

"Gross!" he exclaimed as he launched a little blue goop out of his mouth.

The station was scared. It wasn't able to protect Katie and she lay on the floor waiting for help. Her unresponsive body with her split-open head waited for someone to arrive.

The once warm breeze became a little brisk, the closer he got to the door. Jackson made it into the front doorway of the station and sensed something was wrong. Katie was not at the desk, the radio wasn't on and if she took time to hit the washroom or leave her post, she locked the front door.

"Katie!" yelled Jackson.

"Katie, you there?"

Jackson took a right to head down the hallway to see if Katie was there. Nothing. He poked his head into the washroom and yelled her name. Nothing. No response.

Jackson turned himself back towards the front of the station and yelled out again, "Katie, where are you?"

As before. Nothing. No response. Jackson was puzzled and thought maybe Katie went out back to smoke.

Jackson got close to the front desk. "That's it. She's out smoking those menthol silver 100s. What a shitty cigarette," he said as he passed the front of the desk and made the turn to head towards the back of the building.

Out of the corner of his eye he saw blood. Lots of blood. His stomach sank and his knees got weak. Jackson's eyes searched the floor frantically then he saw her. Saw Katie laying faceless on the ground. What was left of her head held on the best it could. The bullet that ran though her head then put the rest of it on the wall, the floor, and every little crease it could find.

The last thing Jackson saw before dropping to his knees was a red spray exiting his body. He was dead before he hit the floor as his blood started to mix with the other blood that had been splattered around.

Silence was the only thing left in the station that night.

Chapter | 75

The plateau was expecting the boys. It lay awaiting their arrival, following every order that Stocker imposed on it. Its green grass rose to the occasion as the sun shined, welcoming the boys into its peacefulness.

The boys followed the gravel road until it faded away into the plateau. On the edge of the plateau stood the star that overlooked Walcott. And then, the boys saw it, saw what all the stories talked about, saw what they were to stay away from, saw the thing people feared the most—the grave.

In the green plateau was the grave. The grave on Stocker Hill. The boys stopped in amazement and looked onward towards it. Each breath could hardly be heard as fear and excitement entered each of their bodies.

The grave sat in the middle of the plateau waiting. The dark gray, deathly rocks had a warm, inviting tone to them. Pulling the boys closer to the grave with every baby breath they were taking. Inch by inch, the boys slowly worked their way to it. The grave, sunken into the ground, sat in anticipation of the boys' next move. The black, silking dirt on the bottom of the grave moved in excitement waiting for one of the boys to make a mistake.

Brad, who was confident and demanding of his friends, became weak with fear. "Let's take a seat on the rocks and, you know, relax or something."

John sat down without a peep and Rob blurted out in a weird screech, "Yeah, yeah, sit down. Sit down."

Brad and Rob looked over at John as he made his way over to one of the rocks while staring directly at the grave. After looking at John, Brad and Rob's eyes turned to focus on Reed.

Reed made his way to the edge of the grave and was completely focused on the sooty dirt that lay waiting. His eyes burning into the dirt with no expression on his face. His fear that once helped him walk up the road to the grave had turned into empowerment.

"Reed. Reed!" yelled Brad.

No response.

John got his voice back, "Reed. Reed. What are you doing?"

No response.

Rob got up from the rock that had invited him over, walked towards Reed. "Hey, Reed, you alright, buddy?"

No response.

With a forceful push, Rob pushed Reed to the ground and yelled, "What the fuck, Reed?"

Reed fell to the ground a few steps from where he was planted. His face landing on the green, soft plateau awakening him from his trance.

"What was that for?" he barked.

"What was that for you ask?" barked Rob back. "You were in a trance."

"No, I wasn't."

"Yes. Yes, you were."

"Come on," Reed spouted, annoyed, as he got himself up off the ground.

The boys' focus had left the grave and were all on Reed at this point. Reed slowly walked past the grave, gazing at it as he found a rock inviting him to sit.

The boys' focus never left Reed as they stared at him for a lifetime. Reed looked over at all of them, at Rob who blindsided him and was now sitting on a rock of his own. "What?"

"Dude, you were in a trance or something. You were gone," Brad explained.

"No, I wasn't. Stop it."

"You were in a total spell or something. Freaked us all out," Brad insisted as his face showed concern.

"I am fine. Really, I am. I'm fine. Stop looking at me."

The boys all sat on separate rocks. Four separate rocks coddled them as they looked over the grave. The green grass moved in unison as Stocker let the wind flow over the area, the grave and into the boy's face. The agitated feeling of concern for Reed bailed as the warm breeze engulfed them.

"I'm so sleepy," one of the boys whispered.

Another followed with, "Not sleepy, relaxed."

"Yes, that's it. I'm relaxed. So relaxed."

A voice spoke up that startled everyone. "I am home."

Chapter | 76

The morning came in with a thundering crash. The sunlight lit up the bedroom that was housing Dory. His head was pounding, he felt like shit, and woke up to an empty bed. A lonely bed.

"Damn sun," Dory whispered as he wiped the crust from his eyes.

He finally rolled over and landed his weak legs onto the floor. With all his might, he pushed off his bed and stood up to go toe-to-toe with the sun. The sun naturally won as it beamed straight onto his face making Dory's eyes close in weakness.

Dory spun around to hide himself from his defeat and headed for the shower. Within seconds, the shower was on and inviting Dory into its sanctuary. The warm water blasted onto Dory's weak body. With every second that passed, life started returning and he was working his way up to battling the sun again. This time he would not lose.

Dory shut off the shower, dried off and made himself look presentable. The sink started up and the lone toothbrush was picked up from the sink that dove into the flowing waterfall. The toothbrush hovered as his minty friend joined him for the duty at hand. With every brush of his teeth, Dory thought more and more about Harold.

"Where could Harold have gone?" he said as he spit a big, foamy wad into the sink.

The toothbrush was returned to its place and the waterfall was shut down. Dory looked into the mirror, thinking.

"Come on. We have to find him."

Dory left the bathroom, exited the bedroom, walked into the kitchen for an IV of caffeine.

Dory shouted to the empty kitchen, "Got it! I got it!"

– – –

Bill had the same problem as Dory that morning. Sunlight wanted to battle; Bill wanted nothing to do with it.

"Have fun yesterday?" Katherine asked in her annoyed, loving-wife manner.

"Yep and no."

"Having fun this morning?"

"Nope."

Katherine looked at Bill as he lay there. "What do you mean no? You, Dory, and Harold at the bar is always a good time."

"That's it. No Harold. We couldn't find him anywhere," Bill replied.

"That's strange."

Bill pushed himself up. "Yep, very strange."

Just as Bill was about to exit the bed, the phone rang with excitement. *Me, me, pick me up, me, my turn to talk to!*

"What son of a bitch is calling—oh, hey Dory. What do you mean you know where Harold is? Yeah, yeah, I remember that place, but that was years ago. Okay. Pick me up."

Bill officially got up and showered. Made his way downstairs to the kitchen where Katherine had the coffee brewing and cut up some pastries for consumption.

"Dory knows where Harold his."

"Where?"

"He thinks down by the trains where we used to hang and drink."

"Really," Katherine questioned, "you think so?"

As Bill was responding, "It's worth a try," there was a horn blast signaling Dory's arrival.

"Be careful. Don't do anything stupid and no drinking."

"Yes, dear, no day drinking," Bill replied as he made his way out the door.

The entire time the coffee was brewed, drank, and pastries were eaten, Buster lay in waiting for one morsel of something to hit the floor for him to jump on.

"*Nothing!*" barked Buster as he watched Bill leave the house and Katherine head out to the garden.

Bill jumped into Dory's truck and off they went.

"Hair of the dog?" Dory asked.

"Definitely," Bill replied as he reached into the cooler and pulled out a couple beers, "one for you, one for me."

"Thanks."

"So, you really think Harold is out by our old stomping ground?"

"Yeah, he brings it up every once and awhile, so I am thinking so."

The conversation ended and another beer was opened. The truck followed Dory's command and gingerly rumbled down the road until the old train tracks were in front of them. Dory guided his truck down the narrow path near the tracks toward the old docking station that the trains would use.

"Sure enough." Dory pointed with his beer can. "Sure enough."

"Well, holy shit, you were right. He really needs to let the past go."

Dory and Bill exited the truck after it came to a rest and walked towards Harold's truck. They could see Harold's outline through the back window. Both men approached Harold's door and looked through the window.

"No, Harold, NO!" Bill shouted and Dory couldn't speak as the echo of the double-barrel shotgun blast punched them in the face.

Harold was gone with one pull of the trigger.

Chapter | 77

Something changed in Walcott that day. Was it the shift of the wind, how the sun shined down, the peaking of the moon, the star looking over the valley, Stocker Hill?

The boys left the grave, left the plateau, left the green grass, and walked down the Hill. The walk was effortless. No bushes to battle, no thin trails, just a few friends walking away from an adventure that left them speechless.

Each boy's mind was racing. Racing from the memories they just made together. From the fear that entered their bodies. An experience that left them dumbfounded.

As always, Brad was the lead. He led the boys down the Hill as his mind raced with questions, questions he asked himself while keeping his cool demeanor on the outside but freaking out on the inside. His mind questioned, *What did we just do? Did we open something we shouldn't? Are we going to regret this? Who is going to answer for this if things go awry? Who said "I am home"?*

John followed the rest of the guys down the Hill. He just walked with his head down watching his feet go back and forth with every step. His mind was racing with a question or two. No questions on what they just encountered or if they made a mistake. No questions on whether they were in danger or opened something they shouldn't.

No questions like that. John's mind raced repeating two questions, *What was with Reed? Who said "I am home"? What was with Reed? Who said "I am home"?*

As with the other boys, Rob was in questioning mode. His mind would roar, then stop. Roar again, then stop. Stop at the blackness at the bottom of the grave. Roar, stop, roar, stop his mind questioned, *Why am I so scared? It's just a hole in the ground. Is it just a hole? Is it really a grave? The blackness is so mesmerizing. Is mesmerizing a word? Mesmerizing. Of course, it's a word. So black, so scared, what was with Reed? Who said "I am home"?*

Reed did as the others. Walked down the Hill. It wasn't a battle like it was going up. There was no fear running through his body. Just questions in his head. Questions about the time on the plateau. Questions about the grave. His mind wondered into questions, *why was the grass so green? What's with the gray rocks? Why did I end up on the ground? Why am I so at peace right now?*

The bottom of Stocker Hill pushed the boys off ever so gently as they reached the basin. It patted them on the ass and eased their minds. Helped them get their composure, to slow their questioning, helped them towards the place the Hill wanted them to be. As the boys walked from the basin, the Hill whispered, *"be safe boys, I'll see you soon,"* and blew a soft breeze across their bodies.

"That was comforting," John said as the breeze left his body.

"What was comforting?" Brad replied.

Rob looked around and spoke. "The breeze. The breeze was comforting."

Reed said nothing. The boys looked at him as they watched that gaze come across his face again. The gaze that scared them before.

"Reed," cried John. "Reed!"

"What? What's up? Oh, the breeze, very nice. Okay now, I am going to go see Krista. Bye" were the words that left Reed's mouth as he walked away from the boys.

"WTF?" Rob and Brad said in unison.

Rob and Brad looked at each other weirdly as John replied, "I think he's a little spooked. You know how he is. All emotional and shit."

Brad's head nodded in agreement and Rob replied, "I'm guessing you're right. I'm guessing Krista will help our friend."

The boys stood for a moment at the basin of the Hill. They looked up the Hill repeatedly along with watching Reed stroll away from them. When the standing was over, and the acknowledgment of each other was gone, they all turned and headed away questioning in their heads, *who said "I am home"?*

Chapter | 78

The road leading away from Stocker Hill was full of sorrow as Reed slowly walked down it. With every step, the road could sense something was wrong. Something was wrong with the person it was holding up.

Reed's walk was not as jolly as most walks to Krista's house. This walk was different.

Something was different. Reed kept his head facing forward and slowly walked to her house.

As before, Reed went straight for her window and had the window tell Krista he was there. He stood along the side of the house in a daze. Dazed from the day.

As time went by, Reed asked the window again to let Krista know he was there.

The window creaked and rattled a little as Krista finally opened it to see her boyfriend. She looked at Reed and Reed looked at her. She tilted her head, "What's wrong, Reed?"

"We went to the grave."

"You what?"

"Went to the grave."

"Please tell me you didn't. Please tell me that," she whimpered.

"I can't, babe, I can't. We went."

"Damn it, boy. Damn it all to hell. Get your ass in here right now," she ordered.

Reed did his normal display of gracefulness as he climbed into Krista's room through her window. Krista let Reed finish his climb and closed the window. She watched over his face as she held his cheeks in her hand. She watched for a bit with Reed watching back. She held on to his face and said, "Something's different. Something's different about you."

"No, there isn't," he replied as he pushed her hands away from his face.

"Oh, yes there is."

Reed looked back at her and climbed onto her bed. The gaze came across his face again, and Krista watched it happen.

"Reed. You see. You see? Right there. That look. It's a new look. Something is different with you," she said as her eyes welled up with tears.

"Babe. Seriously. There is nothing different. I'm fine."

"I do not think so."

"Yes. Really, I am. I am—I guess?" he questioned.

"You guess?"

Reed looked back at Krista and responded, "I'm scared about one thing."

"What is that?"

"I am scared that I'm not scared."

Krista looked over at her boyfriend as her body began to shake. The tears exited her eyes with a soft roll. They left her beautiful face and slowly fell to the floor. The floor caught the tears and could feel her sadness in every drop.

Reed watched his girlfriend cry in sadness. He didn't understand why she was crying like she was. He didn't understand what was happening. Didn't know what to do.

As Krista cried and cried, Reed finally got up from the bed and held his girl as she whispered into the crevice of his chest, "The old Reed would have jumped off the bed and held me instantly."

Reed held Krista closer and apologized. Apologized for not being compassionate. Reed held Krista and whispered to her, "I'm sorry. Really, I am. I'm just dazed from the day. It will be okay. I'm still the same old Reed."

"You promise?"

"I promise."

Krista finally let Reed go then climbed into her bed. Exhaustion flowed over her body while sadness entered her eyes. Tears ran across her bloodshot eyes as she watched Reed climb out the window. Off he went and she could do nothing to stop him. Nothing to stop the sadness from overtaking her body.

Reed jumped from her window as he had done countless times before. Countless times before where he rarely ever landed on his feet. This leap was different. This leap was graceful. Gracefully landing on his feet. With authority.

Before Reed knew it, he was home. He opened the front door to the house. The house was quiet. Quiet from Buster's paws running across the floor to greet him.

"Where is my buddy?" he questioned into the air. "Buster?"

A whimper went through the air as it left the kitchen floor. Buster looked across the kitchen floor towards the front door. He slowly shook as he watched Reed walk towards him. He shook because he knew something was different.

Reed bent down and peered under the table looking at Buster, "Come here, buddy."

Buster resisted.

"Come on, buddy. Come here, Buster. It's me."

Buster resisted.

"Come on, Buster. Come here."

Buster resisted.

"Well, fuck you, then!" he shouted as anger shot through his body. "Fuck you…."

Buster backed up from his current place and whimpered under his breath. He was scared. Scared of Reed.

Chapter | 79

The softness of the breeze was gone, and the boys scattered from each other. The Hill was behind them, and Reed had left their sides. Each boy wandered in their own direction home, in the direction of comfort, of safety.

John left Rob and Brad in his rearview; once they were out of sight, he ran. Ran hard to a place he knew would hold him tightly, he ran all the way to Suzy. His winded body came to rest outside of her neighbor's house. There he sat on the curb and caught his breath.

Like most nights at this time of the evening, Suzy was in her room listening to music; wondering if this was a night that her boyfriend would visit.

Her favorite song came on and she held her pillow tightly wishing it was her man.

Bam, bam, bam! shouted the window.

"Holy shit!" Suzy yelled as fright ran through her body from the window's shout.

Again, the window yelled out, *bam, bam, bam!*

Suzy threw her pillow to the ground and stormed to the window. She opened the window to see who was making her window yell so loud and there stood John in an unbearable cry.

"Oh no," she exclaimed, a softness in her voice coming out. "Oh no. John. What's the matter? Please get in here."

John climbed into Suzy's room and fell to the floor in a puddle of tears. He shook and gasped, he cried and moaned as emotions exited his body in force.

Suzy knelt down next to John and laid her head on him. She whispered to him and held him closely. Her affection was breaking through to him as John slowly got his composure back.

"I am sorry," John whimpered out.

"Oh, darling, it's okay."

Another whimper exited John, "I am so sorry."

"John, no need to be sorry for crying. Crying is okay, your body needs a good cry every once in a while."

A pause entered the room and there was no word from either of them. Suzy had her head on John, and he looked at her yellow wall wanting the silence to go away.

Suzy lifted her head, and as she began to stand up, she grabbed John's arm and forced him to his feet. She looked into his eyes and then hugged him. She lifted her grip on the hug as she looked into his eyes once more. "Sit."

John was emotionally wrecked and followed her directions. He slowly planted his behind on Suzy's bed while he held on to her. His head lay against her belly as his arms wrapped around her body.

Suzy let him in and held his head while stroking his hair. "What's wrong? What's wrong? I've never seen you so emotional."

John lifted head and started to stutter, "W-we went to the grave."

Suzy paused before shouting out, "You did what? Why?"

"We've talked about it. We've been planning it. We just did it."

"You know all the stories about the grave. The Drucker murders happened up there. Rumors of your father, Reed's dad, and Harold from the garage. Why?"

"Reed," John slowly said. "Something happened to Reed. He says he fine, but he is different."

Suzy looked at John. "Goddamn it. The group of you sometimes have your heads up your asses and this is one of those times."

"I know," responded John.

"Where is Reed now?"

"Krista's house. I think. Well, that's where he said he was going."

Suzy stormed away from John as he started to cry again. She went right for her phone and called Krista."

"Hello," a crying voice came through the phone.

"It's Suzy. John is here. Is Reed with you?"

"No, he left a bit ago."

"Is he okay? Are you okay?"

"No and no," Krista responded.

Suzy sat for a moment before asking another question, but she could hear Krista's whimpers through the phone.

"Krista, what do you mean he is not okay?"

Krista cried a little more and watched her tears hit the phone, then jump off onto the carpet. "He's different. There is something wrong with him." Krista's voice became quieter as she said while she hung up the phone, "There something wrong with him."

Suzy's eyes welled up and she hung up the phone. She looked at John who was lying on the bed now and slowly walked over to him. She lay down next to him and cried ever so softly. In her muffled cries, she said, "You're right, there's something wrong with Reed."

— — —

Brad and Rob chatted for a moment as they watched John walk away. They stood in the street and watched the dark moon hover over Stocker Hill.

Rob looked from the Hill to Brad, "I didn't like that."

Brad looked back over to Rob. "Me either. I think we fucked up."

"Yep."

"And Reed," followed Brad, "he got really weird, didn't he?"

"Yep."

"First thing in the morning, let's grab John and head to Reed's. Sound like a plan?"

"Yep."

"Damn, Rob, you are a man of few words at the moment."

"Yep. So scared."

Brad replied as he put his hand on Rob's shoulder and gripped it for a moment, "So am I, buddy. So am I."

Brad and Rob went their own ways as the dark moon watched over them as they walked away. They were scared. They were scared and they had every right to be.

Chapter | 80

The room was quiet where Brad lay. The window was letting in a little light and the covers kept him cozy. A rustling was starting to brew though; the air hovered thickly in the room, a world of hurt was coming Brad's way.

The covers slipped off Brad's legs as he shuffled around a bit in his bed. The coziness was dispersing, and the bed wanted him gone.

"Alright, alright!" he stated as his feet hit the floor before he got himself into a standing position.

After a minute or two of rearranging his T-shirt collection, Brad threw on a T-shirt and made his way downstairs. As Brad made the turn into the kitchen, he found his mother standing looking outside with a cup of coffee in her hand.

"Let me guess," she questioned, "you and your friends were a bunch of fricking idiots last night?"

"Mom. Language," Brad replied in total shock as the words hovered in the air.

"You never talk like that mom. Why would you think we were idiots?"

"It's in the air, son—it is in the air."

Brad stood in the middle of the kitchen with a puzzled look as he thought to himself, *does she know? No way, she doesn't know. Does she?*

Brad's mom turned around and looked at her son. Their eyes met, sadness flowed from her eyes and Brad caught every drop. The room was silent.

"What?" he finally was able to say after the uncomfortable communication that just happened.

She stood and stared at him.

Brad's levity of humor came to the forefront as he cracked a joke to save himself from the situation.

"So, Mom, how about you whip me up some good fixings? Your boy is hungry."

Brad's mom turned away from her son and looked off into the distance as she said, "Nope, your father is outside waiting for you."

The color in Brad's face leapt from his body and hid somewhere safe. Brad's next few steps were in hesitation as he knew something bad was going to happen.

"Mom, what does Dad want?" he stammered.

Silence was the only word said.

"Mom? What is it?"

Silence was still the only conversation coming back at Brad.

The floor creaked with every step that Brad made, leaving the kitchen on his way outside to find his father. The backdoor slammed closed, breaking the silence, but Brad preferred the silence over the next conversation.

Brad made his way around the corner of the house and headed towards the garage where he thought his dad would be. He opened the garage door and stepped into more silence.

"*Whoof!*" bellowed Brad as a right hook entered his belly and the air rushed from his lungs.

Brad hit the garage floor with a mighty blow as he gasped for air while ending up in the fetal position. The tears started to flow from the pain as his breath came back. Looking up from the floor through his watering eyes he could see his father standing over him.

"Didn't I tell you… didn't I tell you to stay away from Harold and the Godforsaken Hill? Didn't I?" Brad's father yelled down at him.

Brad lay in shock as he was trying to understand the situation, why his dad hit him, and wondering how he could know anything.

"Dad? What?" Brad grumbled.

"Sir!"

"Dad?"

"You will call me sir. Do you understand me?"

"Yes, sir," Brad said as he tried to stand up, his weak legs and aching belly fighting him.

As he made it to his feet another right hook landed on his chin and Brad flailed, landing on his back. All sense of reality was gone as he looked up from the ground at his father. Several minutes passed before Brad even thought about saying something.

Brad's father walked away from his son and made his way to his favorite seat in the corner of the garage. On the bench, next to his little sanctuary in the garage, was a pack of cigarettes, a lighter and an ashtray. He took a seat and lit up a smoke.

"Dad, what the fuck?" Brad finally said.

"Sir! I said!"

"Sir, what the fuck?"

"Harold's dead."

"What? What did you say?"

"I said, Harold is dead!"

Brad looked up from the ground in total disbelief, "There is no way Harold is dead. No way he is dead. You are lying to me."

"I am not lying to you, son. I am not lying. I got the call early this morning from Dory. They saw Harold take his life."

"No. It's not true. It's not true at all."

"Well, son, it is true. I told you to leave it alone, and you and your friends couldn't let it be. You woke up a secret that should have never been woken. Now Harold is dead, and it's you and your friends' fault."

Chapter | 81

As with most nights for Rob, sleep was not in the picture. He gazed up from the couch and looked deep into the ceiling of the trailer. The ceiling was stained from cigarette smoke.

Rob's mom came home and headed back to her room to get some sleep. Most early mornings, Rob would make some kind of contact with his mom, a hug and a kiss, a little conversation or just sitting next to her watching a little TV. Not this day. Rob lay there while faking to sleep. He couldn't handle the sight of looking at his mom and seeing the disappointment in her face.

Thoughts flew through Rob's head. He worried about what they did, the consequences of their journey and Reed. Since he couldn't control his thoughts, his belly started to flip with all the worrying and he began to dry heave. He jumped up from the couch and grabbed the closest towel he could trying to muffle the sound of his body retching. *Don't wake up Mom, don't wake up mom.*

His prayer for silence was not successful and Rob's mom jolted out from her room to check on her son. Rob now was sitting on the couch hunched over with his face hiding in the towel.

"Oh, son," she moaned, "you okay? What's going on?"

Rob peeked his head up from the towel and whispered, "It's nothing, Mom. Really, it's nothing."

"Son, don't tell me it's nothing. What's going on?"

"Mom," he said while he looked into her sleepy eyes, "it's noth—" The dry heaves came back and took control of body.

Rob's mom rushed to the kitchen to get a washcloth and soaked it in cold water. She rang it vigorously, the water spritzing from the washcloth into the sink. She rushed back to Rob and started wiping down his face and forehead.

As Rob brought himself back to have a little composure, his mom pulled him into her and held him closely while still wiping his face.

"Son, I haven't seen you this bad since your father... well, since he passed."

"It's bad, Mom. It's really bad."

"Well, tell me. I can't help unless you tell me."

"Can I tell you later?"

"Son. Spit it out. You're a wreck, and you can't hold it in. It destroys your body. Look at your face—it's glowing red."

"Mom, I'm scared. So scared."

"Of?"

"What we did."

"What is it, Rob? You're talking in riddles."

"Mom, we went to the Hill, we went to the grave, we needed to know, and things changed," he spit out and he began to sob.

Rob's mom lost all expressions in her face. She stopped wiping his face and forehead and just sat there. Sat in silence. Rob didn't notice since he was still in a belly-flipping, mind-wandering cry.

The silence become overwhelming as Rob got his composure and realized his mom was no longer motherly, "Mom?" he questioned.

There was no answer from his mom. Rob pushed himself up and away from his mom then looked at her face. Her eyes were pooling up with tears that were waiting to leave before heading down her rough face. She looked at Rob as the tears finally started to flow. With every blink, more tears exited her eyes, which put Rob into a panic.

"Mom? Mom. I am sorry."

Rob's mom got up from the couch, walked into the kitchen and grabbed a smoke. She lit the cigarette up and added more smoke stains to the ceiling. Rob watched from the distance scared to say anything. His eyes focused on the bright glow with every large inhale his mother would take.

"Rob," she said as the last small drag happened, "Rob, I am going to pray to God that you will be okay."

"God? Mom, God?"

"The Hill, that grave, Stocker, it's all evil and for some reason the evil attaches it to someone, and that person is never the same."

"Oh my God, Mom!" came shooting out of his mouth. "Oh my GOD!"

"What?" she replied as tears began to well again.

"Reed, it's Reed. He changed when we were up there, he changed."

.

Chapter | 82

Hanner finished his cup of coffee and waited to solve his next problem. A problem that was driving him to leave the station and head somewhere else. Hanner dropped his coffee cup and let it shatter on the floor.

A slight murmuring echoed through the air whispering, *"The Hill, go to the Hill."*

"Yes, sir," Hanner replied as he left the kitchen to walk out the front door. His path to the front door included walking over the bloody mess of Jackson and Katie that he created.

Hanner's car was ready and waiting for Hanner to give the order where to go. He climbed into his car and instantly his car knew. The car knew where to go and fired up all its cylinders on its own. The gas gauge pointed to empty but the murmuring whisper of, *"go to the Hill,"* gave Hanner's car enough power to get to where it needed to be.

The rip from the police station was quick and easy for the car as Hanner smelled a slight whiff of copper as he wiped off more of Katie's blood.

The Hill was talking to Hanner and after every few sentences Hanner would reply, "yes, sir—I understand."

During the entire conversation, the car drove effortlessly to the Hill, up the gravel road and found itself right next to the grave. The car sat on the green plateau as Hanner exited the car and stepped away to sit on one of the awaiting rocks. As he sat down and looked at his car, the grave started to feed. With every breath the grave took, the car slowly started to dissolve into it. A few more breaths and the car was gone.

Emotionless, Hanner watched his car go away while the last morsel of metal dissipated, Hanner stood up, walked around the grave, and went back to his resting spot. Hanner waited until his next set of orders came in from Stocker.

— — —

On the other side of town, Reed lay in his bed after his visit to see Krista. He was alone and wide-awake staring into the night. His best friend wouldn't join him, and he was angry with Buster, the one that loved him and gave him affection no matter what, was not in bed by his side.

"What did I do to him?" Reed asked into the darkness. "Nothing at all but give him love."

Reed's temper was starting to flare and his feelings for Krista were unemotional. His drive to see her and take care of her and love her were gone. As he thought some more, *Do I even love Buster?*

"What is going on?" He reacted to his wondering thoughts, "Of course I love Buster and Krista, without a doubt I do."

As Reed lay on his bed trying to hold back his temper, a slight murmur entered the room, *"The Hill, go to the Hill."*

Reed jumped up from his bed and landed on his feet. "What was that?" he shouted. Reed surveyed the room to figure out what just happened. As he got his composure and settled down, another murmur entered the room, *"The Hill, go to the Hill."*

Reed was startled but more at ease as he questioned the sound, "What? Go to the Hill? Is that what I heard?"

"Yes," whispered the murmur.

"Yes, yes I will, yes I will go to the Hill" came out of Reed's mouth.

"Wait a minute. Wait. Did I just say I would go to the Hill?"

Reed was on high alert as panic set in. He walked over to his desk and opened the top drawer. There, under a few magazines lay his prize possession that was a total secret. His beechwood handled, six inches of pure shiny steel—his beautiful, sinister knife.

"You are a beautiful piece of power. No one is messing with me," he said as he pulled the knife out of its holder.

Reed replaced the knife to its home and slid the knife into the back of his pants then covered it with his shirt. The power the knife gave him made Reed feel safe and he sat on the side of his bed. All was quiet now as he sat in silence.

As soon as Reed was calm and under control, the murmur entered the room with a stronger whisper this time, *"Go to the Hill!"*

As the words disappeared into his ears, Reed jumped up and headed out the door. He left his home and headed down the street. As he started to walk away, the front door slammed shut and sent a loud echo ripping through all the rooms and into the town of Walcott. Buster jumped up and whimpered as he ran into Bill and Katherine's room. Bill woke and looked around while Katherine's eyes were wide open.

"Did you hear that?" Katherine said.

Bill started to lay his head back down, "Sort of."

"Well, go check."

"Why?"

"Well, dear, Buster is in our bed shaking life a leaf and I heard something."

"Why is he in our bed? Is Reed home?"

"Well, dear, I really don't know. I'm kind of scared at the moment and the only thing besides me that thinks something is wrong is Buster."

Bill pushed himself up off the bed as he politely responded, "Yes, dear."

Bill made his way out their room down the hallway towards Reed's room. The only thing joining him on his little walk was the creaking floors. He slowly opened Reed's door to find his bed empty. He entered and felt a coldness lingering in the room, an emptiness with Reed not being there.

"That damn—"

The trip back to the room was brisk and loud as the hallway reacted to his every step. Bill entered the room. "He's not there."

"At this time of night? Where is he?"

"I don't know, and I really do not care at the moment. My friend is dead, I am tired, my mind won't stop, and I just want to sleep."

"I'm sorry dear, so sorry about Harold. Reed is probably hurting and wanted to walk in off. Everything will be okay, everything will be."

Chapter | 83

The night embraced Reed as he exited his house with authority. The slamming of the door sent a message to the Hill. A message that Reed was on his way.

The once sorrowful evening turned itself around and sent joy through the night air. The Hill, standing powerfully over the town of Walcott, guided Reed's way. It directed the breeze to be at his back to push him through the streets. The moon took orders from the Hill and lit Reed's walk. The Hill nurtured and caressed the town as it held its power over it.

Before a flicker of his eye, Reed was standing at the bottom of Stocker Hill. He looked up the Hill, up the gravel road, up into the sky and asked, "How did I get here?"

A murmur whispered down from the top of the Hill and blew ever so gently on Reed's face, *"I told you to."*

"Told me to? Who?"

"I did. I told you."

"Brad, are you messing with me? Who?"

A slim figure stepped out of the darkness and walked towards Reed. It was peaceful and welcoming to Reed. It made Reed feel loved and comfortable.

"Hi. Hello. Hi, fine, sir," Reed mumbled.

"Hello Reed," said the figure, "I've been waiting a long time for us to finally meet."

"You have?" questioned Reed as a big smile landed on his face. "I feel so nice right now. What I nice night."

"Well, yes, it is, Reed. It is a very nice night."

"Why do I know you?"

"I have been watching over you for a very long time. I have helped and guided you over every step of your life."

"But we've never met," Reed said as his warmth started to turn to fear.

"Reed, it's okay," said the slender figure. "I am here to help you."

"Help me? How? Why am I here? What's going on?" The questions raced out of Reed's mouth. "Where did you go? I can't see you, but I can see you?"

The figure reached out of the darkness and laid his hand on Reed's shoulder then pulled Reed a little closer. The figure's outline appeared in sight again. The fear raced from Reed's body and was replaced with warmth and love.

"So nice. So nice it is. What a wonderful night," said Reed as calmness overtook his being.

The figure pulled Reed even closer and whispered in his ear.

"Yes, sir," Reed said.

The figure turned away and disappeared back in the darkness. Reed looked up the Hill, looked up Stocker Hill and began the walk up the gravel road. Step by step he walked up the Hill, with the breeze at his back and the moon guiding his way.

Reed made his way to the plateau and stopped. He gazed over the green grass, over the grave and gazed at a man sitting silently on one of the gray rocks. Standing next to him was the figure. His hand resting on the shoulder of the man sitting and his faceless eyes staring directly at Reed.

The emotion left Reed's body and instinct kicked in. *Run*. He turned and with all his might, he ran from the figure, from the sitting man, from the grave and off the plateau. Nothing happened, though. He tried. He tried very hard. He tried with every ounce he could put into it, but no luck. He stood still.

A sweet whisper left the faceless figure and rushed across Reed's ear. "Yes, sir," Reed said as calmness returned to his body.

Reed gazed over towards the grave and began to walk towards it. As he got closer, he recognized the man sitting on the rock.

"Hanner, is that you?"

"So, you're him?" Hanner replied.

"Him, him who?" he questioned.

"You will learn very quickly. I knew this day would come, but never thought it would be you."

Puzzlement flashed across Reed's face as he looked in Hanner's eyes. The once-powerful man was a shell of himself as he stood next to the faceless figure.

"It's time," the figure murmured, "it is time."

Reed, without thinking, stepped closer to Hanner, closer to the figure and pulled his knife from his back then sunk it into Hanner's belly. The knife punctured the skin and blood started draining from his body. Every drop of blood got quickly soaked up by the grave.

"Feed me," the figure stated.

Reed looked into Hanner's eyes and pulled his knife up towards the moon. Blood poured out of Hanner's body and was consumed by the grave. With every beat of Hanner's heart, blood would rush from his opened belly and into the awaiting grave. The black soot soaked up every drop that it was given.

As Hanner's face started to lose its color and with his last breath, he said, "I used to be you."

With minimal effort, Reed reached up and grabbed Hanner by the throat, lifting the large man off the ground and tossed his blood lost soul into the grave.

"You are with me now, son," said Satan.

Chapter | 84

The morning dew put a pleasant aroma in the air that captured the peacefulness of Walcott that morning. The slight breeze rushed from the top of Stocker Hill and pushed its way into every household in town. Wakening everyone to a new day.

Stocker Hill stood proud that morning as it oversaw the changing of the guard. Things were changing for sure, and all the town could do was sit back and wait to see what was going to happen next.